CW00602112

CLOUD SHADOWS

Further Titles by Elizabeth Webster from Severn House

THE ACORN WINTER
HOME STREET HOME

CLOUD
SHADOWS

Elizabeth Webster

SEVERN SH HOUSE

This first world edition published in Great Britain 1995 by
SEVERN HOUSE PUBLISHERS LTD of
9–15 High Street, Sutton, Surrey SM1 1DF.
First published in the USA 1995 by
SEVERN HOUSE PUBLISHERS INC of
425 Park Avenue, New York, NY 10022.

British Library Cataloguing in Publication Data
Webster, Elizabeth
  Cloud Shadows
  I. Title
  823.914 [F]

  ISBN 0-7278-4791-0

To all aid workers in whatever field,
because they never pass by on the other side.

All situations in this publication are fictitious and
any resemblance to real persons, living or dead, is purely coincidental.

Typeset by Hewer Text Composition Services, Edinburgh.
Printed and bound in Great Britain by
Hartnolls Ltd, Bodmin, Cornwall.

If no man is an island,
where does the mainland begin?

Grateful thanks to Hazel Hendry of The Tear Fund, and to various Intrepid Lorry Drivers who prefer to be nameless but who gave me the benefit of their expert advice.

Part One

The Island

There were icebergs in the bay again. They sailed past, drifting slowly southwards on the spring tides towards the warmer waters of the Gulf Stream. One huge, translucent ice tower almost blocked the entrance to Tom's little cove. Not quite, though. For there was a small boat nosing its way cautiously past the magnificent frozen mountain, through the narrow tickle into the quiet reaches of his hidden sanctuary.

Tom sat on a rock and watched it coming, but his eyes kept straying to the marvellous blues and greens, shimmering jades and indigos, purples and azures and lapis lazuli deeps of that incandescent floating fortress.

Beautiful, he thought. Beautiful and dying, shrinking hourly in the melting seas – all that miracle of glowing light . . .

He sighed. He loved this small island of his – the winter ice and snows, the storms and tearing Arctic winds, the pounding seas, and the swept, enormous skies . . . And the slow thaws of spring.

It wasn't lonely. Even in winter there were the birds – thin and hardy, their feathers puffed against the cold, but still alive. And a few fish (he had learnt to fish through ice-holes when the shore was frozen) and a cormorant or two to dive after them, even a fish eagle now and then . . . And a few seals wintering on the rocks, or swimming deep under the ice and coming up for air through the holes. And of course there was Ollie.

Yes, Ollie. Tom had found the abandoned seal pup down on the rocks one summer evening, crying like a baby. He hadn't known in the least what to do with it, but it cried so that he

1

simply picked it up in his arms and took it home. Then, of course, he had to think about feeding it, and he gambled hopefully on the assumption that if its mother had abandoned it, the pup was probably nearly weaned. Fortunately, the caplin had come into the cove that summer, and he just scooped up pailfuls of the tiny silver fish and persuaded the seal pup to swallow them. That was where the name Ollie came in, for the hungry baby seal was always asking for more, but Tom was patient, and in time Ollie learnt to fish for himself. By the time the winter came he was independent, but he still hung around hoping to be fed and apparently liking Tom's company. Often Tom would find him waiting for him on the rocks, or he would see the intelligent questing head thrusting up out of the pack ice in the cold sea to look at him.

Oh, there you are, he would seem to say. *I'm glad you're still around.* And Tom would smile and feel like saying: "Likewise!"

Yes, there was always something living, something struggling to survive in the bitter cold, fighting to keep the spark of life going till the warmer days of spring. He understood that fight. He respected it. Out here, with only the implacable cold, the hard grip of the ice, as the common enemy, life became very simple. There were no problems – no guilts and regrets, no agonies of right or wrong, no duties or cowardly evasions – only the simple desire to stay alive.

Till the spring. Well, it was spring now, and the ice was melting. There was slush on the shore – "shish", they called it here – and faint green fronds among the lichens on the rocks.

And a boat coming in. A small, unobtrusive boat . . . but the world was out there behind its back.

He didn't want the world. He had turned his back on it long ago – or it seemed long ago now, far away from these cool, remote, unsullied spaces. He was happy here in his hidden fastness among the black rocks and fierce cliffs of this little island. It was so small it hadn't got a real name, but they called it Little Reward because it was near Reward Cove – and also because, in the sardonic eyes of the local fishermen, it really had little to offer. There was only the old abandoned lighthouse to live in – though Tom found it quite adequate for his needs – with one freshwater spring for drinking water and a broken jetty where a small boat could just about tie up –

2

and the tall sea stacks that were home to a myriad birds in summer.

They would be here soon, the puffins and golden-headed gannets, squabbling and fighting for house-room on the rocks, and his quiet retreat would be filled with the sound of their voices. But he didn't mind their voices, shrill or gruff and always ceaselessly crying on the wind – they were just company, the voices of friends busy with their own lives. They did not tug at the heartstrings like those other voices of long ago . . .

But the seabirds were not here yet, and there was another voice calling from below the rocks, and he had better see to it.

He got to his feet and stood looking down – a tall, rangy man, thin in spite of his thick jacket and heavy seaboots, but somehow strong and braced for endurance, or for trouble in whatever form it came. Above that squarish face, weathered by summer suns and bitter winter winds, two very bright blue eyes looked out from under bushy eyebrows, and a shock of curly hair, prematurely touched with frost at the edges, escaped like a shaggy halo from his old peaked cap.

"Hallooo!" called the voice. "Tom Denholm, I know you're there. Come down, you varmint!"

Tom laughed and began to clamber down the rocks to the broken jetty on the shore. It was only when he moved that the stiffness in one knee became apparent. It gave him a slight limp, but he paid it no attention and seemed nimble enough on the rocky shore.

The little boat was bobbing close to the rotting timbers of the jetty, and as Tom came forward, a rope shot out towards him.

"Tie her up, can't you?" rasped the voice. "And give me a hand. I don't trust them *strouters* an inch."

Tom tied the snaking rope to a fairly solid-looking post, and leaned down, grinning, to offer a hand to the figure in the boat.

It was a woman who stood there, foursquare and sturdy under her oilskins, glaring belligerently up at Tom out of snapping brown eyes which had nonetheless a decided gleam of mischief about them.

"Come on up, Sally Maguire," said Tom, heaving her on to the flaking planks of the ruined jetty. "Welcome aboard."

"Huh!" she snorted, pulling her woolly cap further down

over her ears. "Don't know as I dare set foot on this old wreck."

Tom simply tucked her arm through his and led her off the precarious wooden structure on to the rocky path beyond that led up to the old lighthouse.

"I'll make us some coffee," he promised, and then glanced at her with faint enquiry. "It's not time for the stores . . .?"

"No, it ain't. And I didn't bring any." Her glare was worse than ever. "Becos I aim to take you back with me."

Tom looked at her. He knew that little bobbing boat meant trouble. "Why?" he demanded, trying not to sound as belligerent as Sally.

She did not answer at once but concentrated on putting one foot in front of the other on the steep path. "It's a bit of a tale, Tom. Wait till I get me breath back."

He nodded, and went on ahead to heave open the ancient wooden door that kept the flying sea spray outside the old lighthouse walls. They went inside, and Sally stood looking around her as she shrugged herself out of her oilskins and slung them over a nearby packing case. Tom, for his part, was regarding Sally with a mixture of affection and respect, reflecting that she made a staunch and resolute friend, but that she would be a formidable enemy.

Sally Maguire was at this time about fifty years old (she thought), wiry and "tough as old boots" (she said), and Responsible with a capital R (she reminded everyone), as befitted the keeper of the village store who was also the postmistress (when there was any post and the snow let it get through). Besides all this, she was the wife of the leading fisherman of the outport, who was skipper of the little fishing fleet, no less, (what was left of it these days) and a man to be reckoned with. Sally was someone to be reckoned with, too, and she didn't let anyone forget it – least of all Tom Denholm, for whom she had quite a soft spot, though she would never admit it.

"Sit you down, Sally," said Tom, going over to the old wood-burning stove where an ancient blackened coffee pot sat permanently on the hot plate, "and tell me all about it."

Sally sat down on another packing case (there weren't any chairs) and had a closer look at the old lighthouse. The stone

4

walls were still thick and strong, built to withstand the winter gales and keep out the cold. There were no trees on the island, only a few stretches of bristly tuckamore on the headland, and a useful clutter of driftwood from old wrecks and storms on the shore, so Tom had to go over to the mainland to bring in a boatload of wood when he needed it. The little outport usually had some, brought up from Lewisporte or Campbelton where the sawmills still flourished. There was still an endless supply of timber in the forests of the Newfoundland central highlands – great stands of spruce and pine, birch and aspen, where the caribou herds still wandered in undisturbed freedom. Fetching logs was a bit of a chore for Tom's little boat, but it was worth it, for the old stove warmed the place up and cast a cheerful glow on the bare stone walls.

Sally noted this approvingly and admitted to herself that Tom seemed to have made the old place reasonably habitable. There was a table, and even a bookcase knocked together out of two packing cases. It was difficult to fit anything to the circular walls, but there were a couple of rather rickety shelves near the door.

"D'you want to see what I've done to the place?" asked Tom, since Sally seemed a bit uncertain how to begin. "You haven't been over since I settled in."

She looked a bit embarrassed at that. "Yeah, well, it was easier to send Danny over with the stores."

Tom laughed. "I'm not grumbling. I'm offering you a tour of inspection."

She grinned, accepting a lifeline. "Don't mind if I do."

He led her up the narrow stone stairs that wound round the lighthouse walls. On the next floor was one round room with a bunk bed built into a niche in the wall, and one wide, curved window of double thickness glass. The winter storms flung spray hard against those windows and they had to be strong.

Sally glanced round the bare room and made no comment except a grudging: "Seems snug enough," and followed Tom's long legs up the last of the stone steps to the room at the top.

"The Lantern Room is mostly as it was," explained Tom, "but it makes a marvellous studio – the light is so good." He waved a hand upwards at the glass dome above their heads, the wide circular windows, and the encircling metal balcony and platform outside the glass. The huge old metal lantern still hung in the airy space of the dome, mounted on its own supporting sprawl of metal struts, with a jumble of levers and handles below.

"No good now," said Tom sadly, "but I daresay it served its turn."

"Saved a good few lives, I reckon," nodded Sally. "But the new light out on the Point is right on up to date."

She turned to look at the walls of the Lantern Room, and her eyes went wide at the sight of Tom's paintings spread all round them. He had managed to hang some of them on pegs set in the stone, but there were others leaning against the walls, stacked in careless heaps, propped up on books or bits of driftwood . . . and a couple on portable easels set as near to the windows as possible so that the pure light streamed on to them from the wide sky.

He seemed to have painted every aspect of his island sanctuary – the rocks, the tall sea stacks scoured by the storms of winter, stark and unscalable to a mere human, but a safe nesting place to a ceaseless flurry of wings in summer; and the sea itself in every mood from black anger to beguiling calm. Then there were the birds, dozens of different kinds, and the seals hauled out on the rocks or diving in the sea; and, of course, Ollie. Ollie in all sorts of moods, like the sea, gazing out at him with great liquid eyes. And, latest of all among his recent efforts, the great translucent towers of the icebergs floating by . . . It was all there – a loving tribute to the place he loved. But in some curious way, each picture seemed to be more a quintessence of the subject in his mind's eye, rather than a mere reproduction. More vivid and perfect than reality itself, so that each cresting wave, each flying bird or diving seal or small summer flower on the edge of a rock, had a strange, pulsing life of its own. Even the cold icebergs seemed to glow and gleam with interior light.

Sally went across to look more closely at these and said approvingly: "Spot on, Tom." Then she gazed round her again, shaking her head in disbelief. The walls of the old building positively shone with life and colour. "You got it all," she murmured, sounding almost awestruck at so much richness. "So that was what all those parcels and things you ordered from St John's were for! I did wonder."

Tom laughed. "Only paints and bits of paper and canvas."

6

"You sure made good use of 'em," she told him, smiling.

"Let's go down," growled Tom, seeming almost embarrassed at her unexpected praise. "Coffee'll be ready."

Sally made no demur, no more excuses to herself. She couldn't put it off any longer. Whether Tom got angry or not, she had to say what she'd come to say. So she followed meekly after him down the twisting stone stairs and went back to sit on her packing case while Tom fetched the coffee.

"It's your friend, Greg," she said abruptly, holding on for dear life to the mug of coffee Tom had just given her.

Tom looked astounded. *"Greg*? Greg Selwyn?"

"That's the one."

"Well? What about him?" Tom sounded dangerously crisp.

"He called me."

"Where from?"

"London, he said."

Tom almost seemed to sag with relief. At least Greg wasn't over here. For a moment he had thought . . . "How the hell did he know where I was?"

"Dunno." Sally shrugged broad shoulders.

Only Tom's English bank knew he was in Newfoundland, and even they only knew about transfer arrangements to a bank in St John's. How had Greg managed to track him down?

"Well, go on," he said, sounding crosser than he meant to.

"He says he must talk to you. It's urgent. Some family trouble."

"I haven't got a family," snapped Tom.

"Yes, you have, too, Tom Denholm." Sally was undismayed. "He told me. You got a sister, he says, and a nephew, and a niece in the States. That's family, isn't it?" The glare was back. "And he says there's trouble at home, and you've got to talk to him."

"I haven't *got* to do anything," growled Tom. "I haven't seen them for years. I don't owe them anything."

Sally just looked at him. "It's not a question of *owing,*" she said flatly. "Family is family. You can't deny that."

"Can't I?" Tom's growl was even deeper, but he was losing ground.

"No, you can't." Sally was at her most commanding. "So just you get your boat out, Tom Denholm, and follow me

7

over and call your friend. Or I'll – I'll clout you with one of me oars."

Tom shook his head in despair. "Sally Maguire, you're a terrible woman to cross!"

She began to grin. But she didn't altogether trust Tom, especially when he seemed to give in. "Well – are you coming?"

"All right, all right. Let me finish my coffee first."

"I promised him, Tom," she said, her voice suddenly warm and serious. "I promised you'd come. Don't let me down."

There didn't seem to be any answer to that, and if Tom was surprised at the sudden depth of feeling in Sally's brisk voice, he didn't say so. He merely got up and laid a friendly hand on her arm.

"Let's go then," he said.

It wasn't a long trip to the little outport, but it was the first time he had taken his own boat out since winter. There was still ice in the bay and the going was treacherous unless you knew the ins and outs like Sally did. So he followed Sally's more powerful boat with careful attention, edging his way through the narrow tickle and zigzagging as she did to avoid the more lethal-looking chunks of ice.

He would have to stay the night, he realised, for the days were still very short and darkness would soon be settling over these dangerous waters. He did not mind staying with Sally and her fisherman husband, Ned; they were friendly enough but not effusive, and they didn't insist on making it a social occasion with all their friends dropping in to meet him. They knew he liked peace and quiet, and that living alone on his island had made him almost allergic to noise and chatter. It actually made him feel ill. Antisocial, he supposed he was. But the slow, spacious days on Little Reward were what he needed – what his soul craved.

Oh well, he would be back there tomorrow – and talking to Greg would be no great hardship. After all, he was his oldest friend, and they usually understood one another.

They arrived at the jetty in Reward Cove, tied up the boats, and made their way past the small group of ochre-coloured wooden houses round the little harbour to Sally's general store and post office. Her house was not much bigger than the others, except that

8

it had a long, built-on room for the shop with an outside wooden verandah for displaying vegetables and fruit in the summer.

"You get on that phone," ordered Sally. "And I'll make coffee."

Tom calculated that it would be three hours on in London, which would make it about seven o'clock in the evening. He hoped Greg would be in. Well, he could only try. The phone rang for a long time, but eventually Greg's crisp, alert barrister's voice came on the line.

"I'm glad you had the decency to call," he said drily. "That battle-axe of a postmistress of yours must pack a powerful punch."

"What is this?" Tom protested mildly. "When is it indecent to live quietly on my own?"

"When your family need you." Greg's voice was uncompromising.

Tom blinked at the flat, angry voice. "Greg, you know I haven't been in touch with Becky and Derek for years. I couldn't keep up with all their jet-setting and gold-plated film-star homes and such . . . They are way out of my league."

"*Were*," said Greg succinctly.

"What do you mean?"

"I mean Derek has swanned off with a girl of twenty – and all his current salary which is, I am told, astronomical. Leaving Becky with the choice of two apartments to sell and no other income."

Tom whistled. "That's outrageous."

"Oh yes, it's that all right, considering what he's earning." His voice was even more clipped and angry.

"How has Becky taken it?"

"That's the trouble, Tom. She *can't* take it. She won't make any decisions. She won't accept that it's over, or face up to a divorce – or try to work out what to do next. All she can do is wring her hands and say: 'How can I pay the bills?' – over and over again. She's really a little – er – unhinged at the moment."

Tom sighed. (He seemed to be doing a lot of it lately.) "What about Kit and Jenny?"

"Jenny's in California. Well out of it, she says, and has no intention of coming home."

"And Kit?"

9

"Gone."

"What?"

"Gone off on some sort of aid agency trip."

Tom groaned. "Not another of us. Is he old enough?"

Greg permitted himself a small, dry laugh. "You've been away too long, Tom. He's twenty-three – nearly twenty-four. Older than Derek's latest dolly bird." His angry voice softened a little as he added: "I think he wanted to escape the hassle. Divided loyalties are hell to live with."

Tom agreed. "How do you come into all this?" He wondered, as he spoke, whether he was being tactless. But Greg and Marian had a good, stable marriage, he knew – unlikely to be rocked by any side issues.

"I don't really." Greg sounded entirely unruffled. "I kept in touch with them vaguely when they were home in London – more because of you than anything."

Was there faint reproach in his voice? Tom couldn't be sure, but he was beginning to feel guilty anyway. "I see . . ."

"And then she rang me, asking for the name of a lawyer. I suppose she thought I'd know a good one – and then it all came tumbling out . . . She really is in a state, Tom."

There was silence on the line for a moment, and then Tom said slowly: "I don't see what I can do about it."

Greg sounded exasperated this time. "You could *talk* to her, Tom. You could even talk to Derek."

"I don't suppose I could persuade him to ditch his new girlfriend and go back to Becky, though, could I?" He paused, and added as an afterthought: "Does she *want* him back?"

"I don't know." There was almost the feel of a shrug behind Greg's voice now. "One minute she rages and says not, and then she weeps and says she can't do without him."

"You sound as if you've had a basinful."

"I have," said Greg. "It's your turn now."

Tom drew a shaken breath of terror. "Greg, *I can't* come home. I can't face it. All that noise – all that grabbing and pushing and shoving . . . All those money-grubbing morons intent on cutthroat mutual destruction. It's obscene."

"I know," agreed Greg, surprisingly. "But that's the way life is."

"It isn't like that out here," said Tom, already a bit ashamed of his outburst. But even as he said it, he thought: Isn't it? The gannets and the puffins fighting for territory, pushing each other off the cliffs and destroying each other's eggs? The bull walruses battling almost to death for the cows? Even the gentle seals fight over their wives . . . And the black bears come down to catch the spawning salmon, don't they? It's all a war – a ceaseless, all-out bloody war in which the strongest and the wiliest live and the weakest go to the wall. Is it so very different from us?

"You don't understand," he said, slowly and painfully putting long-buried thoughts together. "I'm happy out here . . . There are no pressures. I've learnt to – I've more or less found a modus vivendi. It's calm and quiet and undemanding, and I've begun to – I'm beginning to come to terms with the past, and Suzi's death and everything . . ." He stalled there. Not even to Greg could he admit how much all that past agony and regret still hurt. Much more than his smashed kneecap which still ached abominably when he walked on it too much. "How did you find me, anyway?" he asked suddenly.

Faint laughter touched Greg's voice for a moment. "The art shop in St John's. Your bank told me they only had instructions for transfers there, but no personal address – and anyway they wouldn't have given it me. They stretched a point going as far as they did. But I reckoned if you were alive at all, you'd still be painting."

"Very clever."

"Are you?"

"Am I what?"

"Still painting?"

"Oh. Yes – a bit. It's . . . wonderful country to paint." There was sadness in his voice, and Greg could not miss it.

"Tom," he said, sounding oddly gentle now over those long, Atlantic miles, "I don't want to disturb your peace. I know the world over here is a bloody jungle, but you can't turn your back on it for ever."

"Why not?"

"Because you're a member of the human race," Greg told him, and allowed another faint fleck of laughter to creep in. "Or so I understand."

11

There was another silence between them, and another sigh from Tom.

"At least phone her, Tom. Maybe she'll listen to you. She always did look up to you, you know. I'm sure you can sort something out."

"All right." Tom sounded weary. "I'll talk to her. But you'll have to give me her number. I don't even know where she is."

"She's in a suburb out towards Uxbridge," said Greg, and gave Tom her address and phone number.

"Well, I'll try," agreed Tom. "But I can't promise anything."

Greg knew he had to be content with that – for the time being. And if his heart ached for his old friend who had cut himself off from all human contact – from all comfort – he did not say so.

"Good man," he said, sounding painfully jovial. "I knew I could rely on you . . ." and he rang off before Tom could change his mind.

Good man? thought Tom. Am I? . . . Perhaps he's right about the human race! Out here, I suppose, I'm scarcely a man at all . . . With a heavy heart he got International to get him Becky's number. She answered at once, sounding distraught and tearful from the start, and not very rational, either.

"Oh Tom," she cried, "what am I going to do? How am I going to pay the bills? . . . The telephone – I mean, even this –?"

"I'm paying for this call, Becky. Be sensible."

"How can I be sensible? I don't know where to live – I don't know what to do . . ."

"What does your lawyer say?"

"It's just the local solicitor – I don't think he's much good. Derek can make rings round him."

"But I thought Greg recommended a good one?"

"He did, but Derek wouldn't let me see him."

"*Derek* wouldn't?" He was dumbfounded. "But it's your decision, Becky, not his. He has no right to interfere."

"I know," she wailed, "but he's so difficult to deal with. He's much cleverer than me about money. He's always telling me I'm a fool . . . We had a joint account, you see, and he stopped all my credit cards . . . and then there's the insurance, and BUPA – and how can I decide about where to live if I don't know how much it'll cost, or what either of the properties will fetch . . .?"

12

The stream of anxieties went on pouring out and Tom, wearily hanging on at the other end, almost stopped listening. In the end he interrupted her quite sharply. "Becky, this is all nonsense, you know. You'll have enough to live on – more than enough by most people's standards. It's just that you have been used to too much."

"*Too much*?" she yelled, getting angry now. "It's *all* too much! I've spent twenty-five years of my life with that – that creep! I've brought up his children, and hosted his damn company dinners, and made homes for him in whatever benighted country the bloody oil sheiks sent him to, kept house for him, cooked for him, paid the bills for him, and made his life run as smoothly as his damn computers. And what does he do? Leaves me without a backward glance for a scheming, uneducated little floosie younger than his own daughter, whose only aim in life is to grab a rich husband . . ." The tirade died down then, and Becky began to sob.

Tom sighed. (Again.)

"Look, Becky, this is all perfectly true, but it doesn't do any good. Let's be practical. I just want to know if there's anything I can do to help." He took a deep breath and added: "Do you want me to come home?"

"I don't know," she wept. "I don't think so. You'll only argue – or go and thump Derek or something, and that would only make it worse. He shouts at me enough as it is. You never liked him, did you?"

"No," admitted Tom, "I didn't." And maybe, he thought privately, thumping him would be a good idea. "Well, at least use Greg's good lawyer," he pleaded. "Take Greg's advice – and pay no attention to Derek."

"All right." She capitulated all at once. "I'll do what you say."

"And – hang on, Becky. Keep your nerve. It'll all work out if you give it a chance."

"Will it?" She sounded curiously flat and defeated now.

"I'll – I'll ring again in a few days," he said, knowing he was taking the cowardly way out. "Shall I?"

"Yes. Yes, do that, Tom." She took a quivering breath. "It was good of you to call."

But even after she had put the phone down, Tom sat staring into space, wondering if he had done the right thing – and knowing very well that he had not.

"Coffee," said Sally, plonking it down in front of him, and ignoring his troubled expression. "Ned'll be in soon."

She left him in the back office where the telephone was, while she sent her shop-minder, Millie, home and closed up for the day. Tom could hear her bluff thanks and her added remark: "We'll be over later. Not sure about Tom, though."

She came through then, carrying a mug of coffee for herself, and looked entirely innocent when Tom enquired: "What aren't you sure about Tom?"

"Most everything," she retorted, and then relented, smiling. "They're having a jig down at Millie's." She looked at him apologetically. "Old-style, like a ceilidh. Most of us'll aim to be there – but you don't have to. If it's peace and quiet you want, you'd best stay here."

Tom was on the point of agreeing when he suddenly realised that he was being offered solace for whatever unsettling thoughts Greg had stirred up in him, and that it would be downright curmudgeonly to refuse. The little fishing community took their local functions and celebrations seriously – even if the young ones did prefer discos and the television pop programmes – and it was an honour for him to be asked to share in them. What had become of him, that he was so prickly and unwilling to join in a small community's cheerful rejoicing when he was asked?

"No," he said at last, sounding rather gruff and shy. "I'd like to come – if they'll have me."

Sally gave him an approving glance. "That's more like it. 'Fish in summer, fun in winter', as they say."

So when Ned came in from the day's fishing (grumbling about the small catch, as usual), Tom politely asked if he could go with them to Millie's jig. Ned Maguire was a big, burly man with a slow smile and very few words. Now he looked at Tom for a moment in silence, and then gave a cheerful nod.

"Why not? A bit of a jig never did anyone any harm."

Tom wasn't sure if that remark was as innocent as it sounded, but he caught the faint gleam in Ned's eye and forbore to make any comment. So he humbly followed him and Sally down to Millie's house by the harbour, where the fiddler was playing wildly and various people were showing off their heel-and-toe skills, skirts flying and boots stomping, and the food and drink seemed absurdly plentiful considering it was just after winter when the stores were low. Someone plied Tom with a glass or two of something alarmingly fiery and potent, and the evening passed in a haze of laughter, clapping and singing, dizzying jigs and reels, and so much general bonhomie that he seemed to be drowning in goodwill.

But though he found himself hazily saying goodnight to a host of new-found friends before he staggered back arm in arm with Sally and Ned through the dark village street, when he finally got into the spare bunk bed in the store room, he could not sleep. Greg's words kept going round and round in his head, and images of his sister, Becky, young and slim and hopeful as he had known her when she first grew up, kept appearing before his eyes. Becky, auburn-haired, reckless and ravishingly pretty, before she met his tiresome brother-in-law, Derek. (Derek, insensitive and bland, and always too smug and too successful, whittling away at Becky's self-confidence with his constant jibes about feather-brained women who didn't understand finance and had to have their lives made popsy-proof.) Should he have seen the danger signs even then? he wondered. But it's not my problem, he kept telling himself (without much conviction). They'll have to work it out for themselves. I can't interfere. It's never a good idea to interfere in a marriage break-up. I'll only make things worse.

But Becky's voice kept repeating itself behind his thoughts, crying out in desperate bewilderment: *"I don't know what to do!"* and he knew his own arguments were very hollow.

Besides his small boat, Tom also possessed a car – an old, battered estate which he had driven across Canada before crossing from Labrador to Newfoundland on the ferry. He had really been driving away from the Furies, but they had pursued him until he came by chance upon the small outports of Notre Dame Bay and Exploits, and his final choice of sanctuary in the disused lighthouse on Little Reward.

When he decided to live on the island, he more or less gave the

15

car to Sally and Ned. They had somewhere to keep it in the winter, and it would be useful to them when the roads and causeways were open – and Tom could always borrow it back for any occasion when he might need it. The arrangement worked very well. Tom didn't often go anywhere – except to collect stores and logs from time to time. He was content to live in uninterrupted seclusion on his small island and watch the birds fly up from the tall sea stacks and the slow seasons pass.

But this morning, after Greg's unsettling phone call and the even more distressing one with Becky, he felt restless. His peace was disturbed, and he decided to take off for a few days into the forests of Exploits and try to walk off his unease.

"What are the roads like?" he asked Sally, who always knew about weather and transport.

"OK. And the causeways are open. But there'll still be snow in the woods and on the hills. Take skis – or snowshoes or something." She saw Tom look a bit nonplussed at this, and added: "We can lend you some."

So he packed up the old Ford estate, and accepted a flask of coffee from Sally and a bottle of whiskey from Ned "to keep the cold out" and set off. They didn't try to stop him. That was the nice thing about these people. They accepted what you chose to do without comment, and offered what practical help they could with the minimal of fuss and the utmost generosity.

He didn't quite know where he was going, or why he needed to go anywhere, except that all the old doubts and despairs of his own earlier tragedy had risen up again to haunt him, and he could not take them back to his quiet island retreat. He would have to deal with them first.

He drove down to Campbelton and then on to Notre Dame Junction where he took the road to Bishop's Falls and Grand-Falls Windsor. The countryside was still snowy under the green of the pines, but the roads were clear. He went on through the old logging town of Badger, and down to the Buchan Junction, and finally to the Mary March camp site on the shores of Red Indian Lake. It was the wrong time of year for tourists and camping but there were still people about. They told him that here he would be camping on the site of the Beothuk Indians' winter camp ground.

He left the car there, picked up his pack and walked off into the trees.

The snow was not deep here, though the lake was still mostly frozen except at the slushy edges, and at first walking was not difficult. But later on, Tom's feet began to sink into deep drifts among the tall spruce and pine trees, and he stopped to strap on Sally's bear-paw snowshoes. (He didn't trust himself on skis with his damaged knee.) The silence around him was somehow immense and awe-inspiring, and he was suddenly conscious of the oldness of the earth beneath his feet, the thousands of years of retreating glaciers and burgeoning plant life it had taken to make this snowy landscape with its mountains and lakes and tall green forests.

Yes, he thought, it puts my small anxieties in perspective . . . I suppose the Beothuk Indians who lived here, hunting and fishing, long before us, had their own small worries and tragedies, too . . . an arrow in the dark – a child lost in the woods – an attack by a bear – a loved companion gone . . .

His thoughts shied away from that, and then he said to himself: No. Face it. You faced it on the island and more or less came to terms with it. Why run away from it now? It should be no harder here, among these ancient rocks and forest trees and tumbling falls . . . Suzi is dead. You did your best to save her, but you couldn't. Just as she did with the child. It is a dreadful waste of young lives – but it is over. You can't put the clock back. And you've got to go on living. She would be the first to tell you that. And she would say: Stop skulking in the shadows, too. It won't bring me back.

He plodded on gamely, putting one heavy foot in front of the other, hoping that physical exhaustion would finally cancel out thought . . . and found himself lost in admiration of the scene around him. The tall stands of blue–green spruce and pine stretched ahead of him, rising in long swathes towards the higher ground of the central plateau and the mountains to the south, and stretching down to the shores of Red Indian Lake which glimmered in silver–blue flashes between their dark trunks on his left-hand as he walked.

But there were sudden openings in the thick forest where groves of birch and aspen gave a softened lightness to the landscape with

17

their winter filigree of delicate branches, and it was through one of these fronded clearings that Tom caught his first glimpse of a caribou herd. The animals were moving quietly among the trees, grazing on the lichens and dried grasses that pushed through the melting snow. One tall stag turned his head in Tom's direction, snuffing the wind and looking sculpturally handsome with his splendid antlers and alert, twitching ears. But he did not seem alarmed and merely moved on with his harem of wives behind him, and disappeared into the shadows of the trees.

Lovely, thought Tom. So poised and elegant – so unafraid and free . . . He wondered as he walked on whether he would meet a moose – there were plenty of them about, he knew – and whether he ought to be frightened if he did. Probably not, he thought, unless something has annoyed it first.

It was now late in the day and the sun was setting behind the trees. Tom had meant to circle round and walk back to the camp site and his own car for the night, but it suddenly seemed too far for his aching knee, so he decided to make his way back to the shores of the lake and make camp there. He was an old campaigner and had his sleeping bag and his small igloo tent in his pack. There was plenty of kindling for a fire, and it was the wrong time of year to worry about starting fires in the forest. He wouldn't be cold.

When he got to the edge of the lake, he caught his breath in wonder – for the whole surface of ice and water was flushed with flamingo pink from the setting sun. And there were birds – hundreds of them – on the open water in the centre of the lake. Not flamingos, of course, but geese – the white-faced barnacle geese, the Brents and Canadas – on their way back to their arctic breeding grounds for the summer. And the eider ducks, that Newfoundlanders like Sally called gammy-birds, were gabbling away in the reeds . . .

He watched them settling down for the night in the fading afterglow of sunset, and with the oncoming dark a curious feeling of mindless tranquillity seemed to descend on him. It was all right. There was no need for him to do anything. He could just sit here in the quiet night and watch the stars and the white moon climb the sky . . . The world out there need not encroach, need not disturb his hard-won peace, need not touch

18

him at all. If he stayed here long enough, it would probably cease to exist at all . . .

Dreaming, he stayed still, while the moon laid white fire on the snow, the sleeping lake, the pale trunks of the birches, and the dark silhouettes of the pines against a silver sky. But presently he became aware that the temperature had dropped sharply and he was very cold. He got up then and built a fire with dry cones and twigs, and when it had caught, piled it high with the flotsam of broken branches from the winter gales, dead spruce branches, hairy with moss – what they called blasty boughs and old man's whiskers. He was soon warm, and his old camper's billycan made him a strong cup of boiling coffee.

He didn't really want to creep into his tent and shut out that miraculous, shimmering night. It was too beautiful to miss – all that pure, unbroken light pouring down out of a flawless sky. So he stayed there, gazing and dreaming, until at last weariness overcame him and he very nearly fell forward into his own fire. At this, he finally gave in, but he still couldn't bring himself to turn his back on the silver night, so he merely crawled into his sleeping bag and lay down by his own fireside with the moon and the stars above him, and finally fell asleep.

In the morning he was woken by a cacophany of croaks, honks, "arks" and trumpetings from the geese on the lake, and when he opened his eyes he found himself looking at the moose he had wondered if he would be lucky enough to encounter. Several of the great, majestic creatures had come down to the lake to drink, smashing the thin ice at the edge with their powerful hooves. They were on the opposite side of the lake to him, and didn't seem to be in the least interested in him, if they saw him at all . . . He watched, spellbound, while they splashed about in the shallows and finally moved off again into the dark, secret aisles of the forest.

There was mist on the lake at this time of the morning, and it curled and drifted in cobweb wisps and swirls, half shrouding the farther shore, lit into sudden gleams and iridescent veils of light from the rising sun. Really, Tom reflected, it is just as magical by daylight as by moonlight, and just as mysterious . . . I don't know how I can be expected to get up and leave it!

But he got up, relit his fire, boiled more coffee, and neatly folded his sleeping bag and the little inflatable tent and stowed them inside his pack. He wouldn't go back to the car yet. He had still got plenty of coffee powder and a couple of rolls and some cheese, and the lake was probably teeming with fish. He would be sure to catch something with an improvised line and some bait . . . He had become quite expert at "ice-hole" fishing in winter, and rock fishing in spring and summer. This was a bit of both, he thought, for the ice was thin now and melting fast at the edge, and there were plenty of rocks to sit on . . . He would go on for another day and another night. It was so spacious out here, so silent and calm . . . even quieter than his own small island, for there you could never escape the sound of the sea. It followed you everywhere, calling and cajoling, so that you had to go back to it, however hard you tried to ignore it. But out here, in the wide, empty spaces of this pristine wilderness, the silence was almost tangible – and curiously reassuring.

Before the third day he knew, really, that this trip of his was by way of saying goodbye to his wilderness days. Somewhere or other, deep down, he had made up his mind to go back to the world he had rejected. The busy, teeming world with all its delusions and deceptions, its soulless disregard of human frailty, and the colossal loneliness of its inhabitants, struggling to meet its demands. Yes, loneliness, he thought. For out here where I am totally alone except for the wild geese and the caribou, I am not lonely. On my island of Little Reward, where there is nothing but rock and sea birds and seals, I am not lonely. But in London – in the world of work and ambition and fierce, unrelenting competition, I was always lonely. Bitterly lonely. Till Suzi came along. And then, for a time, my world was filled with perfect company, abrim with fulfilment. Until that last fatal journey . . . And after that, the loneliness of a big city was unendurable . . .

Here, he thought sadly, looking round him, there is peace in solitude. But there –? Have I really got to go back to that? I suppose I have . . . For he remembered then his sister's desperate voice crying: "*I don't know what to do!*" and he knew he must go back.

So, on his last morning, he looked at the tall spruce trees and snowy hillsides with loving eyes, and turned for one more glimpse of Red Indian Lake and its myriad birds flying up and settling, calling and crying, and the long shadows of the trees stretching like dark fingers across the ice-strewn surface – and then resolutely set his face towards the camp site and his old estate car, and the road back to the isles.

When he got back to Sally's house, it was too late to reach his own island that day, so he parked the car and went inside to use her telephone.

"So you're back," said Sally, and plonked some more batter in the frying pan for extra pancakes.

Tom grinned and went through to pick up the phone. There was no reply at all from Becky's number, and after some thought he tried Greg again. There was no reply there either, but after Sally had persuaded him to eat some supper, he tried again, and this time Greg answered.

"No, she's not there at the moment," he replied to Tom's worried enquiry. "She's gone north to try to see Derek."

"Is that a good idea?"

"I shouldn't think so. The lawyers were against it. But I think it's a last-ditch attempt to persuade him to come back."

"I suppose it's worth a try."

"Possibly. But she's very overwrought." Greg's dry, barrister's voice expressed unmistakable disquiet. "I'm afraid she may collapse altogether if this effort fails."

Tom, remembering the despair in Becky's voice when he last heard it, could understand this. "I'm coming home, Greg," he said, his mind made up. "I don't know if I can do any good, but I'll try."

"That's good news." Greg sounded suddenly closer, the warmth of approval in his voice.

"It'll take a few days to sort things out here," Tom explained. "But I'll be in touch as soon as I get back."

"Good. I'll wait to hear from you . . . It'll be great to see you," Greg said. "It's been too long." And Tom was surprised to hear genuine affection in Greg's voice.

He rang off then, full of determination to put his own small house in order and get home as soon as possible. *Second-hand*, he told himself, contemptuously. You're living life at second-hand. All these phone calls and faint promises. It's time you got back

21

to reality, Tom Denholm, and made yourself useful . . . But even as he thought it, another side of him longed to stay in his quiet, undemanding wilderness and never go home at all.

He shut his eyes, ashamed of his own weakness, and when he opened them again, found himself looking into Sally Maguire's shrewd, knowing gaze.

"You going, then?"

He sighed. "Looks like it."

She nodded. "Thought you would." Then she laid a consoling hand on his arm. "Got some coffee brewing. Dessay Ned and Danny'll help you pack up, if you need a hand."

"Thanks." Tom was suddenly aware of how much he was going to miss Sally and her bluff kindness. Nothing was ever said, but he knew that no one in Reward Cove would ever refuse help if it was needed.

Sighing, he turned away, finding no words to express his thoughts. In the morning, he remembered to fill the fuel tank on his little boat and take an extra can of gasoline with him in case of emergencies. It might take more than one trip to bring his stuff across. Not that he had many possessions, but there were the paintings. He supposed the best thing to do with those would be to give them to Sally to sell to the summer visitors.

He puttered back to the island and made his way up to the old lighthouse. Better make a start, he said, right now – and collected an armload of books and a couple of his smaller paintings that he thought maybe Becky would like, if she liked anything at present.

He was just starting down the path to the shore, when he heard Ollie calling. It didn't sound like his usual cheerful bark of welcome – it was somehow distressed and urgent, more like the cries the little seal had first uttered when he was abandoned by his mother. Puzzled, Tom stood looking this way and that, and then followed the cries across the rocks away from the path.

In a few moments he saw the seal below him, wedged immovably between one jagged rock and a pile of new-fallen boulders. He was struggling frantically to get free, but making no headway against his prison of stone, and each desperate heave of his supple body only brought more cascades of loose shale and rubble down on top of him.

It must have been the thaw, Tom thought. The ice melting must have loosened all that lethal heap of boulders and sent them crashing down on top of him. But why didn't he have the sense to move away in time? Perhaps he was dozing on the rocks and never saw it coming . . . He put down his pile of books and canvases and began to make his way cautiously down the slippery rocks towards the imprisoned seal.

"I'm coming, Ollie," he said. "Keep still. It'll be all right."

At the sound of his voice, the young seal stopped crying, and even stopped his desperate wriggling and waited quite patiently and confidently for Tom to set him free. It was a difficult job because as Tom moved one boulder, others tried to fall into the space, threatening to hurt the helpless animal still further. But at last he got the heaviest of the stones shifted sideways so that Ollie could move.

"Now!" said Tom, giving the seal's warm flank a swift push forward, and Ollie gave one convulsive heave and threw himself clear, slithering down the rocks between Tom's widely straddled legs.

But as the seal escaped, yet another cascade of heavy boulders shifted behind the pile of loose stones and fell in a roar of flying pebbles and lumps of sharp rock into the gap the seal had left. The impact made Tom's precarious position shift slightly. One foot slid sideways on the slippery surface, and as he teetered, trying to regain his balance, his smashed kneecap suddenly let him down and refused to take his weight. Unable to save himself, he fell over backwards and crashed heavily down on to the jagged rocks below. For a few seconds he continued to bounce and slide down the steep, rocky slope, the impetus of his fall dragging him on, until his helpless body came up hard against a sharp-edged boulder and he lay still.

He came to eventually with the curious impression that someone was persistently washing his face with a wet sponge. But when he opened his eyes he found himself looking up into Ollie's alert, questioning face, and the wet sponge was Ollie himself trying to lick some life into his inert, unconscious friend.

"Oh Ollie," he groaned. "What have you done to me!" But it wasn't Ollie's fault, he told himself. He should have been more careful of his balance. He knew that knee of his was dicey.

23

And anyway, wasn't the clever little creature doing his best to revive him? How could he be cross with him? "Thanks . . ." he murmured, slightly hazily. "Brought me round a treat."

Then he began, cautiously, to assess the damage. There was a sizeable lump on his head, and a cut that oozed a bit stickily, but nothing serious. One arm, his right one, seemed OK and could lever him up a bit. But when he moved, pain shot through him in so many places he didn't know which one to explore first. The other arm was underneath him with the shoulder somehow pushed out at an angle . . . Dislocated, I should think, he said to himself. Not a broken collarbone, though . . . Wants pushing back, but I can't do it by myself . . . He tried to feel down his legs. The good one seemed intact, but the bad knee had developed a fiery agony all its own.

Can't lie here, he told himself. Not all day. Too cold. And no one will come. They're not expecting me back at the outport at least till tomorrow . . . He considered the matter, feeling unexpectedly lucid and clear-headed for a moment or two.

Can't climb up that path again, he said. Not like this. The only answer is to slide *down*, and get myself into the boat . . . He tried to move again, and this time sharp knives seemed to attack his ribcage. Couple of ribs gone, I shouldn't wonder, he said. But I can still breathe.

At this point Ollie pushed his wet nose against Tom's face consolingly, and the flexible, sinuous body and clever flippers tried to nudge his two-legged friend upright to his normal position.

Tom groaned again and said: "Leave off, will you? I'll take my time, thank you."

He took his time. Yard by slow yard, he slithered and edged his way down over the rocks until he was lying, spent and breathless, on the flaking wooden planks of the ruined jetty. He peered over the edge and saw his little boat bobbing invitingly just below him. But how to get into it . . .? I've got one good leg, he told himself. What I want is a crutch – or a prop. Any long bit of wood would do . . . He felt along the rotten boards under him till his fingers found a broken spar lying across the edge of the broken platform. It was only vaguely attached to something – maybe the disintegrating wooden piles below the water line – and it came off quite easily when he wrenched at it with his good hand. He got the thing under

24

his arm and heaved himself to his feet, but he promptly fell over again, and all his aches and bruises hurt more than ever.

No good, he said. Not that way. The bad shoulder won't support it, and the good one is the wrong side! What now? Better *fall* in. If I can, without capsizing the boat.

He leant over to have another look at it, and then decided to take a chance and let himself fall slowly forward, rolling over the edge and somehow managing to land inside the wildly bobbing craft. Good thing I didn't miss it altogether, he thought. I'd probably have drowned. The thought amused him and he tried to laugh. But everything flared up again like angry fire, so he lay there until it all died down, and then thought about starting the motor.

Good thing I filled it up, he thought. And the can is still there if I run out. So long as I can keep my wits about me and steer straight.

Behind him he heard a splash and he saw that Ollie had dived in after him and was swimming enthusiastically round the boat. *That's better*, he was clearly saying. *If you can move about in the water with that boat thing, you'll be all right. The sea is much the safest place to be* . . .

But Tom was not so sure. He had no time to stop and look at the weather. He just had to take his chance and get back to the outport harbour as best he could . . . He started the engine, settled himself as comfortably as he could, half sitting, half lying next to the tiller, and steered for the mainland, praying he wouldn't pass out before he got there.

What a fool! he thought. So self-sufficient, so proud of my solitude and independence, and here I am, a helpless wreck at the first sign of trouble, and a perfect nuisance to everyone . . . Why did I ever think I could manage entirely on my own? And how can I tell them I was *rescuing a seal*!

But his thoughts would not stay on that dark pattern of self-reproach – they kept flying off at tangents, and he let them drift as he picked his way across the narrow strait between his island and the outport cove, between the melting chunks of ice and the huge bulk of the drifting icebergs beyond him in the open sea.

He didn't remember much more about that journey – only that the little motor kept on gamely chugging, the water kept

25

on sliding past his hull as he struggled to keep the tiller straight, and the various pains in his limbs seemed to become one deep, unremitting ache . . .

But he also had a vague impression that Ollie's inquisitive face kept appearing in the churning water, first on one side and then on the other, keeping him company until he got safely near the mainland shore.

Then there were shouts from the fishermen mending their nets on the jetty, and hands reaching out to help him just as a mighty wave of blackness descended on him and he sank into oblivion.

He woke to find himself all neatly tucked up in a white hospital bed. There was a bandage on his head, one arm was strapped to his side in a sort of sling, and his bad knee seemed to have something like a splint holding it straight, but otherwise he thought he was intact.

"How are you feeling?" said a voice, and a young and ridiculously pretty face leaned over to have a look at him.

"Confused," said Tom. "Dare I say 'where am I?'"

The young nurse laughed. "You're in Twillingate Hospital. And by all accounts you're lucky to have got here at all!" She straightened the bedclothes with a flick of her wrist, and added, "Lie still. Dr Grant will be round in a minute."

Tom did as he was told and dozed.

Presently a cheerful young doctor arrived (they all seem absurdly young, thought Tom. Does that mean I am getting old?) and cast an assessing eye over Tom's various bumps and bruises.

"Well?" Tom asked. "What's the damage?"

"Not too bad." The pleasant face was smiling. "We pushed your shoulder back. It's strapped for a day or two to give it time to settle, but it'll be all right." He was watching Tom with an alert, observant gaze, and did not fail to notice the slight catch of pain in Tom's breathing.

"Yes," he nodded. "A couple of cracked ribs – but they'll mend. We don't usually strap them these days. You'll just have to take it easy and not laugh too much!"

Tom grinned, but he didn't try to laugh at all.

"As for that knee . . ." went on the young doctor, "I don't think you've done any more damage than there was already, except some extra bruising." He paused then and added cautiously, "What happened there?"

"Blast," said Tom shortly.

There was a distinct gleam of humour in the young doctor's glance, but he forbore to ask for more details. "How long ago?"

"Oh . . . two years or so. Why?"

"There are things we can do, you know, these days. Replacements. Haven't they told you?"

"Yes . . ." Tom sounded reluctant to talk about it. "They wanted to give it time to heal first – and somehow I never went back."

"Well, you should." Grant spoke firmly. "When you get home, get someone to have another look."

"Yes," agreed Tom. "When I get home . . ."

Grant was smiling again. "I take it your departure is imminent? Your friend – Sally, is it? – was very fierce about it. 'Patch him up good,' she said, 'he's going home soon. Needs to be all in one piece.'"

"Did she now?" Tom found himself grinning again, albeit rather weakly. Then a thought occurred to him. "How exactly did I get here?"

"Search and Rescue helicopter. They run a service to all the islands. It's quicker than anything else."

Tom nodded. "Lucky for me."

"Lucky for everyone round Notre Dame Bay," said Grant.

"I didn't even know there was a hospital at Twillingate."

Grant laughed. "Yes, indeed. Very up-to-date and very useful. And we're very proud of it."

Tom smiled at his enthusiasm. "And I'm very grateful." Then he added, puzzled, "But if I came by chopper, how did Sally come into it?"

Grant's laughter grew. "Oh, she didn't *come*. She merely called from that post office of hers, insisted on speaking to me in person, and then gave me a right lecture!"

Tom forgot to be cautious and tried to laugh. "That sounds like her."

"Put the fear of God into me."

"She does to me, too," grinned Tom. Then he began to consider practicalities. "When will I be out of here?"

"Soon."

"How soon is soon?"

Grant's eyes were full of amusement. "A day or two. You had quite a bashing, you know – including a bang on the head." He pretended to look severe. "We always take concussion seriously."

"But I feel perfectly all right."

"Well, you don't look it," Grant told him, still smiling a little. "More like a rather battered pirate who has been in a scrap, at the moment." He patted Tom's good shoulder kindly. "We'll let them know as soon as you're fit to travel. By order of Sally Maguire."

Tom recklessly began to laugh again, and then wished he hadn't.

"Give yourself a chance," said Grant, hurrying off. "I can think of worse fates than being waited on hand and foot by Nurse Julie Brown."

"So can I," admitted Tom.

It was three days before they let him go, and then Ned came to fetch him. "It's post day," he explained. "Sally can leave the shop to someone else, but not the post."

Tom immediately felt guilty. He was causing these kind, hard-working people nothing but trouble. "What about the fishing?"

Ned grinned, and gave a cheerful shrug. "Not much doing anyway. Glad of an excuse for a day on the town."

But Ned didn't seem to want to linger in the town, and soon they were crossing the Main Tickle Causeway on the way home to the little outport and Tom's island. *On the way home*, Tom thought sadly, *and I'm going to leave it all behind me – this small place that I love, and go "home" to a noisy, busy world that I hate.*

But he shrugged it off (as much as he could shrug without wincing) and put down his gloom-ridden mood to "post-accident shock", hoping it was true. So instead of brooding about the future, he gazed around him as they crossed the causeways with the sea on either side, and marvelled at the changing colours of

28

the ice-strewn waters and the shimmering magnificence of the icebergs floating in the bay.

I didn't get all the colours right, he told himself. There is so much light in them – all those blues and greens and violets and purples, they are translucent as well, and the light is somehow *inside* the ice. How do you paint light? And he sighed to himself with the true artist's despair at the impossibility of ever reaching his goal.

"Smiling face now," said Ned, waving a dismissive hand at the calm seas and small sun-gilded islands and coves around the bay. "Come winter, can't cross at all, except by snowmobile, and that's dicey."

Tom nodded, picturing the darkening skies and wild storms of winter, the freezing fogs, and the huge Atlantic waves towering over the fragile causeways that linked all the islands. It must be terrifying to watch, cut off and marooned until the snows and ice melted or the seas abated.

He had often watched storms sweeping across the bay beyond his little hidden cove, and felt his own small shoreline shake under the pounding of the surf, or the annihilating blanket of fog creeping across the sea towards him, blotting out all landmarks, all contact with the farther shore . . . "It's a wild landscape," he said, almost to himself, "but I shall miss it." He sighed, and added in the same half-absent tone: "England is so – *full*."

Ned didn't see the need to respond to this, but concentrated on his driving. He knew it was going to be a wrench for Tom to leave his chosen way of life and the little island he had come to love. Ned was used to this land and the way it somehow wove itself into your very sinews, and how the sea that surrounded it tugged at your heartstrings and never let you go. After all, he was born and bred here, and he'd worked with the sea all his life. He couldn't imagine leaving it or going anywhere else.

But for Tom, now, it was different. He had found a place where he was peaceful, and had managed to settle down and fend for himself very well. But he didn't really belong here. However quietly he lived and however well he fitted in, he was a stranger in a strange land, and in the end he would have to go back where he belonged. That was how Ned saw it. There were old hurts that still troubled Tom, he knew – and not only that damaged knee, either.

29

He had clearly been running away from old memories. But Ned didn't think Tom was an *angishore*, which was what local people called someone weak and whining. No, Tom was a fighter, really, he felt sure. Look how he had managed to handle that boat when he was half passing out after his fall. He coped somehow in spite of his injuries. Ned respected that. He was sure Tom would get on top of things in England, too, when he got there.

"Won't be long now," he said, avoiding a pothole with a wrench of the wheel. "Hope you're not feeling all shook up?"

Tom grinned at his anxious face. "I'm fine. The old banger's still got a few springs." A thought struck him then, and he decided to make things clear to Ned while he had the chance. "I was thinking, if you could drive me down to Gander when I go, I can hop on to St John's from there and you could keep the car for good. I can't take it with me."

Ned went on driving calmly, but he was clearly pleased. "Won't say no. Comes in very handy – specially when the fish van's broke!"

"Might as well be used," agreed Tom.

Ned considered. "I ought to pay you some."

"No." Tom was quite definite. "What about my rent for the lighthouse?"

Ned laughed. "It's not mine, anyways. Don't know whose it is."

"But didn't summer visitors use it sometimes?"

Ned scratched his head. "I guess. Now and then. And a fisherman or two, up for the summer fishing . . . But it's too derelict for most."

"Well then. Didn't they pay you?"

"Sometimes." Ned's grin was mischievous. "Or gave me a fish."

"Which you didn't really need!"

"Sure," said Ned in his tranquil voice, "we could always use a salmon!"

They were both smiling as they came down the hill to their own little outport.

"Sally says you're to stay with us," Ned announced, as they arrived. "Till you're fit to manage on your own."

Tom was about to protest, but he suddenly realised that Sally

30

was right, as usual, and he would be even more of a nuisance if he insisted on being independent and something went wrong.

"All right," he agreed. "Just till I'm steadier on my pins. And don't you go giving me any more of that 'screech' – whatever it was – or I never will be!"

Ned's laughter rang out as he helped Tom out of the car, and at the sound Sally came through the shop door and stood with hands on hips in her familiar belligerent stance, looking them up and down with her fierce, observant gaze. "So there you are. Come on in. Coffee's up."

After giving him and Ned a hearty meal and time to get their breath back, Sally sat herself down squarely at the table and went into the attack.

"We didn't know what you wanted done with your things over there, so we let 'em be. And you're in no fit state to go sorting and carrying – or walking about on those rocks, either, come to that." She glared at him with mock ferocity. "I reckon it'll all keep for a day or two, won't it?"

Tom put down his coffee cup and sighed. He felt altogether helpless and stupid, sitting here, unable to cope with his own simple arrangements. "I suppose so – yes. But I ought to get moving soon. I promised Greg."

"As to that," Sally told him, "your friend Greg called again."

"Did he? When?"

"When you were at Twillingate."

Tom looked at her glumly. "And I suppose you told him what a fool I was."

"I told him you needed your head examined – yes!" she retorted. Then she relented and added with surprising mildness, "And I said we'd look after you till you were fit to travel, and let him know when you were coming. Any objections?"

"I – no," said Tom, ashamed of his tetchiness. "Of course not."

"See here, Tom," Sally tapped him on his good arm with an imperious finger, "it's no good pretending you can live your entire life without any help from anyone. No one can." The glare was back momentarily, but it seemed to be fading. "We all need each other, one way or another," she explained, as if talking to a favourite, rather dim-witted child. "Out here, where the going's tough, we soon learn to rely on each other – and have a bit of give and take." A curiously sweet smile touched her weather-worn face for a moment. "Besides, Tom Denholm, folks like to feel needed."

Tom was utterly counfounded by that shy, revealing smile. "Sally," he groaned, "you put me to shame!"

It was another three days before Sally would allow Tom to go over to the island and even then she sent her young nephew, Danny, with him to help with the fetching and carrying.

Danny was a cheerful boy with a freckled nose and an impish grin, and he handled Tom's boat with casual skill and seemed to treat the whole excursion like a Sunday School treat.

"What you gonna do about the *bedlamer*?" he asked, as they tied up at the broken jetty.

"The what?"

"The young seal – Ollie, d'you call 'im?"

Tom's eyes went wide. "D'you know about him?"

Danny laughed. "We all know about him. He pinches the fish off our lines sometimes!"

Tom looked embarrassed. "Is he a nuisance?"

The boy shook his head and laughed again. "Nope. We've taken quite a shine to 'im. Ma says he'll be a tourist attraction come the summer."

Tom was mightily relieved. He had been afraid to tell them about Ollie, knowing the outport people's long history of sealing and whaling. It had been their living for many generations, and they would most probably be astonished and not a little annoyed at anyone being sentimental enough to try to save one orphaned seal pup. In the old days it would have been a little extra meat and a valuable skin . . . But since the collapse of the fur trade and the whaling industry, and the growing tourist interest in conservation and wildlife, maybe now they saw things in a different light.

"Well, that's a weight off my mind!" he said happily. "What did you call him?"

"*Bedlamer* . . . a yearling seal . . . well, I guess he's nearly a year old, ain't he?"

"Just about," agreed Tom, surprised at the thought. Was it really almost a year since he had found the abandoned pup on the rocks? Then he must have been here himself almost two years . . . No wonder it felt so difficult to leave.

Suppressing a sigh (in case it made Danny look reproachful) he followed the boy's more nimble feet up the shaly path. His knee still hurt a lot to walk on and still felt stiff and awkward, but it didn't give way any more, and he was all right if he was careful. As for his ribs and the rest of his bruises, he knew they would take time and he must be patient.

But it was good to be back again – even for a little while – and he looked round at his tiny domain with loving recognition. Yes, it was hard to leave it.

However, there was work to do now, and together he and Danny brought down the books and paintings and his few personal possessions, and loaded them on the boat. He had arranged to give Sally the paintings, as planned, and she had agreed that she could probably sell them to the tourists and there was enough room to display most of them round the wooden walls of the shop. This seemed to him the most practical and sensible thing to do with them, and for some reason that he didn't quite understand, he had no desire to take any of them away from this place. This was where he had painted them, and this was where they belonged. So although stripping the old Lantern Room of its stacks of riotous colour made the ancient walls look cold and bare, he did not feel any particular sadness when he stowed his canvases in the boat. Only, at the last moment, he did leave two of them behind on the walls – one, a view from the top of the Lantern Room itself looking out to sea, and the other of the tall sea stacks with their summer clothing of living birds. You can stay there, he told them silently, and keep the old place company.

At last it was all done, and he took one more long look around the empty rooms of the derelict lighthouse, pulled the heavy door shut and locked it with its ancient rusty key, and turned away with suspiciously misted eyes.

"Look!" said Danny, who was far too bright to miss the regret in Tom's face. "There's your friend Ollie. I guess he's come to say goodbye."

Tom shook his head to clear the absurd mist from his eyes and looked down at the sea. And sure enough, there was Ollie swimming close to the shore among the black rocks, and turning and diving

33

in a graceful dispay of gymnastics in the blue–green depths of Tom's hidden cove. He came close to them as they stowed the last few things in the boat, and watched with inquisitive, melting eyes as Danny leapt into the boat and leaned upward to give Tom a hand.

But for a moment Tom hesitated and turned for one last look at the small enclosed world he had loved.

"Tide's turning," warned Danny. "Time to go."

Time to go. Yes, he is right, Tom thought. And I mustn't prolong things by lingering here like a – like a lovesick seal?

But Ollie wasn't lovesick. Not yet. Though his adult mating days were not far off, he supposed, and the young seal would soon be joining his other friends in the wide ocean. Just now, he was merely interested in what his two-legged friend was up to. It looked like a sort of departure to him, and he thought he'd better follow the boat and see where it went.

So Tom took Danny's proferred hand and climbed down into the boat, the little motor sputtered bravely, and they set course for the outport harbour and the busy world beyond.

And all the way across the ice-blue waters, Ollie followed his friend until he was safely landed on the mainland shore. Then the clever, whiskered seal face took one last look and disappeared into the deep waters of the Atlantic ocean.

Well, he's gone, thought Tom. Goodbye, Ollie. I hope you don't miss me. I shall miss you.

"We'll keep an eye out for 'im," said Danny cheerfully. "There's allus leftovers from the catch. He won't starve."

Tom grinned his thanks, and determinedly turned his back on the sea. But he wasn't allowed to be sad for long. A party had been arranged for his last night (even merrier than Millie's jig-night), and he found himself the centre of a dancing, stamping, singing crowd of well-wishers, who all plied him with screech and slapped him on the back (none too gently) and wished him *bon voyage*. They were used to partings in the outport; people were always coming and going, to sea or back from the sea, to mainland Canada, to the United States . . . always across the sea, and always coming back. Or nearly always.

"'Fair weather to you and snow to your heels', is what we say out here," said Ned, smiling. "And spring will be further on in

England." He was holding out a large conch shell in his hand as a parting gift, and he added softly: "You can allus hear the sea in her." To Ned this was the most important ingredient in a happy life, so of course he had to pass it on to Tom.

As for Tom, he was rapidly becoming incapable of answering, what with the fiery screech and the open affection of these lively friends of his.

Danny gave him a piece of blue stone which he said was Labradorite and had come from Tom's own beach. Someone else gave him a tiny boat carved out of whalebone, and one of the other fishermen produced a polished pebble shining with intricate soft colours that Tom immediately wanted to paint. Then one of Ned's crew from the fishing fleet gave him a hand-tied salmon fly and told him he'd never get better salmon fishing than here, so what was he going for? And yet another fisherman – the champion squid-jigger, no less – gave him a piece of moose horn carved in the shape of a puffin.

And last of all Sally came up to him, and everyone stopped singing and shouting for a moment because they all knew what she was going to say. She was holding in her hand a silver ring, curiously carved and winking dully in the light.

"This here," she said, addressing Tom in a slightly softened version of her usual brisk manner, "is what we call out here a two-hander." She paused, and then went on to explain in more detail, "A kinda friendship ring, d'you see? Hands across the sea, and all that." She held it out so that Tom could see the two clasped hands carved into the curving band of silver. "It's made of Newfoundland silver," she told him, "and if you think I'm propositioning you, Tom Denholm, I guess I'd like to, but Ned might have something to say about it."

There was a cheerful burst of laughter at this, but then Sally went on steadily with what she had to say. "It's not from me, anyways, Tom, but from all of us here, hoping you'll remember us, especially when the wicked old world out there seems a terrible place to be."

Why, she knows! thought Tom, amazed. Bluff, no-nonsense Sally knows all about me, and why I came here, and why I'm so reluctant to go back! How could I ever have thought these people were too naïve and simple to understand? They know it all!

Smiling, he held out his hand to Sally. "Put it on for me. Of course I'll remember you – all of you – always. Let's drink to it."

So the ring was pushed on to his finger, and everyone cheered and clapped, and the fiery screech went round again, and Tom lifted his glass and said: "Hands across the sea!" and everyone yelled and clapped even louder, and the fiddle and accordian hastily started up again before everyone got even more sentimental.

At some time in the evening, when the fiddler's fingers got tired, the young ones got together and put on a tape of the latest dance craze from New York and the room was filled with a different kind of sound, and differently gyrating bodies, while Tom and the older ones sat down and rested their feet and ate steaming clam chowder from someone's kitchen. The dancing went on very late, one way and another, but all good parties must come to an end, and at last Tom was weaving his way home (again) between the comfortable, steering arms of Ned and Sally, and the moon was low in the sky.

"Look!" said Sally softly. "The northern lights . . . You don't often see them so clear."

Tom gazed in awe at the pulsing colours reaching out in fingers of glowing brightness from the northern horizon. It was somehow the final seal of magic on this night of strange comradeship and parting.

"I've never seen them before," he breathed.

"They'll still be here when you come back." Sally's voice was warm and half filled with laughter. "And so will we – if you don't leave it too long!"

And before he could answer, she and Ned had slipped into the house through the white wicket gate, and left him to make his last farewells alone.

For a long time he stood there, gazing out to sea at those flickering lights in the sky, and if he fancied he saw a small dark head bobbing out in the swell, he could not be sure he was wrong.

But at last those beckoning mirage-fingers of light began to fade, the stars grew pale in the sky, and he turned his back on the mystical night and went back to reality.

Part Two

The Mainland

Heathrow was the usual nightmare, but to Tom it seemed quite terrifying. He had forgotten the crowds, all pushing and shoving in tight, impatient knots, one way or the other, the noisy tannoy, and the perpetual feeling of rush and collective anxiety. Everyone seemed to be in a hurry, in a rage about something, or seized with a fearful terror of being left behind, or simply lost. No one seemed disposed to talk to anyone else, or to offer help or advice. They were all bent on their own pursuits, all heedless of other people's problems, all focused on their own fragile, easily upset arrangements, their frantic attempts to get from one place to another in the shortest possible time. They looked at him (or through him) with blank eyes that saw nothing, and they seemed to spin faster and faster in gyrating circles like an accelerating top.

Talk about Gadarene swine, Tom thought, viewing the whole frenetic scene with a jaundiced eye. All rushing headlong to destruction . . . Is this what I have come home to?

He was filled then with an awful reluctance to go any further. He wanted to turn round and take the next plane back to where he had come from . . . to turn round and run.

"Tom!" called a voice. "Over here!" And he looked up, his eyes clearing from their moment of panic and saw the familiar face of his old friend, Greg Selwyn, smiling at him over the heads of the crowd.

Greg was a tall man, distinguished in his understated, barrister-smooth way, and that well-shaped, faintly greying head stood out against the throng of milling people round the arrival gate, mostly because it was calm and unmoving.

Tom smiled back, feeling his own terror subside at the sight of that formidable head, and made his way across to his friend's outstretched hand.

"God, am I glad to see you!" he said, and was surprised when Greg laid his other arm round Tom's shoulders and gave him a brief, hard hug.

"That makes two of us," Greg said. "Come on, I've got a car waiting."

Tom acquiesced gratefully and followed Greg out of the airport building. It had suddenly dawned on him that now he was home, full of good resolutions about being useful, he hadn't the faintest idea where he was going.

"I think you'd better stay with us," Greg told him, negotiating the departing traffic, "until you get things sorted out. Marian's expecting you."

"Oh." Tom was a bit uncertain about this. "That's very good of you," he added, in case he sounded churlish.

"Or had you other plans?" Greg changed gear and dodged an aggressive taxi.

"N–no. Except I wondered if I ought to see Becky straight away?"

Greg was silent for a moment, still edging his way through the maze of airport traffic, and then said in a carefully guarded voice: "Tom, things have been happening since we spoke last. That's why I tried to ring you again at Reward Cove."

"Yes?"

Once more Greg seemed to hesitate. "Only, when I heard about your own accident, I thought it had better keep till you got home."

"My *own* accident?" said Tom, with misgiving. "What's happened?"

"Becky took an overdose."

"Oh, my God. Is she all right?"

"She will be. But it was touch and go for a while."

Tom looked at him, appalled. "I should have come sooner."

"I doubt if you could have prevented it." Greg's voice was weary.

"Where is she?"

"She *was* in the local hospital in Leeds."

"Leeds? What was she doing up there?"

"I told you, she'd gone north to try to confront Derek. I don't know what happened but it was clearly a disaster. She went back to her hotel, ordered a bottle of vodka from the bar and took every pill she could lay her hands on, including her tranquillisers."

Tom shook his head in disbelief. "Appalling . . . Who found her?"

"The hall porter." He glanced at Tom, almost apologetically. "As a matter of fact, I was responsible. I knew she was having this difficult interview and I was worried about her. So I rang her, rather late, in her hotel room. When I couldn't get any reply, I got the hall porter to open her door with a pass key. They got her to hospital just in time."

Tom gave a long whistle of relief. "Thank God you rang her when you did." He shot Greg a fleeting smile. "And then what happened?"

Greg's mouth got a little sterner. "They found Derek's address on her, so they got him round to see her. I gather he stayed to make sure she was out of danger and then went back to his girlfriend."

"Could he be that callous?"

Greg shrugged eloquent shoulders. "I expect he was trying to play it down as much as possible. I don't suppose he wanted a scandal or a tragedy any more than the hotel did."

"But she meant it to be final? It wasn't just a –?"

"Bid for attention? No. She meant it all right." Greg's voice was grim. "She was in a coma for several days, I believe."

"The poor girl," groaned Tom. And then, ashamed of his own failure to grasp the situation, he added, "I didn't realise she was that desperate."

"We none of us did," said Greg, kindly letting Tom off the hook. "I made the mistake of thinking her hysteria was just hot air . . . But I'm afraid it goes much deeper than that."

Tom nodded, privately resolving that he would not make such a mistake again. "You said she *was* in Leeds. Where is she now?"

"In a private hospital in the countryside near York." He glanced a shade warily at Tom, not sure of his reaction. "She asked to go there herself, Tom, and the Leeds General Hospital recommended it. She was still very distraught and she recognised

the fact that she wasn't entirely rational and needed treatment."
He paused again, swinging the car off the slip road on to the
motorway, and then tried to reassure Tom. "It's a good place
– very high reputation. Small house units set in green lawns,
very spacious and peaceful. Not a bit institutionalised. And the
specialists are first-rate."

"Did you talk to them?"

"Only briefly, when Marian and I took Becky there. I told them
you were coming and they were content to wait."

"But she'll be all right?"

"Oh yes. They seemed fairly confident of that. But they did
say that these anxiety neuroses are very deep-seated and hard to
dislodge. She needs a lot of time."

Tom was silent for a moment, trying to take in everything Greg
had told him. "I'd better go and see her right away."

"Yes. Tomorrow, Tom. You'll need a night's sleep first."

Tom sighed. "I feel pretty useless."

"You'll have plenty of time to be useful, believe me. There's a
long haul coming."

Tom realised that, and wondered what would be the best way
to put his sister's broken life together again, and how he could
cure her desperate hurt. He fell to remembering again how she
had been as a child – brave and adventurous and not at all afraid
of life. How had she come to this?

"How old is Becky exactly?" asked Greg, negotiating a round-
about on the slip road to his own part of London.

Tom considered. He was rather horrified to think they had
drifted so far apart and he had been away so long that he had
almost forgotten birthdays and how time passes . . . "She must
be forty-four. A year younger than me."

Greg sighed. "That's absurdly young to write herself off as
finished."

Tom agreed. He was still thinking it out. "That would make Kit
twenty-three, as you said, and Jenny would be just twenty-one."
He paused a moment, and then added with some bitterness: "She
married Derek very young."

"And chased round the world making homes for him for more
than twenty years." Greg's voice was very dry.

"Exactly."

40

"It's so unfair," said Greg, trying in vain to sound suitably neutral. "If the man must have a mid-life crisis, I don't see why it has to be so permanent."

"Nor do I," agreed Tom, not trying to sound neutral at all. He would gladly have strangled his brother-in-law at that moment. "Perhaps the girl wouldn't settle for anything less!"

Greg grunted at this, and a dark glance of wry amusement passed between them. Then he seemed to decide it was time to be practical. "Here we are," he announced, pulling up in front of a tall terrace house in a pleasant London square. He laid a kind hand on Tom's arm. "I'm sorry to drop you right in it the minute you arrive."

"It's got to be faced," said Tom, giving him a lopsided grin.

"At least you can relax for this evening. Marian's got a meal laid on, I know, though I daresay you could do with a stiff drink first!"

Talking gently, he led Tom up the steps and in through his elegant front door.

During dinner they discussed immediate plans, and Marian volunteered: "I'll drive you up to Yorkshire, if you like."

Tom looked at her in smiling astonishment. "All that way? What's wrong with the train?"

Marian glanced warily at Greg. "Nothing. It's just that – you don't look too fit yet for dashing about all over the place."

"I'm fine," said Tom. "You mustn't spoil me!"

In truth, Marian liked spoiling people. It was what she was good at. She and Greg had married fairly late and had no children, but she kept a good table and a shining house, and ordered Greg's busy life as smoothly as possible, as well as being on various useful committees herself. She was a tallish, competent woman, with the kind of unremarkable looks that were pleasantly reassuring, like her impeccably understated clothes; but she was, in fact, extremely intelligent – Greg would never have tolerated anything else – and could hold her own in any argument about knotty points of law that might be bothering her distinguished husband. But behind all this, there was an innate good nature and kindness about Marian which made her a very good wife and a very good friend.

41

"I shall have to find somewhere to live," Tom said, pursuing his own anxious thoughts. "Or, I suppose I could go to Becky's house?"

"You could, but you wouldn't like it," Greg told him.

"Why not?"

"It's one of those modern pseudo-folksy leaded-window jobs, in a highly desirable up-market garden suburb. All neat, separate houses and gardens, and no one speaks to anyone; or even knows who anyone else is."

Tom shuddered. "Doesn't Becky have any friends down there?"

"Not really." It was Marian who answered. "She has never had time to settle in one place for long enough. It was always Dubai or South Africa, or Kuwait or California . . . I believe she did have a few good friends out there."

Tom sighed. "It's a pity she can't settle out there, really."

"It's the money," Greg explained. "An apartment in a condominium is fine if you have the income to live in it – and the English house isn't easy to sell just now . . . And then there's the health problem. I think she feels safer with the NHS to fall back on."

"You must be joking!" murmured Marian.

"But she's paying for private treatment at the moment, isn't she?" Tom pointed out.

"Yes. But not for much longer. She tells me her BUPA insurance runs out soon, and Derek won't renew it for her. It's up to her now – that's part of the problem."

Tom nodded. He saw very clearly how it was. He also saw how blessedly cut off from all these tangles of finance and property and possessions he had been in his quiet retreat – and how lucky he had been to be free of them. And as he thought this, a great wave of longing came over him for his little lonely cove and the endlessly moving sea, and the small black head of a bobbing seal . . .

"What are you going to do now, Tom?" asked Greg, getting down to the most important question. "Apart from dealing with Becky, I mean?"

Tom looked doubtful. "I don't know . . . I resigned from the advertising agency after – after all that mess, and I swore I'd never go back . . . But –" He sighed, and then added: "I don't suppose it's that easy to rejoin the rat race, anyway."

"Can you afford to just paint?"

He hesitated. "On my own, yes. I was perfectly happy, with no overheads and no possessions at all . . . Life becomes very simple. Suited me down to the ground. But now, with Becky to consider, I don't know . . ."

"Are your parents still alive?" asked Marian suddenly.

Tom looked surprised. "No, I'm afraid not. We lived on a ranch in Argentina, you know, when we were children. Plenty of space and lots of riding for Becky . . . It was an ideal existence. I'm afraid we were rather spoilt. But of course we both of us came to England eventually to be educated." He made a slight grimace of distaste at the thought. "We hated every minute of it . . . And the parents stayed out there and had us back for the holidays . . ." He sighed a little. "But after my mother died, my father took off and went to live on a mountain in the Andes, and one day he fell off. He was a bit of a recluse by then – liked empty spaces . . . I must take after him." He saw Marian's faintly disappointed expression and said: "Why do you ask?"

"Oh, I just thought . . . it would have been nice for Becky to have some family to talk to . . . especially a woman." She sighed. "She's so rootless."

Tom agreed sadly. "I know. That's part of the trouble, isn't it?"

They were all silent for a few moments, considering the next move, and then Greg said firmly: "That's enough worrying for one night. It will all keep till you come back. We can talk again when you've seen Becky." He got up then and grasped Tom's arm, leading him from the table towards the warm, fire-lit sitting room. "You must be dropping with fatigue. What about a brandy and an early night?"

"Thanks," said Tom. "I don't mind if I do."

The taxi put him down by the first of the modern-looking house units that dotted the hospital grounds. Tom got out and stood looking about him. Greg was right – there were green lawns all round him, and the general appearance of the complex was one of space and tranquillity. There were tennis courts in the distance and what looked like a miniature golf course, and on a nearby slope of gently curving turf, there was a small, open-sided coffee house where several of the convalescent patients were sitting in the spring sunshine.

Well, she couldn't be frightened or unhappy here, thought Tom, could she? It doesn't look like an institution. Then, sighing, he went in search of Becky's whereabouts.

He found her lying listlessly on her bed, looking fragile and unexpectedly young. Becky was still slim and auburn-haired, though there were flecks of silver in the red–gold hair now, and she still had the long-limbed, slightly coltish grace of the girl he used to know. But at this moment she looked heartbreakingly vulnerable, and somehow quenched by all the events that had overtaken her.

"Becky?" he said gently. "Oh, my dear girl, what's been happening to you?" and he folded her in his arms and held her close, while great tremors of grief and despair shook her thin body.

"I'm sorry," she kept saying. "I'm sorry, Tom, so sorry . . . But I did want to die."

"But you've got everything to live for," he told her, still keeping his arms round her. "You're still young, Becky. Young and pretty – and healthy, when you give yourself a chance, with a whole life to live . . ."

But she shook her head helplessly. "What life? . . . Where? The family has gone, and Derek has gone. I don't know where I belong any more."

"You belong with me," said Tom, consciously giving away his freedom. "It's going to be all right."

"But I won't have enough to live on, unless I sell the London house . . . and then I'll have nowhere to live . . ." Her voice began to rise into a wail.

"Becky," he said firmly, "you'll have *plenty* to live on – more than most people, however mean Derek is. And we can rent a flat together, or anything we like. It'll all work out, you'll see . . ."

For a long time he talked to her, and coaxed her and cajoled her into thinking ahead to some sort of future – but he felt that he did not really succeed in convincing her. She seemed to listen to what he was saying, but as soon as he paused for breath, another spate of anxieties and objections spilled out, and though she tried hard to pay attention to his arguments, her concentration kept slipping and her eyes seemed to dart to and fro with a kind of restless disquiet which he could not dispel.

"But the house . . ." she said. "The money . . . The divorce proceeding . . . And then there's the furniture . . . And there's Jenny in the States – how will I ever see her? And Kit – he's not really self-supporting yet, and I don't even know where he's gone . . ."

Finally, Tom persuaded her to leave her room for a little while and go over to the small coffee house and sit outside on the lawn in the sun.

For a time she seemed quite normal and reasonable, and sat sipping her coffee while Tom told her about his life on Little Reward and his friendship with Ollie the seal. But all of a sudden she began to cry, and the tears poured down her face in a piteous stream. "He doesn't want me," she said. "No one wants me . . . D'you know, he said I never –" she gulped, "never held his hand in public, or kissed him in front of everyone and told him I loved him, like Moyra does . . ." She looked at him bleakly. "How could I, Tom? After twenty-five years of marriage? It's . . . absurd."

Tom privately agreed, and thought how clever Moyra was at catching her man, and how incredibly insensitive Derek was to tell Becky all this.

"D'you know," Becky went on, in a suddenly bright voice: "She actually came to see me in hospital." She began to laugh hysterically. "I'm afraid I threw a vase of flowers at her."

"I don't blame you," growled Tom, his mouth twitching with faint mischief.

But Becky couldn't stand any more. She suddenly clutched Tom's arm and whispered: "Take me back inside, Tom . . . I can't bear it out here."

So he took her back to her room, where she lay down again on her bed and turned her wet face to the wall.

"I should leave her now," said the duty nurse, when he asked her what to do. "She still gets very tired. Tell her you'll come again tomorrow. She'll be all right then." She looked at Tom with kindly concern. "And maybe you could see Dr Bradley tomorrow – if that would put your mind at rest?"

"Yes," agreed Tom. "It would."

*   *   *

45

Tom spent a restless night in a rather airless hotel bedroom, his mind not at rest at all. He kept wondering how he was going to get through to Becky, how to get past her immediate neuroses and find the warm-hearted, rational, courageous girl he used to know. She was still there, somewhere, he knew, and occasional glimpses of her came through from time to time in a rare, sweet smile or a chance remark of sudden self-awareness – but for the most part her real personality seemed swamped by the enormous weight of her own anxieties . . . How to dispel them? What could he say to her? The whole fabric of her life had been destroyed by Derek's actions. He had dumped her without a backward glance, as far as Tom could understand it, and how did you put hope for a future or belief in human loyalty back into someone's empty days after that?

He tossed and turned, opened the window for some air, and finally fell into a fitful doze where he dreamed vividly of Sally Maguire's tough, uncompromising voice saying: "*We all need each other, one way or another.*" Yes, he thought, we do. I can't deny it any longer . . . He sank into deeper sleep then, and woke to a bright morning and the sound of birdsong.

Birdsong? He had forgotten it was an English spring he had come home to. I'd better go out and look at it, he thought, while I've got the chance. I'm not due at Becky's till the afternoon.

So he strolled out into the streets of York, where even amidst the morning traffic the scents of spring assailed him. There were cherry trees in blossom, tubs of bright polyanthus in doorways and window boxes, and crocuses in the park – and a thrush was singing, loud and clear, above his head.

He went first, dutifully, to the Minster, because he knew he ought to see it, and stood for a while marvelling at the soaring arches and shadowy echoing spaces, and the way the whole airy structure took his eyes and his soul upwards. He said a halting, uncertain prayer for Becky to that unseen Presence who might or might not be there behind the slanting shafts of light. Please make her well again. She's still young. She's got a whole life left to live . . . You can't mean her to be finished yet . . .? There was no answer, of course, but Tom's spirit somehow lifted a little, especially when he looked at the amazing colours of the rose window with the sun behind it.

But then, all at once, the enclosed space seemed to press on him, and he went out again into the open air, through the narrow medieval alley of the Shambles. The North York Moors, he said to himself, catching sight of a bright tourist poster on a notice board. That's what I need – airy space and room to breathe. I'll go and look at some moors. But can I get that far this morning? I've got to get back to Becky in the afternoon . . . He found that he was standing beside a window full of more bright posters of local tours and events, and went into the little office to enquire.

"Why not take the tour bus to Rievaulx Abbey?" suggested the smiling girl behind the counter. "The moors really begin there. It's quite quick – only half an hour or so, and you can always get a later one back."

Tom thanked her and was soon on board a smooth tours bus, running through the green and gold fertile vale of York towards the high moors beyond Hemsley and Sutton Banks.

He got off with the rest of the tourists and decided to look at Rievaulx Abbey first, following along the tumbling water and glistening pebbles of the little river Rye and the newly greening belt of trees till the road turned the corner and he saw the incredible rising arches of Rievaulx's famous Choir. He hadn't expected it to be so magnificent and heart-lifting in its ruined splendour, but something about those dauntless arches and flying buttresses, still standing unshaken under the spring sky, caught his imagination, and he found himself almost too enchanted to leave.

But the hills enclosing the ancient Abbey stones in their sheltering embrace were beckoning to him, and eventually he turned away from all that brave glory and began to climb up the winding track to the wide, peat-scented spaces of the rolling moors beyond.

This is more like it, he said, gazing round at the ever-widening curves of moorland stretching to the horizon, the racing cloud shadows on their pale flanks, and the huge empty skies above. A faint grin of rueful memory touched his mouth as he took in these limitless unspoilt spaces. To think I told Ned Maguire England was too full! he said. What a fool I am. And he walked on happily across the springy turf. This would be wonderful country to paint, he thought. I could stay here and gaze and gaze and paint and paint. Everywhere I look there is a new, enormous vista, and a new set of fantastic colours . . . Enthralled, he wandered on.

But towards midday he began to worry slightly about getting back to civilization, and turned to look down and check where the main road might be. He caught a glimpse of it winding up a distant hill, and thought if he took a slanting path downwards, he would probably meet it in the valley below. There were a lot of sheep on the hills, dotted about in peaceful white clumps, and there were many twisting sheep tracks among the stones and streams and heathery slopes of the moors. He took one likely looking one and plunged downhill. The cloud shadows still raced before him, and a lark shot up almost at his feet and climbed, singing, into the blue air above his head. He had a sudden sense of extraordinary exhilaration, as if the world had turned on its axis to somewhere new and strange . . . There was a spice of magic in the air, and he wanted to run and climb, and sing like the soaring bird.

He came down the last few yards of the steep track to the road, and found himself looking down at a lopsided, stranded lorry, and a furious girl kicking one of its wheels.

"Can I help?" he asked, going across to the angry girl.

"Not unless you're Atlas," she said. "The jack keeps slipping – and the wheel nuts are welded solid."

Tom laughed. "Maybe we could wedge it with stones."

The girl pushed the tawny–gold ruff of hair out of her eyes and glared, looking rather like a belligerent lion cub. She was, Tom observed, not only cross but out of breath, as though she had been pushing and shoving at the offending lorry for some time. And, despite the glare, her clear grey eyes were somehow laced with laughter, and totally undismayed by adversity. This girl was used to trouble – and used to getting round it somehow.

"I'm sure we can manage together," he said, and for some reason his words echoed and made rings on the air, like pebbles dropped in a pond.

The girl looked at him hard for a moment and then said: "OK. We'll try."

Tom surveyed the collapsed tyre and the obstinate wheel nuts for a moment in silence. Then he suggested: "Stand on the wheelbrace and jump. I think it'll stay upright!"

She jumped several times, the unruly tongues of hair bouncing in sunny glints round her face, and finally the first of the wheel nuts gave a little.

"Now the others," praised Tom. "You're doing fine."

Once more she brushed the hair out of her eyes with a dust-streaked hand and gave him a fleeting grin. "Yes, sir."

"I'd do it myself," explained Tom, "only I might bring the whole thing over on top of us."

She nodded and went back to her furious jumping. Before very long, the rest of the wheel nuts were loose enough to move, and they could begin to prop the lorry up somehow, in spite of the slipping jack.

"Good," said Tom approvingly. "Now for the stones."

Together they carted stones and piled them under the lorry's sagging chassis, lifting it bit by painful bit with the faulty jack and the combined strength of their two straining backs. At last the wheel was nearly off the ground, and Tom said breathlessly, "Only a couple more and we'll be all right."

And after one more heave and a couple of extra stones, they were – and then in no time at all, it seemed, the wheel was changed.

"Well, thanks," said the girl, wiping her hands on a grubby cloth. "I don't know what I'd have done without you."

Tom looked into those grey, dauntless eyes and said, "You'd have done it somehow, I've no doubt."

She laughed, and held out a friendly hand. "I'm Daisy. Mostly known as Crazy Daisy. Can I give you a lift anywhere?"

"Tom," he said, grasping her hand. "I was aiming at getting back to York."

"Going that way myself," said Daisy. "Got a few calls to make on the way, though. You in a hurry?"

Tom hesitated. But the chance was too good to miss. "No. Not till after lunch."

"Hop in, then. One good turn deserves another." She climbed up into the driver's cab and Tom climbed in beside her. "I'll kill that rotten so-and-so," she muttered, starting up the engine.

"Who?"

"Ted Wilkes – owner of the lorry. Lent it me for the collection; all smiles, perfect working order, so generous!" She slammed in the gear and set off up the hill with an angry lurch.

"Don't take it out on the lorry," protested Tom, smiling. "It might bite back."

Daisy laughed again. "It already did." Then she relaxed and allowed the lorry to settle down to a steady run.

"What collection?" asked Tom, intrigued.

She shot him a brief, assessing glance. "Relief Aid. We take out lorry loads from time to time."

"Where to?"

"Oh . . . Bosnia . . . Somalia . . . Rwanda . . . Wherever the need is most urgent. Mostly Bosnia this year."

"Not in this thing, I hope."

"No fear." She grinned at him cheerfully. "This is only for local fetching and carrying from the collection points. But it's even fallen down on that!" She laughed. (Misfortune seemed to make her laugh, Tom reflected.) "Honestly! I've changed wheels on everything from ten-ton Tessies to Jeeps, and this pathetic wreck can't even stay up long enough to fetch a tin of corned beef!"

"Do you get a lot of stuff handed in?"

"Oh yes. People are very good. They do what they can."

"Not as much as you," murmured Tom, remembering far too well those long, dangerous roads through mountains and snow and clogging mud, and endless checkpoints and sniper fire – or shells . . .

"Oh well, I'm footloose and fancy-free," smiled Daisy. "What have I got to lose?"

Your life, thought Tom sadly. But he did not tell her so.

They stopped at various farms on the way, where boxes of donated goods had been stored in conveniently empty barns, and Tom helped Daisy stow them in the back of the lorry.

"That's the lot, I think," she said after the last stop. But instead of driving back on to the main road, she continued on past the farm until she came to a small village square and an inviting-looking pub called The Woolpack. "I don't know about you," she said, "but I'm starving. Let's pick up a ploughman's."

So they pulled up in the square, and Tom ordered two ploughman's lunches and bought Daisy a cider.

"Only a half, mind. I'm driving that plaguey thing. And the local brew is lethal."

Tom glanced at her laughing face, and thought strangely: I

know this girl . . . Somehow, even the planes of her face and the freckles on her nose seem familiar . . . She's not exactly pretty, but there's something extraordinarily compelling about her, I suppose it's the mixture of impish good humour and strong reliability. I could trust that face . . . In fact, I already do . . . she reminds me of a younger version of Sally Maguire.

"Sit down," said Daisy, "and stop analysing me. Tell me why you were walking way beyond your capacity on that gammy knee. What did you do to it, anyway?"

"I –" Tom actually blushed. "I – er – damaged it."

"I can see that," retorted Daisy. She was looking at him shrewdly. "Hazards of war?"

He stared. "How did you know?"

She shrugged fluid shoulders. "Dunno. You get to recognise it." She was still looking at him, and suddenly leant forward so that her eyes looked clearly into his. "I think I know you, anyway, don't I? Weren't you mixed up in that mercy dash that went wrong? Tom Denholm and his intrepid partner, cameras rolling, bullets whirring."

"*Don't!*" said Tom sharply.

She paused then, and something gentle and compassionate came into her face. "I remember all the fuss . . . Someone got killed, didn't they? And you got shot up trying to get them out."

Tom cleared his throat. "It wasn't quite like that."

"How was it, then?" She seemed in some deliberate way to be forcing him to talk about it.

He sighed. "It's a long story, Daisy . . . and not a very nice one."

"I'm listening," she said.

Tom shook his head slowly. "I don't know quite where to begin . . . I was a commercial artist then, working for a big agency, making far too much money doing far too little . . ."

"That's the way of big business," agreed Daisy.

"One of our clients was a firm of pharmaceuticals who wanted to up their image. So they hit on the plan of sending supplies to a Bosnian hospital and bringing out a couple of casualties . . . All that media hype stuff."

Daisy made a kind of growling noise into her cider.

51

"They weren't really that concerned with Bosnia," Tom said bitterly. "Or with the safety of the team. Only with their own benign image . . . so they sent one of their own staff – the youngest and prettiest they could find – to join me on the trip. I was supposed to do the talking and help get things through, and to observe what went on and then illustrate it for their next advertising campaign . . . The company with a heart of gold stuff . . . and Suzi was supposed to hand over the goods, smiling, and receive the casualties, still smiling."

Daisy looked at him in disbelief. "Hadn't they any idea what it was like out there?"

"Not much. You've no idea how cut off from reality you can be in a glass-and-chrome high-rise office block in central London."

Daisy made a face. "I can imagine." She looked at him with sympathy, and when he failed to continue, prompted him gently. "So?"

"So they gave us a small back-up team and a spare driver – but no real instructions, and no official backing, of course. The kind of one-off venture that the UN most dislike."

"Yes," agreed Daisy grimly. "They do!"

"I knew Suzi anyway," Tom said, sounding curiously driven now. "Back in London, I mean . . . we met through work, and sort of went on from there." He took a gulp of his own beer and tried to go on calmly. "I tried to persuade her not to go. But she was young and keen on her job, and – and idealistic, too. She'd no idea what it was all about . . ."

He stalled there for a moment, and Daisy pushed him again, still gently. "So what happened?"

"Suzi was new to it, you see." He seemed to be making excuses for her, even in his own mind. "But no one had the right to be foolhardy in that dangerous war zone . . . She didn't obey the rules."

"And –?"

"They were shelling the square, off and on. But a child saw us coming and ran out. I suppose it was desperate for food or something – they are usually so disciplined about staying indoors when the shelling gets bad."

Daisy nodded. "So – he ran out?"

"And Suzi ran after it. She knew she shouldn't, but she did.

52

How could you blame her?" He paused and shut his eyes for a moment, seeing the littered square, the broken buildings, the fire and smoke, the rubble all round them, and the child lying on the stony ground . . .

"The next shell hit them both," he said, "just as I was running out to them – breaking the rules as well . . ." He could not say any more just then, but Daisy picked up his drink for him and put it in his hand. "It was so *stupid*," he muttered. "She couldn't save the child. And I couldn't save her."

Daisy's face was still softened and gentle; so was her voice. "More than just a colleague, was she?"

He nodded. "I – we were pretty close, yes. But she was very young still, and quite ambitious, really . . . we were thinking of getting married in the summer." He paused, and then burst out angrily: "They never should have sent anyone out there so young. It was such a waste." His voice faltered then, but he controlled it.

"I don't know," said Daisy stoutly. "I can't think of a better way to die."

He looked at her in astonishment.

"Trying to save a child." She spelt it out for him. "I mean, you've got to do *something*."

Tom was silent. But he understood a lot more about what kind of a person Daisy was. And he felt ashamed, all over again, that he had allowed his own sense of grief and loss to make him turn his back on all that high endeavour.

But Daisy was smiling at him now with sudden extra warmth; and their lunches had arrived.

"I don't know why I'm telling you all this," he said lamely.

She laughed. "Because I asked you to." She pushed the plate of bread and cheese towards him cheerfully. "Come on, eat up. What's done is done. And there's plenty more to do yet!"

Tom felt an extraordinary sense of relief. She understood him. She did not blame him. And she had the good sense to hold out an immediate lifeline. *There's plenty more to do yet.*

"Cloud shadows," she said obscurely, with her mouth full.

"What?"

"I live on these hills – when I'm home. My Dad's a sheep farmer." She waved a hand at the sunlit moors outside the pub windows. "Cloud shadows come over it, and it's a darkened landscape for a moment. But it passes."

A darkened landscape, thought Tom. And he remembered not only Suzi, but his sister, Becky, too, and all her problems. *But it passes*.

"You're a funny mixture, aren't you, Crazy Daisy," he said, smiling at her over his bread and cheese.

"Why?"

"So tough and practical one minute, collecting stores and driving lorries into war zones. And then you go all poetical about cloud shadows!"

"Being practical doesn't necessarily mean you can't see!" retorted Daisy, reaching for the pickled onions. "And war zones make you appreciate quiet open spaces. *Don't they?*" She shot at him.

Tom looked at her, half smiling. "You know too much."

But Daisy just grinned. And presently, to turn his thoughts to other things, she said: "What are you doing up here, anyway? You don't live here, do you?"

"No." He answered her slowly, only half back in the present. "I don't live anywhere very much at present. I came up here to see my sister in Greenbanks Hospital."

Daisy's expression did not change, but she was clearly aware of the implications of that name. "I'm sorry . . . Can you tell me about it?"

"Can you stand it?"

"Try me," she said.

So Tom found himself telling Daisy all about Becky and her despair, wondering whether he ought to, and somehow being sure that he should and that Daisy might be able to help.

"Perhaps you should take her to Bosnia," Daisy said.

"What?"

"Let her see what it's really like to have no home, not even a broken one, no food, scarcely any water, and no way of keeping warm through the bitter winter, even if the snipers let you."

Tom nodded. "Yes . . . She has been dreadfully spoilt and cushioned all her life, I know. So have we all, really, by those standards . . . But I don't think she's ready to face reality yet."

Daisy shook her head at him. "Don't leave it too long – or she may never come out of it."

Tom privately agreed with her. But he also knew it would take time before Becky could even begin to see herself clearly, let alone anyone else.

"You know," he said suddenly, "I left England on a sort of wave of revulsion, thinking we were all too spoilt and rich and uncaring. I suddenly realised I didn't have to go on making money. I didn't *have* to do anything. I could simply opt out and go away."

"But that wasn't the answer?"

"No," he agreed slowly, "it wasn't. And I haven't been back five minutes, and I've already met several people who are not uncaring or spoilt at all! I couldn't have been more wrong."

"I'm glad to hear it," said Daisy primly. "There's hope for you yet." She gave herself a little shake then and pushed her plate away. "We must go. Things to do in York. Where can I drop you off?"

"Anywhere near a taxi rank," said Tom, suddenly aware that he didn't want this meeting to end.

"I could take you out to Greenbanks, if you like?"

"No," he said, sounding unnecessarily explosive. He somehow didn't want Daisy, with her clear-eyed air of youthful health and energy and good common sense, to be even remotely connected with Becky's nightmare world. "Just – put me down where you can . . ."

"All right." She smiled at him and did not pursue it.

They drove on through the rolling countryside, coming gently down into the wide plain of York, and finally pulled up by a nearby taxi rank in the outskirts of the city.

Tom got out, and was wondering how to say goodbye to her, when she gave a casual wave of her hand and started to drive off.

"Hey!" he shouted, horrified, and started to run after her. "Daisy, I haven't got your address."

"Ditto," laughed Daisy. But she fished in her pocket and brought out a card with a charity logo on it. "Two addresses for final collections," she said succinctly. "Either will reach me." The card said: "Relief Aid. Items to Daisy Bellingham" and gave a farm address in Yorkshire and a street number in the east end of

London. "What about you?" She was leaning out of the window, still smiling a little.

"Haven't got an address yet," said Tom. "But I'll find you!"

"You do that, Tom Denholm," she told him severely. "I'll be expecting you," and she headed off into the moving traffic.

Tom stared after her for a moment like a man in a dream, and then resolutely hailed a taxi and drove out of town to Greenbanks Hospital.

Morris Bradley was a small, wiry man with a narrow, high-domed head, and very penetrating grey eyes. He sat behind his desk observing Tom calmly, and decided he liked what he saw.

Tom, for his part, also liked what he saw, and felt curiously reassured by that clever, observant gaze. "I realise these things take time," he said cautiously, "but I hoped you could tell me what I can do to help my sister."

Bradley sighed. "It's difficult to tell you . . . She is really suffering from a loss of identity – a loss of rôle, if you like. It is a terrible blow to her self-esteem – the humiliation of being rejected by someone she loved and trusted is very hard to accept. It has left her in a sort of limbo where she feels somehow totally cut off from the world she knew."

Tom nodded. "I can understand that."

"The trouble is, "Bradley went on, looking at Tom with a rueful mixture of humour and despair, "the society we live in today gives us all the wrong priorities. We have been taught to care about wealth and position – houses, cars, swimming pools, clothes, high living, expensive tastes, exotic holidays . . . all manner of status symbols. And when these props to our vanity are suddenly withdrawn or threatened, we have nothing else to fall back on . . . we see a lot of it here – since this is a private hospital mostly frequented by the well heeled and insurance holders." He glanced at Tom somewhat wryly, almost apologetically Tom thought. "But I do work in the NHS too, you know. And the problems are just the same – status symbols and props to our fragile egos . . ." He paused, and then asked Tom: "Does your sister have any intellectual pursuits that might counteract her obsessions? . . . Anything that might interest her enough to hold her attention?"

It was Tom's turn to sigh. "I don't think so . . . She was always

56

rather an outdoor, active sort of girl when she was young – loved riding and expeditions and picnics . . . Fun-loving, really." A bright picture came into his mind of a long-legged, laughing girl astride a chestnut pony, auburn hair flying, knees gripping hard against those shining flanks, hands loose on the reins as she galloped fearlessly across the wide grasslands of their Argentinian ranch . . . reckless and laughing, without a care in the world. He sighed again and explained rather awkwardly: "I didn't see a lot of her after she got married . . . She and Derek were always jet-setting about from one glamorous place to another . . . I'm afraid they were out of my league."

Bradley smiled. "What is your league exactly?"

Tom looked startled. "I'm not sure I can answer that. I *was* a commercial artist – but I packed it in a couple of years ago, and since then I've been wandering in the wilderness."

"Why?"

"Why what?"

"Why did you pack it in?"

"Oh, I – didn't much like the commercial world. It's pretty callous and pretty brutal – all that cutthroat competition . . . I just – rebelled."

Morris Bradley was still looking at him. "*Why?*" he said again.

Tom stared. "You're very persistent, aren't you? Why do you want to know?"

"Because if you are going to help your sister, your attitude to life may be important, especially if, as I suspect, it is a great deal healthier than hers or her ex-husband's."

Tom had the grace to grin. "I see your point."

"Well? What triggered it off – this rebellion?" And since Tom still hesitated, he pressed him gently: "I think you should tell me."

So Tom told him. (He reflected somewhat grimly that he had spent an awful lot of time today talking about himself.) He described the agency's ill-fated publicity campaign for the pharmaceutical company in scathing detail, their lack of planning and failure to comply with the UN guidelines for aid convoys, the subsequent muddle and breach of rules in that war-torn country, ending with the unnecessary deaths of Suzi and the child she was trying to save.

"The last straw was when I overheard one of the directors of the pharmaceutical company telling one of my own directors: 'It was very sad about Suzi, of course, but it made wonderful publicity!'"

Morris Bradley snorted. "No wonder you left."

Tom's grin was a bit pale by now. "Yes. Well, I've never regretted it."

"Where did you go?"

"To Canada, mostly. And I ended up on a remote island in northern Newfoundland . . ." He paused, remembering that lovely sanctuary with a sudden wave of homesickness. Oh, for that quiet shore, and the peaceful, empty days . . .

"What did you do?"

"Nothing. Watched sea birds, and seals . . . painted a bit." He looked at Bradley, almost with appeal. "Out there, ordinary preoccupations didn't seem to matter any more . . . I – I didn't really want to come back."

Bradley smiled at him. "But you came."

Tom looked confused. "I – you met Greg Selwyn when he brought Suzi here, didn't you?"

"I did, indeed."

"Well, it was his fault."

"How was that?"

"He reminded me that I was still a member of the human race."

Bradley laughed. "Good for him."

"I suppose so," agreed Tom gloomily. "But I don't much look forward to rejoining the rat race."

"Could you manage without?"

Tom shrugged helplessly. "*I* could. But Becky will need support of some kind."

"From what I can gather, most of her fears on that score are groundless." There was a distinct glint in his eye. "She'll just have to learn to set her sights less high."

A sudden reminiscent smile of extraordinary tenderness touched Tom's mouth for a moment. "I met someone today who said I ought to take her to Bosnia!"

Bradley looked interested. "Who was that?"

"A girl running relief supply lorries. Daisy Bellingham, her name was."

"Oh, *Daisy*," smiled Bradley. "Crazy Daisy? We all know Daisy. She's a great girl."

"That's what I thought," agreed Tom, also smiling. Then he grew serious again. "But what ought I to do about Becky at the moment?"

"She'll be here for another couple of weeks to complete the course of treatment," the doctor explained. "It's easier for her to have antidepressants here where we can regulate the dosage." A bleak smile twitched at the corner of his mouth. "She can't stockpile any that way."

Tom nodded grimly.

"And there are group therapy classes for all the patients who can stand them. It doesn't always help. Some people are so intensely private about their own troubles that they find it hard to share their thoughts with anyone, but your sister seems to respond."

"Ought I to – I haven't planned to live anywhere special yet – should I stay up here where I can visit her every day or something?"

"No, I don't think that would be a good idea," said Bradley, not missing the faint fleck of relief in Tom's eyes. "The trouble has been in the past that she relied on her ex-husband too much and expected him to fix everything in her life for her. Now she has got to come to terms with doing things for herself – including financially. If you make it too easy for her, I'm afraid she will just latch on to you to be the next Mr Fix-It, and that will be no good for her and appalling for you."

Tom looked at him gratefully. "You're very frank."

"No point glossing things over," said Bradley. "I don't believe in easy options. We're here to get to the root of the trouble and build things up again from scratch so that the patient becomes strong enough to cope with her own life. That's the only way." He saw that Tom was still looking doubtful, and added kindly: "Come up and see her once a week. Give her a fixed date to look forward to. Encourage her to make plans for the future, if you can, but don't try to make all the decisions for her . . ." He paused, and then added drily: "Maybe you could persuade her uncooperative ex-husband to make the divorce settlement a little less fraught with difficult decisions."

"Yes," said Tom, his voice hardening. "I intend to go and see Derek when I leave here."

A flick of grim amusement crossed Morris Bradley's face. "Don't hit him too hard," he said.

This time, Tom found Becky up and dressed and waiting for him. She had brushed her hair and bothered to put on some make-up, so he gave her an admiring glance and said: "You look better."

She smiled and it was almost the real, wide, Becky smile he used to know. "I'm a bit more together today," she admitted. "I'm sorry I was such a wimp."

Tom grinned. "I reckon you're entitled to a bit of wimpishness, all things considered!"

They strolled together over to the little coffee house again, and sat at a table on the green lawn just outside it.

"I'm going to sell the house," she said suddenly.

"Which one?"

"The English one. Well, both of them, I think. I don't want them. I don't want either of them." She looked at Tom with a kind of reckless bravado. "I don't want anything that was Derek's any more."

Tom nodded. "sounds like a good idea. Cut your losses and start again."

"Somewhere *new*." She took a deep breath. "I'd like to take all my clothes off and roll in new snow. Does that sound crazy?"

"No." There was a glimmer of mischief in his glance. "Norwegians do it all the time!"

She laughed, sounding almost natural, almost relaxed. "But I suppose there are other ways of shedding a skin?"

"Plenty," smiled Tom. "There's a swimming pool here, isn't there?"

"Yes. I haven't tried it yet."

"Clean and cool," said Tom, rightly interpreting her mood. "I'll come in with you, if you like. I'm sure I could borrow some trunks."

"Would you?" Her smile was curiously childlike and grateful. "D'you know, Tom, you remind me of you long ago?"

"Me long ago? Why?"

"You were always so kind to me – my big brother, always getting

60

me out of scrapes, or helping me down when I got stuck in a tree, or yanking me out of a river when I went in too deep . . . Do you remember the picnics?"

He smiled. "Out on the prairie, miles from anywhere, and you grumbled because we forgot the mustard!" He saw that she was still smiling a little with reminiscent tenderness and added softly: "Those were the days . . ." Then he thought they had been sentimental long enough, and got to his feet and took her hand in his. "Come on. If you want to swim, let's do it."

She held on to his hand, still like a child, and said in a small, suddenly humble voice: "Tom, am I a dreadful liability?"

"Of course not." Tom spoke with instant reassurance. "It was about time we got to know each other again anyway. I've been away too long."

Her glance was still absurdly grateful and it bothered him a little. He didn't want her to feel too swamped by unnecessary gratitude – it was not a good feeling to live with. He remembered that she had rather hero-worshipped him when she was a small girl . . . But that was long ago. It would not do now.

"Here we are," said Becky. "I did look at it once, but I wasn't – wasn't well enough to cope. I was afraid I'd sink like a stone!"

It was a long, low building with a sliding glass roof and wide glass windows which rolled back in summer to make it almost an open-air pool. But now, in spring, the windows were closed, the air was warm and the water was gently heated. There were swimsuits and swimming trunks available for patients to borrow if they had not got their own, and Becky nervously chose a black one-piece costume, hoping, she explained to Tom earnestly, that it would make her feel "more together".

They plunged into the water and both set off on an energetic crawl. Becky was a good swimmer, having always lived the sort of life that had swimming pools and sun-drenched beaches readily available, and even now when she was still ill and tired, she managed a couple of lengths before she tired. But Tom watched her in case she collapsed or suddenly gave up and wanted to sink and drown. He knew the desperation was still there behind her present gentle mood, and might surface at any time.

She had turned on her back by now and was floating peacefully

61

with her eyes closed. "Cool and clean . . ." She repeated Tom's words. "I feel better now."

Tom, swimming close to her, said gently: "When you're out of here, we'll try the sea."

She turned her head and smiled. "That'd be nice." But somehow she didn't sound convinced. There was a curious fleck of doubt in her voice.

They climbed out of the pool together and sat for a moment on the side before going to change, and Tom said suddenly, feeling an urgent need to exact a promise from her: "Becks, you won't ever – try that again?"

She did not answer at once, and this time she did not look at him. But finally she said, almost flippantly: "I can't. They won't give me any more pills!"

Tom was not altogether satisfied with her answer, but he thought he'd better not pursue it further. Instead, he pulled her to her feet and said: "Let's get changed, and I'll buy you another coffee."

While they were peacefully sitting in the swimming-pool lounge, drinking scalding coffee to warm themselves up, Tom thought perhaps it was time to give her something else to think about for the future, and said: "If you get rid of both the houses, where would you like to live?"

Becky seemed curiously vague and dreamy about this. "I don't know . . . somewhere new . . . I'd like to have a horse."

He nodded. "You always loved riding. Haven't you had a horse since?"

"Yes." Her voice was still soft. "In California, I did."

"What happened to it?"

"I sold him. I couldn't bring him over here. His name was Spice."

Tom could hear the regret in her voice, and touched her hand gently. "We can get another one."

"It won't be Spice, though, will it?" she said sadly. Then she turned with unexpected frankness to Tom, and added: "You know, you're right about too many *things*, too many *places*, no roots at all . . . But Spice was different. He was real."

Tom was silent, remembering Ollie the seal, a long way away across the wide Atlantic. He was real, too.

They were looking out at the sunny green lawns and the trees in the park-like grounds beyond where there were several fine beeches, a spreading cedar, and an ancient, sturdy-looking oak, when Becky said suddenly: "You know, a tree fell down here the other day. It was a beech tree."

"Yes?"

"And I asked the gardener why it fell. He said beeches had very shallow roots – they spread sideways instead of going down deep . . . But oak trees, he said, were different. Their roots went down very deep . . ." She turned to look at Tom, her wide, childlike gaze suddenly filled with sorrowful self-knowledge. "You're an oak, Tom. But I'm afraid I'm a beech . . ."

Tom did not answer at once, but he quietly waved a hand at the beautiful silver–grey trunks of the beech trees on the lawns. "Well, they look good for another hundred years or so," he said, smiling. "And so do you!"

Derek had elected to meet Tom in a hotel in Leeds, but Tom, out of a mixture of perversity and curiosity, decided to do a little reconnoitring first. What was Derek doing in Leeds, anyway? A north of England manufacturing town was surely not his usual stamping ground? Not someone like Derek, used to the oil-rich capital cities of the world. It must be the girlfriend's home town, he supposed. She must have insisted on taking him to visit her parents – a famous ploy for making sure he was well and truly hooked.

Tom was a bit ashamed of jumping to these conclusions – he knew he was taking a sour view of the whole sorry affair – so he wandered out into the town to have a look at the address Becky had given him. Sure enough it was a thin, rather cramped terrace house in a faceless red brick suburb of rather mean streets. That figures, he said to himself unkindly, trying to escape from shabby respectability into a high-flying world with a rich husband. Well, good luck to her, but why couldn't she choose a rich *un*married man? I suppose they are not so easy to come by – or to seduce?

There was a small workmen's café on the corner, next to the local shop, and Tom went in to get a cup of tea, and – he had to admit it – to watch that anonymous-looking road for a little while. He didn't quite know what he was expecting but he felt he just wanted to know a little about the background to Derek's extraordinary behaviour. Or was it so extraordinary? A lot of men swapped wives in middle years, getting bored with the last one and frantically snatching at the last chances of youth and renewal . . . it wasn't uncommon. But it was the *way* Derek had done it that was so difficult to stomach. With all that money behind him, he could afford to be generous. And a man with a grain of imagination or understanding would realise that he had left Becky with some impossible choices, and without the financial know-how that he possessed which made them seem simple to him . . . Oh well, maybe he would find out a little more when he met him.

The waitress was chatty, bringing his tea and an unwanted oatmeal scone which she said he was sure to like. "Don't live round here, do you?" she asked, all cheerful curiosity.

"No. Just meeting someone." He smiled at her, thinking he might have sounded too unfriendly. "What's it like to live in?"

"Here?" She made a face. "Like the back of beyond. Dead as ditchwater in the evenings."

"I can imagine," Tom said. "What do you do, then?"

"Go up west most nights." She gave her hair a flick with one hand, and added, smiling: "Bit more lively up near the clubs."

Tom nearly said "I can imagine" again, but just stopped himself in time. He could imagine it, too – the discos and cheap nightclubs and three-D cinemas . . . and bunches of idle, catcalling yobbos clustered round the brightly lit arcades and shopping malls.

"I suppose you know most of the people round here," he said, feeling mean again about his devious probing.

She shrugged plump shoulders. "Some of 'em. Keep themselves to themselves, most of 'em do. Not that friendly."

Tom was watching the road opposite fairly closely, and as he spoke, a smallish, wispy man in a raincoat came down the street, turned into the road and after a few strides went up the steps of the house Tom had been watching, inserted a key in the front door and went inside.

"That one, for instance?"

She realised Tom was after something and grinned. "Private detective, are you? I could tell you a thing or two about that lot! Grabbed a rich bloke for herself out east somewhere, hasn't she, and him a married man and all. Her parents weren't none too pleased at first, I can tell you – respectable, they are. But now he's going to marry her, the poor sap, it's all brisk and Frisco, as they say."

"Why 'poor sap'?"

She snorted. "Bit of a schemer, she is. Known her since school days . . . All soft and sweet, big eyes, holding hands, darling you're wonderful! Gets 'em every time!" She plonked a sugar bowl down on the next table with unnecessary force. "Men! They're such babies! (Saving your presence!) A bit of flattery and eyelash batting, and they're sunk!"

As she proclaimed this damning indictment, the door of No. 22 opened again and two people came out. One was a plumpish, bouncy-looking girl, and the other was Derek. The girl was holding on to Derek's arm and looking up into his face with very obvious devotion, and even as Tom realised who he was looking at, she reached up and kissed Derek there in the street (like a lovesick teenager, thought Tom sourly) before walking on with him, arm in arm.

And then Tom remembered Becky's shamed, disbelieving voice when she told him: "*He said I never held his hand in public, or kissed him in front of everyone and told him I loved him . . . How could I, Tom? It's absurd . . .*"

Absurd it may be, thought Tom grimly, but this wretched girl knows how to twist a man round her little finger all right. How can Derek be such a fool?

"I must go," he said, reaching in his pocket for some loose change. "How much do I owe you?"

"Only seventy pence," she said, disappointed. "You didn't have the scone."

But Tom just smiled at her, left a pound on the plate, and went out into the street. They'll be walking down to the hotel, I suppose, he thought. It's nearly time for the meeting. I wonder if he'll have the nerve to bring her with him? I'd better hurry up and get there first.

So he was quietly sitting in the hotel lounge with a drink in front of him when Derek came in, alone. He looked sulky and on the defensive, but he made an attempt to be his usual bland and confident self.

"Tom. I see you've got a drink." He signalled to a hovering

65

waiter. "Moyra will be joining us later. I think you ought to meet her."

"Oh?" said Tom, and failed to rise to his feet.

Derek sat down in a nearby armchair. It was clearly going to be a difficult interview. He was used to those.

"How is Becky?" he asked, trying to sound solicitous. (My ex-wife is very neurotic . . .)

"Not very well," said Tom. He did not elaborate. What was the use? Emotional blackmail would not win Derek back.

"Did you want to discuss anything in particular?" Derek put on his best behind-his-desk, high-finance voice.

"Yes," said Tom. "Your handling of the settlement."

Derek bridled. "I think I've been more than generous."

"Do you?" Tom's voice was dry. "Two unsaleable properties and no income?"

"The Californian condo isn't unsaleable."

"How do you know? I doubt it will make her enough profit to live on permanently. And in case it's escaped your notice, there's been a recession in England resulting in a depressed housing market."

"I'm sure a sale can be arranged." His voice was as bland and unruffled as ever.

"Well then, arrange it," snapped Tom. And when Derek's eyes went wide, he went on more quietly. "I don't think you quite understand the situation," he said, trying to be patient. "You are used to handling financial deals and taking appropriate decisions on a grand scale. Becky is not."

Derek shrugged. "That's not my fault."

"Oh yes, it is," Tom contradicted. "You never let her find out how to handle her own affairs. You did it all. Is it any wonder she doesn't know what to do for the best?"

"Can't she get an adviser?"

"Yes. She has. A lawyer you tried to prevent her from employing."

Derek looked sulky. "I thought the one she had already was adequate."

"I'm sure you did," Tom said. "A simple local solicitor with no particular knowledge of high finance or international money? You could make rings round him."

Derek did not reply to this. Instead he said, like a truculent schoolboy, "Well, what do you want me to do?"

"Make a proper, steady provision for her future, so that she doesn't have to tear herself to pieces trying to balance seeing Jenny in California with seeing Kit in England. Make it possible for her to make the right decisions."

"I thought I already had."

"Derek, I happen to know the extent of your current salary. Becky told me. It is, I believe, in excess of £300,000 a year. By present law, Becky should be allowed half of that."

Derek looked even more sulky. "I have new commitments now."

"That doesn't mean you can just shrug off the old ones, does it?"

Derek clearly thought it did. "There would be plenty of cash from the property sales. They are all the capital I have."

"Really? It would amount to about half your salary for approximately two years," said Tom flatly. "What about the future?"

"I shan't be earning that sort of money for ever."

"But you are now," pointed out Tom. "And Becky deserves to have a fair and acceptable amount of it."

There was a silence for a moment, and then Tom said curiously: "What did you think Becky would do?"

"I thought she'd stay in California, and Moyra and I could take over the London house."

"Oh, did you?" Tom was astounded. "Very convenient."

"She *likes* California," protested Derek, not really understanding Tom's outrage.

"*With* an income," Tom spelt out. "And health insurance. It's very expensive out there. Becky has to think of the next twenty or thirty years of her life – with no visible support." He looked at Derek hard, and then said, not knowing he was going to be outspoken: "How could you do this to her, Derek? After twenty-five years of marriage?"

Derek blinked. "That's the point, isn't it? After twenty-five years things get stale . . . Moyra makes me feel young again . . ." He seemed genuinely puzzled by Tom's disapproval, and went on into lame excuses. "People do get divorced all the time, you know – it's no big deal."

67

Tom stared. "Isn't it?"

Derek ignored the question. "A fresh start," he said.

"At Becky's expense?"

"I have to think of myself," Derek insisted. "I've only got one life."

"So has Becky," said Tom.

There didn't seem to be anything left to say after that. Tom had done his best to argue Becky's case and put forward her point of view. But it was clear that Derek was so wrapped up in his own best interests, he could not really consider Becky's. Tom doubted if he had the imagination to understand what she was going through anyway.

"Well," he said quietly, "I will advise Becky's new lawyer to be in touch. The rest is up to you. But I think I should warn you that if Becky is put through any more distress, he will be instructed to get very tough." He thought that was enough of a threat to push Derek into doing something positive. He was a bully, after all, and bullies usually caved in when the opposition got tough.

"Very well," said Derek, sounding very clipped and fed up. "We'll leave it at that."

And here, right on cue, Moyra came tripping into the hotel lounge, high heels clacking, bangles jingling, arms outstretched. "Darling," she said, "I couldn't wait any longer. Am I too early?" And she wound her arms round him from behind his chair and kissed the top of his head.

(Going bald, too, observed Tom sourly.)

Seen close to, Moyra was the kind of girl you would call well built. Pink-cheeked, bubbling with health and energy, young and active, insensitive and brash, and determined to make Derek feel young and active, too.

"No," said Derek, his voice fatuously indulgent and fond. "You're never too early!" And he caught hold of her hand and reached up to kiss her.

"Are we going out to dinner? It's Scottish Dance night at the Caledonian. Reels and strathspeys and such. You'd like that, wouldn't you?"

"Sounds very energetic."

"Of course! Lots of fun." She turned, large-eyed and inviting, to Tom. "Are you coming, too?"

68

"No." Tom stood up. "Not my scene." Not Derek's either, I should think, he told himself, eying Derek's slightly thickened waist and middle-aged spread. She'll give him a heart attack before she's finished. Perhaps that's the idea? (But he was immediately ashamed of that thought.)

"Oh, what a pity." She sighed with exaggerated disappointment. "It would have been nice. I do so want us to be friends."

Tom just stared. He did not see how he could answer without being rude. Finally, he turned to Derek and said with apparent innocence: "By the way, was this the hotel Becky stayed at?" Some devil inside him needed to stir these smug, self-satisfied people into some semblance of remorse, some acceptance of responsibility for Becky's suicide attempt.

"No," said Derek, flushing darkly. "It wasn't."

There was a moment's painful silence, and then Moyra plunged in: "I was so sorry about Becky . . . I never meant to hurt her, you know."

"Didn't you?" said Tom. "You do surprise me."

He walked away from them then, before he throttled Moyra and shook Derek like the rat he was. And they stood looking after him, speechless.

But just before he left the quiet lounge to cross the busy hotel foyer, he paused and said over his shoulder: "I shall await results," and walked out into the street.

Tom did not go back to see Becky again after his meeting with Derek. He did not want to raise her hopes about a more workable settlement until he had talked to the lawyers and there had been some practical response from Derek, and he somehow did not like to see her and not mention the painful interview at all. Better wait a week, he told himself. There might be better news then.

So he took the train to London and went back to Greg's for the night.

"Greg's got a late brief conference," Marian explained, bringing in a tray of tea. "But he'll be back later."

She watched Tom settle gratefully into a chair, and noted that he seemed saddened by his visit to Becky but not entirely despondent about it. She also noted that he was still having trouble with that knee of his, though he said nothing about it.

"How did you find Becky?"

Tom sighed. "Very distressed the first day. But she seemed a little more together the second day – more able to make a few tentative plans."

Marian nodded. "That's progress."

"Yes, I hope so . . . though I suspect she may revert to the first stage of – of desperate anxiety from time to time." He looked at Marian rather bleakly. "I don't think it's over yet."

"Did you see Dr Bradley?"

"Yes. We had quite a talk."

"What did you think of him?"

"I was impressed. He seemed to know what he was doing – and he was very compassionate."

Marian agreed. "That was how he struck me."

There was a faintly puzzled expression in Tom's clear blue gaze. "You know, Marian, I've been so wrong about people."

"Have you? How?"

"Well, after the Suzi fiasco, I went storming off, convinced that every benighted soul on this cruel earth was a callous, self-centred bastard . . ."

Marian laughed. "After all, you were in *advertising*!"

Tom had the grace to laugh, too. But he wanted to explain to Marian how things had been across the Atlantic in Little Reward, and how much he had dreaded his return to the hard, uncaring, commercial world he had known.

"I met such warmth and kindness in Reward Cove," he said slowly, "and I was so sure I was coming back to – to –"

"Callous, self-centred bastards?"

He grinned. "And from the moment I set foot on English soil, what with you and Greg, and –" He thought suddenly, vividly, of Daisy and her sturdy, unexpectedly gentle voice saying: "*I'm listening* . . ." "– and everyone I've met," he went on lamely, "I've been confounded at every turn!"

Marian poured him out another cup of tea, smiling. "It's probably good for the soul to be proved wrong!" she said. Then she asked, not without a gleam of sardonic humour, "Don't tell me Derek confounded you with kindness, too?"

This time Tom's laughter was grim. "Scarcely." He allowed a

little of his own furious contempt to creep into his voice, but there was still faint puzzlement too. "D'you know, I really believe he thinks he's quite justified in walking out and starting a completely new life . . .? I don't think he has the faintest idea what damage he's done to Becky."

"Can he be that stupid?"

"Yes," said Tom bluntly. "I think he can."

"Did you get any sense out of him about the settlement?"

"Only by issuing threats."

Marian looked unperturbed. "It's probably the only language he understands. He's a bit of a bully, you know."

"That's what I thought," agreed Tom.

"Did you meet the girlfriend?"

"Oh yes."

"What's she like?"

Tom's eyebrows shot up in comical dismay. "Like a caricature of a predatory young woman on the make . . ." He grinned at Marian again, but it was a rather lopsided grin this time. "Bouncy, demonstrative, possessive . . . drivingly full of self-interest and about as sensitive as a rather dumb sheep." (He thought he might be maligning the sheep, at that.)

Marian looked slightly sceptical. "She must have some saving graces."

"Possibly. I suppose she must be fond of Derek. But he is much too old for her – she's just a rather selfish child, really . . ." He added in a dry voice: "She did say she never meant to hurt Becky."

"Oh, really!" Marian sounded as exasperated as he felt.

"Anyway," Tom went on, "I told Derek Becky's lawyer would get tough, and when Greg comes in I'll find out how to put that into practice!"

And, as if on cue, they heard Greg's key in the lock, and his cheerful voice call out: "Anyone home?"

In the morning, Tom and Greg went to see the chosen lawyer, who, Greg had assured him, was one of the best, clever as paint and toughness personified when he got his teeth into a case. This opinion seemed to be justified when Tom met him. Austen Bennett was lean, sardonic and deceptively mild of manner, but his raking gaze missed nothing and there was a hidden edge of steel beneath the quiet voice.

"So I am to proceed?" he asked, turning a humorous glance from Greg to Tom.

"You are, indeed," Tom assured him. "Ignore the opposition."

A faint grin lit the lawyer's long, pale face. "I must confess," he said, "I was a trifle surprised to be ordered off the case by my client's ex!"

"You wouldn't be surprised if you knew him," growled Tom. But then, wondering if he was being unfair, reported as truthfully as he could on his difficult interview with Derek, relayed as many of Becky's instructions as seemed relevant or sensible, looked anxiously at Greg for a moment and then said: "I think that's as much as I can tell you at present, while my sister is still in hospital. But I think she'll be well enough to see you herself very soon . . . Is that enough to go on?"

"Plenty for the moment," confirmed Austen pleasantly. "I have actually made discreet enquiries about the husband's financial position . . ." The dark, clear glance just flicked on Greg's face again for a moment. "It should not be too difficult to establish a reasonable basis for a settlement – and one which the courts would uphold."

Tom nodded. "I can leave it with you, then?"

"Yes, indeed. It will be a matter of negotiation now between the two sides."

"You will have to be tough," warned Tom.

Austen smiled widely. "Believe me, Mr Denholm, I am. Especially when pushed."

Tom grinned back, feeling unaccountably reassured by that cool, calm smile. And Greg, seeing that the situation was well in hand, took Tom away and bought him a drink in a nearby bar.

"Phew!" said Tom. "I wouldn't like to be on the wrong side with that one!"

"I told you he was a tough customer."

Tom shivered and took a gulp of whiskey. "I'm sorry, Greg. I'm just not used to money. I've been away from it too long. The whole thing fills me with terror!"

Greg smiled. "You're not the only one," he said.

*　　　*　　　*

After Greg had gone back to his chambers for the rest of the morning's work, Tom decided it was time he went down to have a look at Becky's suburban house. She had given him the keys, and a list of vague instructions which she kept on contradicting, but he thought he had better make sure the house was still safe and in good order, and at least pick up the mail.

Becky's house was in a leafy suburb, bright with hazel copses and long-fingered weeping willows. Tidy gardens hid behind neat privet hedges, front doors (studded oak, pale cream with fanlights, stripped pine with boxwood finials) all remained firmly closed, and the windows (old-world leaded or large picture, and mostly covered in floating swathes of net) remained shut. There was no one to be seen in the front gardens (what Tom could see of them over their enclosing hedges), and no one to be seen on the road. A few cars were parked in visible places, but for the rest, the whole place seemed entirely lifeless. It was in the commuter belt, of course, he told himself. Everyone was at work. But did *all* the women work, too? What about the children?

A sudden picture came into his mind of the little group of frame houses round the harbour at Reward Cove, the white picket fences freshly painted for the spring, the doors wide open while everyone swept and shook the murk of winter out of their houses, the cheerful gossip over gates, the fishermen mending their torn nets, the children swooping about like a flight of eager birds, calling and crying, shouting and laughing in the returning spring sunlight . . . How different from this, he thought sadly. All that warmth and careless, unspoken closeness in the little community . . . How I wish I was there!

But he had arrived at Becky's door, and he was just about to put her key in the lock, when he noticed a faint movement in the garden round the side of the house. He hesitated for a moment, and then decided to go and have a look.

There was a man stooping over one of the flower beds, his back to Tom, his hands busy among the thrusting spring bulbs.

"Hullo?" said Tom.

The figure straightened up and turned sharply. "My lord, you startled me." It was not an old face and not a young face looking at him; middlish and brownish and friendly – though a shade wary at the moment.

"I'm Tom Denholm." He held out his hand. "Becky's brother. She asked me to come and have a look at the place."

"Oh." The grizzled head nodded in relief. "Not one of Derek's friends?"

"No." It was clear to Tom that battle lines had already been drawn up.

"No," he repeated firmly, making it clear. "*Becky's*."

The man nodded, and only then reached out to shake Tom's proffered hand. "Bob Nerris – live in the next road – keep an eye on her garden for her when she's away." He paused and added, almost shyly: "How is she then?"

Tom hesitated, not sure how much Bob Nerris knew about what had been happening to Becky. "Not very well at present," he said at last. "But I hope things will be better now I'm home . . ." He paused again, and then realised suddenly that Bob Nerris knew all about Becky's suicide attempt and her transfer to Greenbanks Hospital. It was somehow clear in the concerned, steady gaze of those watchful brown eyes, and the way he waited for Tom to be more explicit. "You know what's been happening?" Tom asked, but it wasn't really a question, more a confirmation.

"Yes, well, you see, Mrs Selwyn, she came down to fetch some clothes and things . . . and my wife, Mary, knew where to find them . . . She does the cleaning for Becky, see? . . . And they are quite sort of close, you see . . . Becky always wrote to her from abroad and such – especially since there was trouble."

Tom saw very clearly that Bob and his wife were a good deal more than just gardener and cleaner in Becky's life. And he was cheered by these unexpected allies.

"I've got to find a few more things for Becky," he said. "Maybe you'd know where they are?"

"I might." Bob sounded doubtful. "But I could get Mary along. She'd be sure to." He added helpfully: "She's at home today . . . I could give her a ring."

"Come in, then," Tom smiled. "And ask her to bring round a drop of milk. Then we can all have some tea."

Bob grinned. "Now you're talking!"

They sat round the kitchen table, drinking tea, and discussed

74

the situation. Mary was a bit younger than Bob, squarish and practical, but with a soft-skinned, gentle face that somehow radiated warm-hearted common sense.

"She never ought to have come here," she told Tom. "Not if she was going to live here alone –"

"Why not?"

"Well, look at it. This neighbourhood." She waved a plump hand at the half-hidden houses beyond the window. "No one knows anyone. No one speaks. They're all off to London to work, or what have you. She could sit here alone and never speak to a soul all day . . . No life for anyone that is, let alone someone like Becky who's been all over the world, like, and had lots of social life before . . ."

"Why did she come here, d'you know?"

"Because Derek bought it for her – when she was ill before, and the doctor said she needed somewhere *permanent*, not to go gadding about all the time."

"I didn't know she had been ill before." Tom was surprised. "When was that?"

"Oh, not that long ago." Mary turned blue, honest eyes to Bob for confirmation. "Two years . . .?"

"Ay," Bob nodded. "Just about."

"She was out in the Middle East somewhere, where Derek's job was – but women couldn't go out anywhere except with a chauffeur, and she hated it . . . so she came home." Once more the candid, worried gaze sought Bob's for reassurance. "In a terrible state she was . . . I always thought that was when the real trouble started . . . I think she knew he was carrying on, even then."

Tom nodded. It made sense, after all.

"Can you understand it?" Mary exploded suddenly. "A lovely woman like Becky? – always elegant and well dressed, keep her end up with anyone – all that entertaining she did for him, impressing the clients – kept a wonderful table – I waited for them at dinners once or twice so I know . . . she always looked smashing . . . And he goes off with that – that vulgar bit of fluff!" She blushed and apologised hastily. "Sorry, I get carried away. But it makes my blood boil!"

Tom grinned at her companionably. "I know. It does mine,

too." Then he returned to the crux of the matter. "So the doctor persuaded Derek to buy this house?"

"Yes. He said she needed –?"

"Stability," said Bob, and then – the gardener speaking – "Roots, like."

Tom remembered then Becky's sad, suddenly lucid voice saying: "*I'm afraid I'm a beech* . . ." And for some reason the memory brought a lump to his throat. She's always been a bit like a beech, he thought. A copper beech, auburn-haired, tall and slender, always reaching for the sky . . .

"They'd always rented houses before," explained Mary, anxious to make things clear to Tom. "Dashing about from place to place. Never stayed anywhere long . . . went wherever the job sent him . . ."

"That's the trouble with oil," pronounced Bob. "Anywhere under the sun . . ."

"And then, as soon as she was settled here, he was off again, d'you see?" Mary went on indignantly. "Said she'd better stay put if she wasn't well . . . But it only made her worse being left here alone – and not knowing what he might be getting up to without her . . ."

"I can imagine," said Tom drily. And he could.

"So I think she tried to get well a bit too quickly and went off after him again before she was really ready for it." Mary shook her head in disapproval, still full of righteous indignation. "To tell you the truth, we weren't very surprised when she got ill again, Bob and me – we were almost expecting it." She looked at Tom with the same mixture of candour and anxiety she had turned on Bob. "When the crunch came, I mean, it was all too much for her, poor lady . . . She couldn't believe he could do such a thing . . ."

Tom could see it all. He understood a lot more now about how Becky's final collapse had come about.

"She will get well, won't she?" asked Mary, her kind, round face filled with concern.

"Of course she will." He tried to sound entirely certain. "Her doctors are very hopeful. But it will take time."

"That's what we thought," agreed Mary, natural common sense coming to the fore. "Well, she's young enough yet. She's got plenty of time left." The anxious eyes smiled hopefully

76

at Tom. "And as for Derek Wade, she'll be better off without him!"

Tom laughed. "I've been trying to tell her that myself!"

"Oh, she won't see it now, I daresay," Mary allowed, "but one day she will."

"Best in the long run," growled Bob.

Tom couldn't agree with them more.

"Well now," prompted Mary, reverting to practical matters, "you'd best tell me what things Becky wanted and I'll see if I can find them." She got up and made for the stairs, with Tom behind her. "D'you know, that man came back here –"

"What man? Derek?"

"Yes. Derek. Mr Wade. While she was out one day – I think she was seeing her lawyers – and I was here cleaning. He came waltzing in with his – girlfriend, and took away the dinner service."

"*What*?"

"Said it was his." She turned round on the stairs and glared down at Tom. "Can you imagine? . . . I couldn't stop him, really – not knowing if it was his or not . . . But it seemed so – so *mean*." She drew in a furious breath. "I didn't know how to tell her when she came home. But she just laughed and said: 'Perhaps he's teaching her how to cook!'"

Gallant, thought Tom. When she wasn't entirely overthrown by despair, she tried hard to be gallant about it . . . That sounds like the Becky I used to know.

"She was always brave," he murmured, aloud. And there was almost a hint of tears in his voice.

Mary did not answer at once. But suddenly she stopped on the stairs and blurted out: "I don't think she'd have tried to do that terrible thing she did if she'd been down here . . . At least she would have had us. But up there, in a strange hotel, there was nobody to turn to."

"I know," agreed Tom. I know. And I should have been there.

"I wish there was something we could do," said Mary, going briskly towards Becky's door. "You will tell us if there is?"

"Of course," promised Tom.

"We can't help being worried about her, me and Bob, d'you see? She's like – well, almost like *family*, somehow."

77

"Yes," Tom said, sounding curiously angry with himself. "And you've done more for her than most of her own family, so far."

Mary looked at him in surprise, not really understanding the self-accusing contempt in his voice, and did not know how to answer him.

But at that moment, the phone rang in the hall.

"You'd better answer it," she said. "Bob and me don't know what to say these days."

So Tom went downstairs again and picked up the receiver.

"Could I speak to Mrs Wade? Mrs Rebecca Wade?"

"I'm sorry," said Tom. "I'm afraid she's not here at present. This is her brother speaking. Can I help?"

"This is the aid agency here. Mrs Wade asked us to enquire about the whereabouts of her son, Christopher. She was anxious about his safety."

"Yes?" Tom's voice was crisp. "She is certainly anxious about him. Have you any news?"

There was a fractional pause at the other end, and then the pleasant woman's voice began cautiously: "I really ought to speak to his mother first –"

"Well, I'm afraid you can't," said Tom. "She's in hospital, and rather unwell at present. I think you'd better tell me."

"Oh." There was another fractional pause. "Then perhaps it's as well to tell you first . . . I'm afraid the news isn't very good."

"What's happened to him?"

"We don't know for certain. Communications are very bad out there, as you can imagine. All we have been told is that they were in a small convoy, and one of the lorries got separated from the others. There were mines on the road, and they had to make a detour or something. Two lorries got to their destination unscathed, but the third one hasn't arrived yet." The friendly voice hesitated a little, and then went on: "We have no reason as yet to be alarmed, you know. It has probably just got bogged down by the weather – or by red tape at the check points. It's always happening."

"Yes, I know. I've been there."

"Have you?" The voice sounded inexplicably relieved. "Oh, then you will understand the situation . . . It will probably be perfectly all right, you know. But we may not hear anything concrete for several days."

"I understand that."

"Perhaps you could explain things to Mrs Wade? We don't think there's anything to worry about. Not yet, anyway. We do try to keep all our aid workers safe, you know. But it's a risky business – there's such chaos out there."

"I know," said Tom again. "I'll – I'll do my best to reassure her."

"I don't want her to be alarmed."

"Nor do I," Tom told her fervently.

"We will ring again as soon as we have any more news," said the voice. "Can I reach you here?"

"Er – no." Tom was thinking furiously. "I may not be here. I think you'd better leave word with Greg Selwyn and his wife, Marian. They will know how to reach me, or my sister." And he gave the worried charity worker Greg's number.

"Thanks," she said cheerfully. "I'll be in touch," and rang off before Tom could ask any more questions.

I can't tell Becky, he thought. Not yet. She can't take this on top of everything else. I'll have to wait for more news. Oh God, I hope the stupid boy is all right.

"Is everything all right?" asked Mary, from upstairs, looking down at his troubled face with anxious eyes.

"Yes, I think so," he said. "I hope so."

And he went back to his task of sorting Becky's belongings, and shut out his own black feeling of foreboding. Nothing had happened to Kit. Of course it hadn't. It was all a perfectly understandable delay. It would be all right. He only had to wait for news.

He only had to wait.

After some consideration, Tom decided to stay one night in Becky's house before he went back to London. He wanted to have a closer look at this green but soulless suburb of hers, and try to find out whether it would really be as lonely and frustrating a life here as his first impressions suggested.

So when he had said an unexpectedly warm-hearted goodbye to Bob and Mary and thanked them for all their help, he decided to go for a walk along the leafy, empty road and see for himself how things were.

It was sunny now, after a brief spell of spring rain, and the air was cool and scented with flowers. Cherry trees sported puffs of pink blossom in the gardens, and daffodils nodded against the well-kept lawns. But nothing stirred. No one came out of their doors, or leant over gates or gossiped over hedges. It was totally silent – except for a couple of blackbirds stuttering out alarm calls, and a lone thrush singing high up in an ash tree.

Well, at least the birds are alive, he thought. But where is everyone else? Don't they have dogs to walk, or children to fetch, or shopping to do? What do they do all day?

He watched a grey squirrel cross the road and shin up a high garden fence. It sat for a moment on the topmost wooden panel and polished its whiskers busily with its neat, clever paws, before disappearing over the fence into the garden beyond.

Becky's own garden did not have a high surrounding fence, but it had trees and a small stream running through it, and backed on to more thin woodland of silver birch and alder . . . Plenty of space for squirrels, he thought. But could she spend all day alone, listening to blackbirds and looking at squirrels? He didn't think so.

He walked on, past more neat, modern houses in neat, quiet gardens. Very quiet. No one was even cutting their lawn. No shops, he thought. No pub. Not even a village hall. (But I suppose these residents would be too posh for a village hall!) Where do they go, then? Up to London for entertainment? To the nearest supermarket for food? . . . There's no sense of community anywhere. How could they live like this? Could Becky?

The more he thought about it, the more certain he became that she could not. It would have been all right if the children had still been at home – or her errant husband coming home in the evenings . . . But even then her days would have been pretty lonely . . . What has become of us all, he thought, that we allow ourselves to live in this soulless way? What has become of neighbours and friends, and aunts and grannies-next-door?

There was no answer to this, and the silent houses seemed to turn their backs on him, hiding behind their high hedges in cold disapproval. He began to fancy, as he walked by, that they actively disliked his presence and were doing their malevolent best to freeze him out. He shivered a little in the warm sunshine, and walked a little faster.

The empty road sloped down here towards a much busier thoroughfare at the bottom of the hill. Cars and lorries whizzed past in a continuous stream. They didn't seem to be cruising along or stopping at local places as residents might, but went on rushing by, intent on frenetic journeys to unknown destinations.

He had just paused to look at all this speeding chaos with some dismay, when on the other side of the road a small fluffy dog trailing a loose lead came galloping happily round the corner, a smile of wicked glee on his furry face as he escaped from whoever was behind him. He did not pause to look at the oncoming traffic, but ran out into the road, dodging the cars and lorries with miraculous agility as he made for the other side where Tom stood transfixed with horror.

"Benji!" cried a child's voice. "Benji! Come here! *Benji!*" And following round the same corner came a desperate small boy in red boots. Like the dog, he did not pause to look at the traffic either, so intent on catching his dog that he thought of nothing else, and was just about to plunge off the pavement after him when Tom shouted.

"*Stop!*"

The child looked up, startled by Tom's roar.

"Stay there!" yelled Tom. "*Stay still!* I'll get the dog."

For a moment he thought the boy would take no notice, but then something about the urgency of Tom's voice seemed to reach him. It was a command, and he obeyed it.

"*Stay there!*" Tom shouted again, to make sure, and then pursued the furry delinquent – now thoroughly frightened and still dodging cars close to the pavement. Tom stretched out a long arm and grabbed the trailing lead just as the scared little animal skittered past. As he straightened up, pulling the dog towards him, he called again to the child across the road: "It's all right. I've got him. *Don't move!*" and as he did so, he saw a frantic, fair-haired girl – presumably the child's mother – come running round the corner and seize the small boy by the hand.

"Oh, thank God," Tom said aloud. Then he waited for the

traffic to ease, picked the small dog up and tucked it under his arm, and walked soberly across the road.

"I d–don't know how to thank you –" she began, and Tom could see that she was trembling with fright. "Adam, you *know* you mustn't cross the road."

"It was Benji – " The boy's voice quavered now, and he looked about to burst into tears. "He ran away –"

"No harm done," said Tom, to both pairs of anxious, tear-filled eyes. "And Benji isn't hurt, either."

They stood there looking at him, both of them almost too overwhelmed with relief to know what to do next. Then the girl seemed to notice Tom's own blazing pallor, and said anxiously: "Are you all right?"

"Of course," he said, summoning a smile. He could not tell her that for a moment he had seen another child run out into another street, and Suzi – young and reckless and ardent – run out after him . . . And the roar and flash and flame of the falling mortar shell, and Suzi and the child – what was left of them – lying still on the smoking ground . . .

"But for the moment –" he added, and then did not go on. The young mother had been frightened enough as it was. She knew, just as clearly as he did, that it had been touch and go whether Adam would stop in time.

"I heard you shout," she said, beginning to smile.

"I should think they heard me in central London," grinned Tom.

She was still looking at him rather anxiously. "Look, we only live just up the road . . . Would you come back with us and have a cup of tea? You look as if you could do with one."

"Sounds like a wonderful idea," said Tom, and fell into step beside her.

"Did you hurt your knee?" asked Adam, who was a bright little boy, and very observant when he wasn't frightened.

"Not today," Tom told him. "That was a long time ago."

"Oh." The puzzled blue eyes looked up at him. "Would you like a plaster on it? Mum could do it."

Tom laughed. "It's all right, Adam. It'll be fine."

"Come on," urged the young mother, smiling. "Tea-time."

To his surprise she walked up to the next pedestrian traffic lights and then crossed over to the side he had originally been on and began to go up the road towards Becky's house.

"I didn't realise you lived in this road," he said.

"I didn't realise you did, either," she returned. "Which house do you belong to? Or am I being nosy?"

He grinned. "I was just thinking no one was in the least interested in anyone else round here . . . Not what you'd call a friendly neighbourhood."

"You can say that again!" she agreed fervently.

He caught the fleck of bitterness in her voice and glanced at her in surprise. "Well, I'm only a visitor . . . I just came down to keep an eye on my sister's house – Hawthorne's, I think it's called."

The girl stared in astonishment. "*Becky Wade's* house?"

"Yes. Becky's. D'you know her?"

She looked suddenly shy, almost embarrassed. "I – yes. Not very well. It's her son, Kit, I really know."

"Kit," said Adam, skipping along with the dog, his fright apparently forgotten. "When's Kit coming back?"

The girl seemed to think some explanation was needed and turned to Tom with disarming frankness. "I'm Holly Ross . . . Kit may have mentioned me? We were at college together. He and I . . . well, when he's home we spend a lot of time together . . ."

"I see," Tom smiled. "I haven't really seen much of Kit recently – I've been away."

"Then you must be Kit's famous Uncle Tom."

"More infamous than famous," growled Tom.

He thought confusedly: Here's another person who is going to be worried sick about Kit if he is really missing. It gets more and more complicated.

"How is Becky?" Holly asked, sounding shy again. "Kit told me there was – um – trouble. Is she all right?"

"Not very," Tom told her. "She's in hospital at present. But she's improving."

"Oh . . . Oh, I'm glad . . . I did wonder – and with Kit away, I'd no one to ask."

She turned away from the main, tree-lined road then went down a small cul-de-sac where there were one or two less pretentious houses and an older, more rambling one at the end which looked like an old-fashioned rectory. "Down here," she said. "I have a flat round the back . . . It's a bit shabby, but it does very well for Adam and me."

She led him past a rather overgrown laurel shrubbery and in through a blue-painted back door into what must have been the kitchen quarters of the old house. But now it had been converted into a smallish, comfortable-looking flat. There was a pleasant little sitting room with windows looking out over a green and tangly garden, a small yellow-painted kitchen, a tiny bathroom with a shower unit, and one toy-strewn bedroom with its door open onto the narrow hall.

"Sit down," she said cheerfully. "You still look a bit shattered, and I must admit I am, too. I'll make some tea."

Eventually they sat opposite one another while Adam and Benji ran in and out, quite obviously not shattered at all.

"It's nice here," said Tom, approving the casual shabbiness and informality of the flat. After Becky's too-perfect house with its deep-pile fitted carpets and glittering modern kitchen units, this seemed much easier to live with.

"Kit found it for me," she said. "It's reasonably cheap because it's not very smart or well furnished, but that's really a good thing with a small boy in tow – and the best thing is, we have access to the garden, which is lovely for Adam and Benji."

Tom nodded and watched the two young creatures scamper in and out across the unkempt lawns at the back of the house. "How long have you been here?"

"Almost two years now. I stayed on in my awful bedsit after I left college as long as I could, but it was too small for Adam really, now he's growing up. He needs the space . . ."

Tom agreed, smiling. "He's a lively young fellow."

Holly made a face. "Too lively by half, sometimes . . . Like today. But he's going to school now, part-time, and that uses up quite a lot of energy! That's where we were coming from just now, when Benji escaped."

"How old is Adam, then?" Tom was beginning to wonder whether the missing Kit could possibly be the boy's father, and didn't know how to ask without seeming unpardonably impertinent.

"He's just five . . . I shall be able to work part-time soon, and that will make things easier all round." She pushed the lint-fair long hair away from her face and sighed. "The DSS do their best – but it's not a lot."

"Don't you get any other help?"

"Like what?" She looked genuinely puzzled.

"Well – from his father?"

She laughed. "Oh, him – No fear. Pigs might fly."

Tom smiled at her irreverent laughter. "But the law can insist on maintenance now, can't they?"

"Yes – if they can catch him!"

Tom joined in her laughter this time. But he persisted. "So what happened there?"

She shrugged fluid young shoulders. "The usual story. Love's young dream. We were both students." She looked at Tom with sudden honesty. "I did love him very much, you know – at the time. It wasn't just a one-off-and-forget-it sort of thing . . . But as soon as anything like trouble came, he was off . . . He wanted me to –" But Adam came running in and out of the room then and Holly did not finish that sentence. "Well, you can guess what he wanted me to do . . . And when I wouldn't – when I made it clear that I wanted to go ahead with it, you couldn't see him for dust!" She looked at Tom with humorous sadness. "Men – they're frightfully good at opting out of commitments and responsibilities, aren't they?"

Yes, thought Tom grimly. I've been guilty of that myself.

But Holly was quick to notice his self-accusing expression. "Not *every* man," she amended swiftly. "I mean, Kit's not like that. He's almost too keen to take on responsibilities."

"Is he?" Tom asked innocently. "I'm glad to hear it."

Holly looked at him and grinned. "I bet you thought he might be Adam's father?"

Tom grinned back, relieved to be honest. "It did cross my mind."

"He says he'd like to be," she admitted slowly. "And I know Adam would love it . . . But –" She paused, and seemed uncertain how to go on.

"But what?"

"He's too young," she burst out, "too young to take on a wife and child and all that . . . I keep telling him . . ."

85

"How old are you?" countered Tom, smiling, for she seemed almost a child to him, with her floating hair and vulnerable smile.

"I'm twenty-four," she said. "I was nineteen when I had Adam."

"That's only a year older than Kit."

She signed. "Yes. In numbers. But in experience – I'm a hundred years older."

"It must have been difficult," Tom said gently, "bringing him up alone . . . on a student grant."

She agreed, but quite cheerfully. "It was. But my mother helped . . . She made sure I got my degree – and I'm glad I did. It may help later . . . And then Kit came along – and he was a tower of strength."

Tom said suddenly, out of more than curiosity: "Why did he go away?"

Holly looked at him very straight, and sighed again a little. "I told him to . . . He had been at home a bit with his mother – in the vacations, I mean . . . But she was in such a state, he didn't know what to do for her . . . And she kept dashing off after his father, to Kuwait or Dubai or wherever . . . He never knew where she'd be or what she'd do next – Kit, I mean."

Tom nodded.

"And I think he felt . . . a bit torn in two, you know." She turned to Tom seriously. "Not that he approved of what his father was doing, but –" She broke off, and then went on in a curiously detatched, reflective tone: "They had a funny sort of childhood, you know, those two, Jenny and Kit. Expensive boarding schools, and jet-set holidays all over the place, but Kit told me he never felt he really belonged to his parents. He was just a rather tiresome appendage . . . He didn't get to know his father at all. He was always away somewhere, or in conference, or entertaining VIPs, with no time for family life . . . I think Becky – his mother – did try to be at home for them as much as she could. But then if she left Derek for too long to his own devices . . . Well, you can see what happened." She glanced at Tom warily.

"I can indeed," agreed Tom.

She smiled at his grim voice. "Kit's very fond of her, you know. He was very angry, too . . . And very – very upset to see her so –

in such a state . . ." She looked at Tom again, almost pleadingly now. "She just took off, you know, the last time, before she was ill again – and that was when Kit decided to – er – put a bit of distance between them."

Tom understood this. "But why *Bosnia*?"

"Oh, he'd already done a bit of VSO work when he was a student . . . He has a conscience, you know – perhaps because his wretched father is so damned rich!" She laughed a little. "Kit lent me the deposit for this flat, you know. Said he could easily afford it, which he could, of course. But I've paid him back now," she added hastily, "every penny."

Tom grinned at her. "I admire your independence. And Kit's, come to that. But Bosnia . . ." He hesitated. "You do realise it could be dangerous?"

"Oh yes," she said. "So does Kit. But the aid agency is pretty good at protecting its own people. And I think he felt – considering what was at stake, I mean – it was worth the risk."

"Yes," agreed Tom sadly. "I suppose so."

"You've been there, haven't you?" Holly said suddenly. "Kit told me. He rather admires his famous Uncle Tom, you know."

"Oh *don't*," said Tom, horrified. "I hope he wasn't influenced by my disastrous exploits."

She smiled at him then, with sudden compassion. "No. You can't be held responsible. I told him he ought to go away and see a bit more of life before accepting a whole lot of responsibilities and commitments he wasn't ready for . . . And Bosnia was his way of 'doing something useful'."

Like Daisy, thought Tom suddenly. *Daisy*! Of course. She's the one I must talk to about Kit. She'll know what to do. Why didn't I think of it before?

But shy, fair-haired Holly was looking at him intently, with a question in her eyes. "There's nothing wrong with Kit, is there . . .? Do you know something I don't know?"

Tom groaned inwardly. What could he say to her? "Er, no, not really . . . I think Becky must have been more anxious than she let on. She seems to have pestered the aid agency people to find out where he'd got to. They rang up today to say there was really no hard news . . . The situation is so confused out there."

Holly nodded soberly. "But they weren't *worried*?"

"No. They didn't seem to be. I think it's quite usual not to know where they are."

He saw the girl relax and accept this fact with a brief, philosophic shrug. "I suppose so."

"Mummy," said Adam, coming to lean against Holly's arm, "can the man stay to supper?"

"He isn't just 'the man', Adam," she told him, laughing. "He's Kit's Uncle Tom. And of course he can stay to supper – if he'd like to?"

"Uncle Tom?" tried out Adam hopefully, fixing Tom with large, soulful blue eyes.

"I'd be delighted," smiled Tom, meaning it. He had no desire to spend a cheerless, lonely evening in Becky's empty house.

"It'll only be scrambled eggs," she said apologetically.

"And bacon?" asked Adam, hopeful as ever.

"And bacon," his mother conceded.

"And baked beans?"

"Well –"

"*Please*?" He turned companionably to Tom. "D'you like beans?"

Tom laughed and ruffled the small boy's hair. "I can eat anything you can eat better," he sang. "I can eat anything better than you!"

"No, you can't!" countered Holly, also singing.

"Yes, I can!"

Delighted, Adam began to sing it, too. "No you can't!"

"Yes, I can!"

They ended up in hilarious discord, with Adam rolling on the floor. Holly left him there, still laughing, and went to start the supper.

"Can I help?" asked Tom, following Holly into the kitchen.

"Certainly not. You've just saved my son's life. We're going to wait on you hand and foot."

"Oh," said Tom, crestfallen. "Couldn't I lay the table?"

"No, I am," announced Adam. And then, looking at Tom, he added kindly: "But you can carry the forks."

It suddenly became a glowing, happy occasion. Perhaps they were all a little light-headed with relief – even Benji the dog seemed on his best behaviour and looked at everyone with shining, devoted eyes.

Adam went to bed soon after supper, making no protest about it, but he did ask for Tom to come and say goodnight as well as his mother. "I like uncles," he announced to Tom, in a voice already slurred with sleep. "They're fun."

Tom's eyes met Holly's with comic dismay. He didn't know whether to laugh or cry. He only knew he didn't want to be made into a small boy's idea of a hero. It was too difficult to live up to . . .

They lingered for a while over coffee, and Holly told him a bit about her degree course and what she might do with it later on. "I expect it'll be teaching – it would fit in with Adam's life best. But I'd have to do an extra year's TT course first . . . Kit says –" She broke off, and added a little breathlessly: "I'm always quoting Kit – but I really have got a will of my own, you know!"

"I know," agreed Tom, smiling at her. "I think you're doing very well. And so is young Adam!" He got to his feet then, and added gently: "But I don't think you should refuse support when it's offered – from Kit or anyone else!"

She looked at him quietly, and answered his smile with a fragile one of her own. "I think I agree with Adam. I like uncles," she murmured.

But as he was going out of her door, she said shyly: "If – if there is anything I can do for Becky, you will let me know? I – I don't suppose we've got much in common, except we've both been let down by an irresponsible man!"

"Oh, I don't know," said Tom. "I think you've got a lot in common – including Kit!" Then he grew serious. "I don't know if she ought to come back here at all, but if she does, she'll badly need a friend. The best thing you could do for her would be to ask her to supper, like me, and introduce her to young Adam."

She looked at him anxiously. "Would it? . . . I don't want to seem too pushy. Or to put Kit in an awkward position . . ." She sounded ridiculously humble.

"Don't be absurd," he said, and gave her shoulder a small, friendly squeeze. "She'd love it." He turned to go then, and added over his shoulder in the dark: "I'll let you know if there's any news of Kit."

He did not wait to see the small, revealing flash of relief in her eyes when he mentioned Kit. But he knew it was there.

On the whole, Tom reflected, the visit to Becky's house had been less depressing than he expected. But that was largely due to the warmth and kindness of Bob and Mary Nerris – and to his unexpected meeting with Holly and Adam. But if he was being honest with himself, he had to admit that it was the decision to go and find Daisy that had really lifted his spirits. He had badly wanted an excuse to look her up, and now he had one. He couldn't think why he needed an excuse, really. He could just go and talk to her anyway, but he fancied Daisy might be a bit dismissive of pure self-indulgence – whereas if he really needed help she would, he knew, do everything she could with the utmost generosity. I'm a fool, he told himself, I'm behaving like a bashful teenager. What's the matter with me? But he knew, really. There was something special about Daisy Bellingham – and her good opinion of him seemed to matter a lot.

So he made his way across London to the other side of the Thames near the Elephant and Castle with a mixture of hope and trepidation. Number Four, Candle Street turned out to be a small office behind a flaky blue door at the side of a metal box factory surrounded by warehouses and derelict building sites.

Tom pushed open the blue door and spoke hopefully into the gloom. "Anybody around?"

"Who's asking?" replied a sharp, suspicious voice.

Tom took a further step inside, and found himself looking into the face of a young Jamaican wearing a highly colourful T-shirt over shabby jeans. He was leaning against a table and looking at Tom over a sea of untidy papers.

"I'm looking for Daisy Bellingham," said Tom.

"Friend of hers, are you?" The voice was still suspicious.

"Yes!" said Tom, hoping it was true.

The young, wary face relaxed a little. "You'll probably find her down at the warehouse. They're loading today."

"Where's that?"

The long limbs unwound themselves and the boy came across to stand at the open door with him. "Down there." He pointed a finger. "Last one in the row – yellow roof – see it?"

"Thanks," affirmed Tom.

"You're not trouble, are you?" The boy was still looking at him with some doubt. "I wouldn't want trouble for Daisy."

"No," Tom smiled at him. "I'm not trouble. I just want to see her."

"OK," the boy said. "I'm Mike." He nearly smiled back at Tom, but thought better of it. "Tell her I've nearly done the lists," he added, and turned back to the littered table.

"I will," Tom agreed, already out of the door and heading for the distant yellow roof.

When he got there, the wide warehouse doors were open, there was a long, heavy lorry inside, and someone was banging about behind it. Tom edged his way round to the back, and found himself looking at the back view of a dishevelled Daisy, more like a lion cub than ever, lifting down an armload of boxes from a pile stacked high against the wall.

"Can I help?" he said. (He seemed to have said this before.)

"Thanks," said Daisy, not looking round. "All these have to go." She backed past Tom, carrying her load of stores, and still didn't seem to register who he was.

Tom picked up another load and followed her round to the open end of the lorry.

"Put them right at the back," she ordered. "This is only the first half . . ."

"Right," said Tom, and climbed inside to stack the stores as far back as he could.

But Daisy suddenly dropped a couple of boxes out of her own load and began to laugh. "Tom Denholm! What are you doing here?"

"Looking for you," said Tom, pushing the last of his boxes into place. He turned then, smiling, and they stood looking at one another, absurd gladness clear in their unguarded faces.

"Well, you've found me," said Daisy at last. "What now?" But somehow she couldn't stop smiling, and nor could Tom.

"I want to talk to you," he began. "In fact, I want your advice. But I'll help you finish loading first, if you like?"

"Done!" agreed Daisy, and turned briskly back to the stack of goods piled against the warehouse wall.

They worked side by side until the whole consignment of

food-aid and medical supplies had been neatly stowed away at the back of the lorry. Finally, Daisy said cheerfully: "That's the lot. Come on, there's a useful caff on the corner."

They crossed the road from the broken concrete of the empty building site, and pushed their way through the door of a steamy café called Joe's Place. It smelled of fish and chips and dough-nuts, and the coffee machine was hissing loudly, but it was warm and welcoming, and not too crowded.

"Hi, Daisy," called the round, red-haired man behind the counter. "The usual?"

"Make it two," ordered Daisy, smiling, and led Tom over to a table by the check-curtained window.

They sat down and waited while Joe himself slapped two bits of bacon into two rolls and brought them over to their table with two large mugs of tea.

"I hope you like bacon butties," said Daisy, laughter making sparks in those far-seeing grey eyes.

Tom was tempted to start singing: "I can eat anything . . ." again, as he had to young Adam (he felt like singing), but he merely took a bite out of his roll and nodded approval.

"Well?" prompted Daisy, knowing there was something serious on Tom's mind.

So he told her about Kit, and about Kit's girl, Holly, and her small boy – and how anxious she clearly was about Kit though she didn't say so . . . And he also told her a bit more about Becky, and how disastrous it would be if she started worrying about Kit's disappearance as well as everything else.

"I can't tell her, Daisy. Not now. I shall have to wait until there's more positive news. But what if there isn't?"

"Then she'll have to face it," said Daisy, being positive herself. "It might even do her good to worry about someone else."

Tom sighed. "You're very tough, Crazy Daisy."

"No, I'm not," she told him. "Not really. But sometimes shock therapy does more good than pussyfooting around." She patted his arm. "Don't look like that. We won't force the issue yet."

"We?" said Tom, knowing he need not say it.

"Of course, we. You came to me for help, didn't you?"

"I don't know what we can do, though."

"Nor do I – yet. But I daresay I'll think of something." She was still smiling at him, full of optimism and energy.

"What d'you think might have happened to him?"

"Several things." She looked at him levelly. "The lorry he was in might have been hijacked. There are still a lot of maverick soldiers – or bandits – about who would be glad of an extra lorry and its supplies. Or he might have hit a mine. Though that would probably have been discovered by now. He might have been shot at – or kidnapped – or escaped . . ." She watched Tom's face grow pale with anxiety as she spoke, and went on more gently: "I'm just telling you the worst that could happen . . . On the other hand, he may just have got lost, and he'll probably turn up a couple of days late, totally unscathed."

Tom nodded, accepting her forthright reading of the situation. "That's rather what I thought." He was silent for a moment, trying to get all the alternatives straight in his mind. "What ought I to do?"

She was still looking at him, head on one side in a considering manner. "You're thinking you ought to go out there, aren't you?"

He shook his head helplessly. "I don't know – the last thing they want is amateurs blundering about and getting in the way. But I do know the country a bit – and I do speak a bit of Serbo-Croat."

She stared at him, startled. "You didn't tell me that."

"No, I –" He made a vague, apologetic face at her. "It didn't seem relevant at the time."

"How come?"

"What? . . . Oh, how did I come to – well, I did a year's course on Slavonic art at Sarajevo University – a long time ago."

"My God," said Daisy. "You *would* be useful!"

He laughed. "Daisy, we don't even know he's really missing yet. Or where exactly he went missing – if he did at all . . . We'll just have to wait."

"Oh, that's all right," agreed Daisy airily. "I've got to go back to Yorkshire for another load first anyway. We should have heard by then."

It seemed to Tom that she had accepted the whole situation and was already making plans for him that he had not dared to put into words even in his own mind.

"Can I come with you?" he said suddenly.

"To Yorkshire?" She grinned at him. "Why not? You could share the driving." Then she looked at him hard and added: "That is, if your knee will let you?"

"It took me all across Canada," he said. "The Rockies are almost as tough going as Bosnia."

"I wasn't –" she protested, half laughing.

"Oh yes, you were. And if I did go with you, I'd insist on sharing everything – the driving, the arguing at checkpoints, the risks, the muddles, the lot!"

"You're very masterful," she said, with a grin.

"Not as bad as you!" he retorted, and they both began to laugh.

So there they were, driving up to Yorkshire together in yet another rather battered lorry, and as they came near to York, Daisy said suddenly: "I want to ask you something."

"Yes?" Tom was driving at that point, and he lifted an enquiring eyebrow in her direction.

"Can I come and see Becky?"

He did not answer at once, and then said abruptly: "Why?"

Daisy touched his arm, as if to allay fears. "Because I want to." Then, to his still doubtful silence, she added: "It may be important, Tom. With you going off, I mean. If there was someone else she trusted . . . it might help."

He nodded then, understanding her very well. "Except that, if I go off, you will too."

She agreed tranquilly. "But I might come back sooner."

Tom thought about the implications of that, and then said slowly: "You think very far ahead."

"Got to," said Daisy. "Practical. Especially if people depend on you."

Tom sighed. "I don't like people depending on me," he said, ashamed to admit it.

"Can't escape." Daisy smiled at him with sudden, unexpected compassion. "You're not a quitter."

There didn't seem to be any answer to that, so Tom kept silent. But Daisy went on pursuing her own line of attack.

"And after we've seen Becky, I want you to come home with me."

"Why?" asked Tom again, though he was half smiling by now.

Daisy's clear grey eyes were grave this time. "Tom, how long is Becky going to stay in Greenbanks? And what's going to happen to her afterwards? Especially if you're not there to take charge. Have you thought?"

"I –" He hesitated. He had thought, yes – a lot, but he hadn't come to any satisfactory conclusion. "It's been on my mind, yes," he admitted lamely.

Daisy nodded. "My mother does bed and breakfast in the summer," she said casually, as if changing the subject. "Well, lodgers you'd call them, really, and they usually want to stay longer . . . It's a farm, see – sheep and such, and a few horses . . . Fresh air, good food – " She looked at him sideways. "Simple, mind. No frills. But lovely hills to walk on, and plenty to do on the farm . . ." She was still looking at him with that oblique, half-smiling gaze.

"Oh Daisy, stop!" he protested.

But she went on calmly. "I think your sister would like it – from what you've told me about her. She used to like the country and riding and such, didn't she?" Her voice softened a little, and she added gently: "She'd be safe there, Tom. You wouldn't have to worry."

He blinked absurd tears out of his eyes and laid a hand over one of Daisy's. "Don't say any more now – or I shall cry like a baby!" But the smile he turned on her was luminous and strange.

"I wouldn't mind," said Daisy, offering him an extra-strong mint out of her pocket. "Tears are good for you." Laughter flickered between them like summer lightning.

"Let's see how she is first," Tom said, trying to come down to earth and be practical like Daisy. And he drove on through the outskirts of York towards the road to Greenbanks Hospital.

Becky was feeling better that day. The shadows and fears that had clouded her mind for so long seemed to have lifted a little, and a small surge of hope and renewal – a flicker of her old, natural optimism and energy – seemed to have arrived inside her from nowhere. The sun was shining outside, the birds were singing, and Tom was coming to see her. He had

95

telephoned to find out how she was and to say he was on his way.

There had been some bad days after his last visit, when the terrors descended on her mind again, and she hid from the light and buried her head in the bedclothes and refused to get up at all. And one day, she remembered, the nightmares had pursued her so hard that she had tried to run away. But she couldn't think of anywhere to run to and the staff had found her hiding in a bed of nettles behind the compost heap. She couldn't explain to them what she had been running from, or why she had ended up in the most uncomfortable, pain-filled sanctuary she could find. It was something to do with punishing herself for being to blame for something – for everything, including Derek's desertion – but she could not quite remember what had driven her to such despair.

Now, it was better, though. She put on a clean silk shirt and a bright tweed skirt, and took trouble over her hair. Maybe, she thought, things will get better soon. Maybe life isn't impossible, after all. Maybe I shall be able to manage on my own, when I get a bit stronger . . .

So when Tom arrived, she greeted him smiling, and said: "I'm much better today. I'm so glad you came."

Tom looked her up and down approvingly, and gave her an extra hug of reassurance. "You do look better, I must say. Where would you like to go? Shall we sit in the sun?"

"Why not? I'd like to get out of here." She glanced round at the pleasant reception room with a faint grimace. "It's nice enough, Tom, I know. But I'm beginning to feel a bit shut in."

He nodded. "I thought you might. But you'll be out of here soon, won't you?"

"In a week or so, they say."

Tom's heart gave a lurch of swift alarm. So soon? He would have to make arrangements almost at once, then. But he did not say anything at that point. He merely took Becky outside and sat with her on a bench overlooking the sloping lawns and the spreading branches of the fine old cedar tree.

He told her then, quietly, of his interview with Derek, and his subsequent talk with Greg's high-powered lawyer friend.

"It's all in hand," he told her, smiling. "No need to worry now. They'll sort things out and make sure you get a fair and sensible deal." He glanced at her face, wondering whether even the mention of financial arrangements would start her worrying again. But Becky seemed to accept it, almost cheerfully, and shrugged dismissive shoulders.

"As long as they can be tough on my behalf," she said. "I couldn't handle it myself. He's as slippery as an eel about money!"

"I know," Tom agreed grimly. "I saw that. But they'll be tough, believe me! And the law's on your side in any case. There are new rules about maintenance these days."

She sighed, fingering the knobbly wool on her skirt with a nervous hand. "I'm not really money-grubbing, Tom. I just want to feel – safe."

"I know," said Tom again. "And so you shall. I will personally guarantee it."

She laughed. "You're such a comfort! I feel better already."

Then he told her about his visit to her house, and how loyal and supportive Bob and Mary had been.

"Yes," Becky agreed. "They are real friends, those two . . . More than most round there."

Tom agreed. "I thought they were lovely people." He smiled at Becky and added gently: "They were so worried about you . . . Mary said you were almost like *family* to them."

Becky was touched by this, and just nodded silently.

At last Tom thought it was about time he mentioned Daisy, who was probably waiting for them by now in the little coffee house on the lawn. She had told him she would have a walk round the grounds first – she could do with some air, she said – and would then make her way to their rendezvous and wait patiently. "It doesn't matter how long, Tom. Take your time. And if she doesn't want to meet me, don't force the issue. Another time will do."

He had accepted her easy arrangements with gratitude – and a smile that said more than words about her enormous tact and kindness. Trust Daisy to make things as simple as possible.

"I've brought someone to see you today," he said finally. "A friend of mine called Daisy. I hope you'll like her."

Becky looked at him in surprise, but without alarm, he noticed. "That'll be fun. I could do with a new face round here."

He rose to his feet, relieved at her acceptance. "She'll probably be waiting for us in the coffee house. Shall we go?"

Becky tucked her arm through Tom's confidingly, and smiled. "I feel like company. Tell me who she is."

"Well," Tom began warily, "she's a sheep farmer's daughter from around here. But among other things, she drives relief aid lorries to Bosnia . . . I thought you might like to talk to her about Kit. She'll probably be able to relieve your mind a bit. I know you've been worried." He did not say anything about the phone call from the aid organisers. He had agreed on this with Daisy, and planned this way of approach to give Becky the maximum reassurance. He felt a bit guilty about withholding the latest worrying information, but he was sure it was the right thing to do – at present.

"That's wonderful," said Becky.

"She won't be able to tell you quite where he's got to," explained Tom swiftly, "but she can explain what it's like out there."

Becky nodded. "I won't expect too much." She sounded entirely rational and reasonable today. "I expect I'm silly to worry – but I suppose mothers always do about their errant sons."

Tom laughed. "I expect our mother worried about us!"

They were still laughing together when they arrived at the coffee shop. Daisy saw them coming, and noted with cheerful relief that Becky looked fairly calm and balanced. She also noted how like her brother, Tom, she was, in a slightly tired and blunted way. The same springy, auburn-glinting hair (more flecked with grey at the edges than Tom's, though), the same tall, athletic build (but held back by a certain lassitude that made her seem less energetic than Tom, in spite of his damaged knee) and the same blue eyes (though still clouded with doubts and anxieties) and the same light-bringing smile that flashed out in cautious welcome.

"Hallo," Daisy said, holding out her hand. "I hope you don't mind my coming to see you. Tom thought I might be able to reassure you."

Becky took her hand, looking with interest into the friendly face before her. She too thought of a playful but slightly dangerous lion cub when she saw the honey–gold tawny tongues of hair framing

98

that fighting head, and felt a curious sense of recognition and relief as she met that unflinching gaze.

"Of course I don't mind," she said, being direct because Daisy somehow required it of her. "It was very good of you to come . . . Tom, can you get us all some coffee?"

Tom sighed with relief. It was as easy as that. When he came back with the tray of coffee, the two heads were close together and Daisy was saying: "It might be a bit of a culture shock for him to see how poor everyone is, and how frightful the conditions are they have to live in –" She glanced round her at the beautiful grounds of this very special hospital, and added: "And how desperately short of supplies and equipment the hospitals are . . . but that won't do him any harm."

"No," agreed Becky, very well aware of what Daisy was actually saying. "I suppose he has been a bit too – privileged and sheltered all his life. I suppose I have too, really."

Daisy grinned. "Life usually gets up and hits you when you get too smug!"

Becky actually laughed. Then she asked the question that Tom had been dreading. "But – you don't think he'd actually be in danger?"

Daisy looked at her straight. "Yes, he could be. We all *could* be. But he's with a team, and he's well protected – as far as he can be . . . All the aid workers are looked after – they are valuable people, after all." She smiled. "A young man has to take risks sometimes, doesn't he? You wouldn't want to hold him back?"

Becky shook her head doubtfully. "I tell myself that – but I'm afraid I would! . . . Being a mother is frightfully difficult!"

Daisy's smile grew gentle. "Yes, it must be . . . Letting go must be worst of all."

Becky sighed. "I don't know . . . I've not been a very good mother to either of my children, really . . . And now, just when I want to be, I can't – because I'm being too possessive!"

Tom thought, amazed, they are talking like old friends – and Becky is thinking about *someone other than herself* for the first time in months. How does Daisy do it?

At this point he decided it was safe to bring in the subject of Holly and little Adam, and their curious encounter on the edge of Becky's faceless, cold-hearted suburb.

"There's someone else anxious about Kit," he began cautiously. "I think you've met her once or twice – a girl called Holly?"

Becky looked startled. "When did you meet her?"

Tom explained then about young Adam's wild dash after the dog, and everyone's instant terror.

Becky shuddered. "Thank goodness you were there!"

"All I did was shout," he said, smiling at the recollection of that enormous yell. "And then they took me home with them and asked me to supper. They were so nice to me, Becky."

"I should think so!"

"No, I mean they were the only ones who were – except your gardener, Bob and his wife . . ." He paused and then added slowly: "I think you'd really like Holly if you got to know her, and young Adam is enchanting."

Becky asked, grasping at essentials: "Is she really fond of Kit, do you think?"

"Oh yes," Tom said, "but she sent him away, you know. She said he was too young to saddle himself with an unmarried mum and someone else's child."

Becky looked surprised. But Daisy said thoughtfully: "She must care about him quite a lot to have sent him away."

Tom shot her a surprised, grateful glance.

"Yes, I suppose that's true . . ." admitted Becky, looking at Daisy with respect.

Tom thought he had said enough about Holly for the time being – and Daisy had, as usual, put the relationship in a real perspective . . . Better leave it now. It could all be allowed to develop later on. Because he was sure in his own mind that Holly and Adam were going to be important in Becky's life . . . He was just wondering what other reassurances he could think of to talk about, when Becky said suddenly: "Tom, I forgot. Dr Bradley wants to see you for a moment. About when I'm coming out, I think." She looked at Daisy and went on, almost shyly: "Daisy and I'll be all right here for a bit. Why don't you go along now?"

Tom looked enquiringly at Daisy, who gave him a quick, smiling nod. "Sounds all right to me," she said. "Let's order some more coffee – and two of those sticky buns."

He left them companionably hovering over the cake display

on the counter, and went off to find Bradley somewhere in the hospital.

"Is she ready to come out?" asked Tom, feeling both anxious and responsible.

Bradley hesitated, looking at Tom with frank uncertainty. "She's certainly ready for a more open-ended existence. This enclosed, safe, ordered way of life is very artificial – and very easy to accept. But whether she is ready to cope all on her own, I don't know . . . I rather doubt it."

Tom nodded. "That's rather what I thought."

"She's had one or two setbacks, you know," went on Bradley. "Did she tell you about trying to run away?"

Tom looked startled. "No. What happened?"

"She just went missing one morning. We searched the grounds, all the rooms, even the cupboards . . . She had taken her handbag with her, but nothing else – no extra clothes or anything . . . We were getting really quite worried when she hadn't turned up towards evening. The gates are open all day, of course, as this is an 'open' hospital – but we close them at night. We didn't quite know what to do about it, in case she was *outside* and wanted to come back in . . . Some of the better patients do go out shopping and so on . . ." He sighed. "It's always a problem – a patient's safety versus a patient's freedom . . . Anyway, just as it was getting dark, one of the gardeners found her, curled up in a tight little ball, half buried in a bed of nettles behind the compost heap!"

Tom shook his head in disbelief. "Why there?"

"I don't know . . ." Bradley was thoughtful. "But sometimes these emotional traumas take the form of self-punishment . . . It's a kind of guilt complex."

"*Guilt*? Why should Becky have a guilt complex?"

"No good reason at all. But it often happens. She feels it *must* have been her fault for her husband to have behaved as he did."

Tom made an explosive sound, and Bradley laughed.

"Yes, I know it's absurd. But I'm sure that was part of the trouble – at the back of her mind . . . That was what was making her feel so inadequate." He grew serious again. "As a matter of fact, I was on the point of contacting you. We are supposed to

101

ask the relatives' consent for a restraining order if patients try to abscond or put themselves at risk."

"What kind of restraining order? Do you mean – certification?" He was a bit horrified at the mere mention of the word.

"Yes. A temporary detention, under the Mental Health Act . . . But in your sister's case it was so borderline, and she hadn't actually come to any harm, so I decided to wait and see . . ." He looked honestly at Tom. "But I took a risk."

Tom nodded soberly. "Is it likely to happen again?"

"No, I don't think so . . . She really does seem much better now." He paused and then added slowly: "The last place she was in, you know, when she was ill before, insisted on giving her shock treatment."

Tom looked at him, appalled. "I didn't know that. Who gave consent for that?"

"Her husband, I believe. It was before the final break-up . . ." He shook his head rather angrily. "But I don't think it did her much good – rather the reverse, and it certainly upset her memory . . . It's a dangerous treatment, and we don't much like using it here."

Tom smiled at him, a bit wanly. "I'm glad to hear it."

"Yes – but you see the quandaries we are sometimes put in about restraints and consents."

"I do, indeed." Tom was silent for a moment, thinking things out. Then he said: "Would it be all right to take her out for the day?"

Bradley looked pleased. "Yes, I'm sure it would. Why?"

So Tom explained about Daisy's suggestion, and the sheep farm on the Yorkshire dales, and Daisy's hospitable mother. "What do you think?" he asked, anxious to have Bradley's approval.

"It sounds ideal," agreed the doctor warmly. "And she would be within reach of us here if the need arose." He thought about it and added slowly: "We would like to keep her on the antidepressants for a bit longer, but we are a bit concerned about giving her too big a supply . . ." He glanced at Tom out of shrewd, knowledgeable eyes. "I don't think she would try that sort of thing again, but we have to be careful . . . If what you suggest could be arranged, she could come back here once a week for a check-up and a week's supply . . ."

"Would that be safe?"

"It wouldn't kill her. She took a whole bottleful before, as well as aspirin and vodka!"

Tom nodded sadly. "I can't guarantee that Becky will like the idea, of course. She may insist on going home. But I don't think she should stay in that lonely suburban house on her own, and I – I may have to be away myself for a while."

Bradley looked at him sympathetically. "You can't disrupt your whole life, I know. But perhaps she will like the idea of living on a Yorkshire farm. I know I would!"

Tom grinned. "Peace and quiet. And no demanding patients with traumas!"

They laughed together, and left it that Tom would come tomorrow and take Becky to look at the farm. They would take it from there.

On his way back to find Daisy and Becky, Tom had to pass through the open foyer of the pleasant unit where Bradley's office was housed, and he was confronted with a curious little incident.

A tall, thin boy with a shock of pale hair and rather desperate eyes, came up to him and said: "You're Becky's brother, Tom, aren't you?"

"Yes," Tom admitted, smiling. "I am."

"I like Becky," said the boy. "She's real." He looked at Tom rather earnestly. "Some of them aren't, you know."

"Aren't they?" Tom looked round at the few people sitting around and talking among themselves. They all looked real enough to him. But then, he reflected, I'm not living among them. And when you're ill, sometimes nothing seems real.

"Can I ask you a question?" asked the boy, fixing Tom with those fierce, desperate eyes.

"I should think so," Tom said easily. "Though I may not know the answer."

The boy nodded, and drew a deep, angry breath. "That's what they all say," he muttered, and seemed all at once to be unable to go on.

"Well?" prompted Tom gently, knowing he was asking for trouble.

"*Do you believe in God*?" The boy's hot, seeking gaze was fixed on him in anguished entreaty.

Tom thought to himself in swift terror: What am I to say to him? He needs reassurance so desperately. But how can I say "Yes" when I don't know the answer? I can't lie to those imploring eyes.

But then he suddenly remembered Daisy – and her sublime belief in everyone else's goodness, and how much that belief achieved.

"I – yes, I think I do," he said. "I believe in the power of good. That's just another word for God, isn't it?"

The boy stared at him for a long moment in silence. "*The power of good*," he repeated, as if trying out the phrase in his mind. "Does it exist?"

"Oh yes," said Tom with conviction. "It certainly does."

For a few more seconds the burning eyes remained fixed on him, and then they seemed to fill with a kind of exultant relief. "That's all right then, isn't it?" he said, and strolled off, leaving Tom in shaken silence behind him.

Wow! said Tom to himself. That was a near one – and I still don't know if I said the right thing . . . And his heart ached a little for the boy and his bewildered search for certainty and truth in this shifting world of changing values.

I must pull myself together, said Tom. I've got to sound just as certain for Becky. She needs something to hold on to, just as much as that frightened boy.

When he got back to the little coffee house, Daisy and Becky had moved out onto a bench on the lawn and were laughing together in the sun.

"Tom." Becky's face was glowing. "Daisy's been telling me about the farm – they've got lambs there, orphan ones, in the kitchen! And lots more in the lambing pens. And they've got horses, too – one called Bluett, one called Ginger-Nut, and one called –?" She turned to Daisy, smiling.

"Morello. She's black and shiny, see, like a cherry. And you've forgotten Garnet. She's in foal, too."

"It all sounds so lovely," said Becky wistfully. "I wish I could see it."

Tom looked from Becky's glowing face to Daisy's innocent one, and laughed. "Guess what? I've just been fixing with Dr Bradley to take you out for the day tomorrow."

"Oh Tom!" She was like a child being offered a trip to the seaside. "Can we go and see the farm?" She turned to Daisy. "Would you let us come? Would we be in the way?"

"Of course not. You could help feed the lambs. There are never enough pairs of hands at lambing time." She winked blandly at Tom.

Becky was looking beyond them both at the sunlight and shadow on the trim lawns of the hospital grounds. She waved an apologetic hand at it and said: "I know this is all very beautiful and I'm very lucky to be here, but – but some real, open space would be simply wonderful!"

Tom grinned and patted her arm. "You shall have it. Tomorrow."

But Daisy said severely: "You simply *can't* be ill any longer! There's a whole world waiting for you out there!"

"I know," Becky agreed. "And I – I'm nearly ready for it. Aren't I, Tom?"

"Yes," said Tom, sounding positive and cheerful. "I think you are."

"In any case," Daisy remarked, looking at Becky with fierce intensity, "you can't let that creep have the satisfaction –"

"What?"

"Of making you ill." Daisy spelt it out for her. "Why should he? He's not worth it. And you're made of stronger stuff than that!"

Becky's smile was sad. "No. Tom's the strong one. I'm not like him."

"Rubbish!" said Daisy. "I think you're very alike. Only you don't know it!" She grinned at Becky and got briskly to her feet. "We must go now. I have to get home."

Tom got up then, almost too astonished at Daisy's forthright tactics to say anything at all, but he could see that Becky was not dismayed by this plain speaking. In fact she seemed to be cheered by it.

"I think I'll go and play squash," she said suddenly, grinning back at Daisy. "You've made me feel like hitting something really hard!"

"Good!" encouraged Daisy, eyes alight with mischief. "See you tomorrow." And she walked off, tactfully leaving Tom to say goodbye.

"She's amazing," said Becky, laughing. "I'm so glad you brought her."

"Yes," agreed Tom. "It was a good idea." He did not tell her that it was Daisy's idea in the first place, and he had agreed to it with some misgiving. He simply hugged her hard and murmured: "Go on getting well!" before he turned away, saying over his shoulder, like Daisy: "See you tomorrow."

"I don't know how you get away with it," said Tom, laughing, as they drove off into the Yorkshire countryside.

"I'm a stranger," Daisy explained. "I can say things you can't. It may be cheek, but she'll accept that from me!"

"So it seems!" Tom grinned.

"Are you complaining?"

"No, I'm delighted." He glanced at her sideways and saw that she was really a little worried about his reaction. Daisy's fierce confrontations were mostly bluff, he realised. "And the way you got her interested in the farm was very clever."

Daisy blinked. "I wasn't being clever, Tom. Just waxing lyrical about something I love."

He nodded soberly. "I know – but it worked!"

She began to smile. "I hope it works on you, too."

"I don't see how it can fail," he said, watching the hills begin to unroll before him.

They drove on through a dazzle of spring rain and fitful sunshine as the clouds raced over the swelling hillsides. This time they climbed high into the empty moors that he had only touched the fringe of before, and finally came to the cluster of warm stone buildings that was Jenks Farm. There were several barns, a neat milking parlour, and a couple of loosebox stables spread round a wide cobbled yard – and at the far end of this square space stood a long, low farmhouse with a mossy tiled roof. The door stood open, and a couple of collie dogs got up and barked joyfully as Daisy drove in.

"Now, remember," said Daisy, "you're staying the night."

"Casing the joint?" His eyebrows were as quirky as his smile.

106

"Just about."

"Daisy," he said, "you love this place and everyone in it. That's good enough for me."

Daisy clearly didn't know how to reply to this, but before she had made up her mind what to say, her mother came out of the farmhouse door and stood smiling at them in the clean, scrubbed yard.

Ruth Bellingham, forthright and welcoming, was like a slightly more thickset version of her daughter – the same unruly ruff of hair, but more pepper-and-salt than tawny–gold, the same steady grey eyes, and the same infectiously friendly smile.

"Come on in, Tom. I've heard all about you. Tea's brewing."

The big farmhouse kitchen was warm and inviting, and seemed to be full of animals. Beside the sturdy Aga a couple of lambs lay curled up in a cardboard box stuffed with straw, and next to them, protectively, lay an ancient collie bitch, head on paws, eyes watchful and alert.

"That's Nell," said Ruth, stooping to fondle her ears. "She's too old for work now, but she's very good at minding the orphan lambs."

Besides these, there were two cats asleep on a long cushioned settle by one wall, and a boxful of young ducklings in another warm corner near the Aga.

"Lambing's really over now," Ruth explained, "but there are always a few late ones. Jim's out with them now, but he'll be in soon . . . Sit you down and have some tea. It's no good waiting for him!"

Daisy, meanwhile, had also stooped to rub Nell's ears and smile affectionately at the thumping tail. "How's her rheumatism?"

"Getting worse," said her mother. "She won't get up now, unless she has to."

They looked at each other and sighed, knowing that the time was coming when the faithful old collie's life would end.

"I'm sorry about the ducklings," said Ruth, with an impish grin rather like Daisy's. "A fox got the poor mother – but I think one of the hens will adopt them – it usually works."

She fetched the large brown teapot that was standing on the Aga hotplate and set it down on the table. Farmhouse tea turned out to be lavish and homely, and almost more than Tom could eat. There were thick slices of home-cured ham, wedges of white Wensleydale cheese and some of their own as well, hunks of home-baked bread and home-churned butter, last year's heather honey, apple pie and cream, and a large, rich fruit cake.

They had only just begun on this abundant feast when Jim Bellingham came in with two of his farm workers. Jim himself was squarish, solid and imperturbable, with the calm, slow movements of a good hill farmer who was used to handling frightened or recalcitrant animals, and a calm, slow smile to match. His companions were also fairly slow-moving and unruffled, but they didn't have Jim's underlying quiet air of authority.

Mango (he was always just "Mango" – no one used his real name, even if they knew it) was solid and squarish, like his boss, and his face was permanently browned and scoured by the bitter winds of the high winter moors. His eyes, set in a fine net of wrinkles, were brown and tranquil, and seemed to reflect a steady belief that every emergency could be handled if you went about it the right way.

Lacey (also other name unknown) was small and stringy, with the seamed, clever face and light, dancing build of a jockey, which he had once been. His handling of horses was legendary, and though he could turn his hand to most things on the farm, he loved nothing better than to take his charges out on to the windy gallops where both he and they could breathe the spicy air.

Both men had one thing in common – they were devoted to Daisy, and had been her willing slaves since she was a small, imperious girl. Now they looked at her indulgently as their boss turned to question her.

"This is Tom," said Daisy. "Remember, Dad?"

"Ay," Jim answered, holding out his hand. "Glad to know you, Tom," and he sat down in his chair at the head of the table. "Mango and Lacey," he added, tilting his head at the two men. "Mango does the cows and Lacey does everything else, including the horses, and helps with the sheep at lambing, like Mango. Isn't that right?"

"Ay." The two farm hands grinned and sat down at the table, too. They seemed to be men of few words.

"You collecting tomorrow?" Jim asked Daisy, reaching for the cheese.

Daisy hesitated and glanced at Tom. "No, I thought I'd take a day off. I want to show Tom's sister, Becky, round the farm." She looked from her father to her mother for approval. "If that's all right?"

"Fair enough," said her father. "You can show her the new foal."

Daisy turned a glowing face to Lacey, the silent farm hand. "Did Garnet manage it?"

Lacey smiled his slow, gentle smile. "She did that – a gradely little chestnut filly – just like her mother."

"That's great! Any complications? You were worried about her, I know."

"Nay, it all went as smooth as silk."

"Took all night, mind," put in Mango, flashing a sardonic grin at Lacey. "But what's beauty sleep to him?"

Daisy laughed.

The meal progressed cheerfully, with everyone's plate piled high with reinforcements as soon as they were emptied. Nothing of any importance was said, either about Becky's proposed visit or about Daisy's imminent departure on another relief trip. Conversation was calm and leisurely, mostly about farm matters, and not demanding any particular attention. Mostly, they were all too busy eating to talk. And, Tom reflected with a sense of profound relief, there did not seem to be any tensions or undercurrents at all.

But when the last cup of tea and the last slice of cake had been consumed, the two farm workers went off on bicycles, Jim pushed his chair back and went to sit in the old armchair by the Aga, and Ruth waved Tom and Daisy out of the room, saying: "Go and show Tom the view from the top of the Fell before it gets dark."

So they climbed the heathery, scented slopes behind the farm-house, following the old sheep tracks in the springy turf till they stood breathless on the top of Jenks Fell, and looked down into the darkening dales below. Up there, on the roof of the world, the air was as pure and heady as fine wine, and the silence all around them was deep and profound, only broken by an occasional bleat from a distant sheep, or the sudden liquid call of a curlew.

"Wonderful," breathed Tom, gazing out at all that airy space and blue distance. "So quiet."

"Empty enough for you?" asked Daisy, smiling at his enchanted face.

He shook his head in faint self-reproach. "To think I said England was too crowded!"

"Some of it is," she admitted. "But not up here."

He laughed, and turned again to look at the long, smooth lines of the high moors stretching away into curve after curve of rolling hills as far as the eye could see. Twilight was creeping along the valleys and up the slopes of the lower hills now, but up here the sky was still clear and bright, awash with the golden afterglow of sunset, and as they watched, a sudden last gleam of red–gold sunlight pointed an incandescent finger through a cleft in the hills, turning everything in its path to molten gold. It was gone almost as soon as it had come, and behind it the deepening twilight seemed to draw the hills together to face the oncoming night.

"Let's go down," said Daisy softly. "Can't stay on the peaks for ever."

Tom did not answer. But he took her hand in his and they went down the hill together like two children going home.

Later that evening, when Daisy had shown Tom to a pleasant, whitewashed bedroom overlooking the fields beyond the farm-yard, there was a gentle tap at the door, and Ruth Bellingham put her head round it. "Can I come in, Tom?"

"Of course." Tom smiled at her, thinking how like Daisy she was, though perhaps a little shyer at putting words to her thoughts.

"Are you comfortable up here? Is it all right?"

Tom looked at her, amazed. "*All right*? It's lovely – so airy and cool and open . . . Just what I like best. No unnecessary clutter!"

Ruth laughed. "That's a relief. Got no time for clutter myself!" But there was more to her question than mere hospitable concern, and Tom knew it, so he simply waited for her to go on.

"About your sister, Tom – Daisy told me all about it. I hope you don't mind?"

He began to say "No, of course not", but she cut him short, intent on what she had to say.

"I just wanted you to know that I'd be glad to have her here, if she took to the idea, that is." She looked directly at Tom then, smiling and anxious both at once. "There's plenty to do on the farm, if she felt like helping . . . and plenty to see, if she didn't . . . Good walks all round, and we'd be company for her, of a sort – though Jim gets too tired by evening to do much but snore!"

Tom grinned at this, but he still waited for Ruth to finish.

"And then there's the horses – if she really likes riding, they do need exercising, especially now Daisy is away so much . . ." She paused, and then added with disarming frankness: "What I'm trying to say is, there's plenty to occupy her, and we'd keep an eye, of course, but it's a pretty simple existence up here, a farm has no use for frills – so would it be *enough*?"

Tom shook his head at her in despair. "How can you ask that? It has everything she could wish for. She was brought up on a ranch, you know. That's not very different. Becky has been rather spoiled and overburdened with possessions recently, but she's not like that underneath . . . She'd love this place, I'm sure – and she couldn't fail to find the moors simply beautiful . . ." His smile was almost tender as he looked at Ruth's anxious face. "And with you to look after her as well – what more could she ask?"

Ruth sighed, a kind of rueful compassion in her answering smile. "We women," she said slowly, on another sigh, "we always expect too much of life, you know . . . And people don't realise we need to keep our own self-respect, our own independence . . . no matter what our lives are like . . . It's going to be hard for her to start again . . ."

Tom nodded quietly, enormous relief flooding over him as it became clear that Ruth Bellingham understood very well what was at the root of Becky's troubles.

"You do realise that she might be – a bit of a responsibility?"

"No farmer's wife can afford to be afraid of responsibility!" retorted Ruth. "We live with crises every day!"

Tom looked at her with respect, but he still felt obliged to warn her. "She might have a relapse – or something."

"Well, the hospital isn't far away," said Ruth tranquilly. "Her doctor will know what to do."

111

He met her level gaze with humility. There wasn't much more he could say.

"Of course, she might take against the place," said Ruth impishly, "and then all our plans would come to naught!"

Tom laughed. But he realised something else about this conversation. Behind all their plans was the unspoken assumption that Tom himself would be going away and leaving Becky in their charge. Going away? . . . With Daisy? To Bosnia to look for Kit? . . . It was not certain yet that he would need to do so, but Ruth and Daisy seemed to think it was already decided. Perhaps it was, he told himself wonderingly . . . Perhaps we already knew how it would be . . .

"Do you worry about Daisy?" he asked suddenly, out of the thoughts churning round in his head.

Ruth looked at him without surprise. "Yes, of course. But she's grown-up now – her own woman. It's like I said, you've got to find your own self-respect and your own independence . . . And anyway, no one could ever stop Daisy doing something if she set her mind on it!"

They found themselves laughing companionably together as Daisy came up the stairs behind them. "Cocoa in the kitchen," she said. "Time for bed. Dad's orders!"

Meekly, they followed her down to the welcoming warmth of the farmhouse kitchen, and the glorious jug of old-fashioned cocoa on the stove.

Becky's day out at the farm was more successful than anyone had dared to hope.

To begin with, she was in a cheerful mood and feeling much more confident because Bradley had come round and told her he was pleased with her progress. "You are much stronger now," he said, smiling encouragement. "I think you're almost ready for the big bad world outside."

"Am I?" Becky sounded doubtful. But then, with sudden surprising fervour she added: "Oh, I do hope so!"

And Bradley patted her arm approvingly and said: "That's the way to look at things!"

So when Tom and Daisy came to fetch her (in one of the farm cars instead of Daisy's rattling lorry), she had made up her mind to be positive and enjoy every moment of the day, and waste no more time on fruitless anxieties about the future.

"We're lucky with the weather," said Daisy, grinning a welcome. "The moors look fine in this kind of light . . . Nothing dark about them today."

They drove up into the hills under a clear spring sky, and Tom sat back, sighing inwardly with relief as Daisy pointed out landmarks and favourite places to an appreciative Becky, looking as wide-eyed and eager as a child.

Then there was coffee in the big farmhouse kitchen, with Ruth Bellingham at her warmest and most welcoming, and everyone coming in from their farm chores to have a breather. They were all introduced to Becky, and Lacey, with his gentle smile, said softly: "You'd likely want to see the little foal, I reckon?"

"Oh, *please*," Becky begged, and followed the quiet, unhurried figure down the cobbled yard to the stables. Tom and Daisy looked at one another and smiled, allowing Becky to go on ahead before they joined the inspection party.

Lacey did not open the loosebox half-door, but he let them all look over the top into the warm, straw-filled stable within. The mare, Garnet, stood proudly over her offspring, her ears alert, the beautiful burnished head still a little tense, and the big, liquid eyes looking anxiously from one visitor to another.

"'Tis all reet, lass," crooned Lacey in his soft, caressing voice. "We've only come to admire her . . ." and he pointed a gnarled finger at the spindly-legged little foal standing unsteadily in the straw.

"Oh," breathed Becky. "Isn't she lovely!"

The small head was alert and poised, like her mother's, and the chestnut coat was almost as silken and glowing, now that the dishevelled dampness of new birth had been licked away. But the long legs were still a bit shaky, and the little foal lurched cheerfully after her mother, trying to balance in the rustling straw.

"We'll have to give her a name," Daisy mused. "What goes with Garnet? . . ." She looked from Becky's enchanted face to Tom's almost equally fascinated one, and added gently: "Becky, would you like to name her?"

Becky turned quickly to Daisy, not sure if she really meant it. "Can I? . . . But I'm not sure what would be right . . . to go with Garnet? . . ." She paused, considering. "How about Jewel? . . . Or Gemma?" Instinctively – used to dealing with her own horse, Spice – she put out a gentle hand to the anxious mare, Garnet. "What do you think, mother? Isn't she a little Gem?"

The mare eyed her suspiciously for a moment and did not move.

"Or would you rather call her your little Jewel?" Becky asked, in a softened tone Tom scarcely recognised.

This time the mare whinnied softly in answer, and to everyone's astonishment, came forward and nuzzled Becky's hand with her velvet nose.

"Well, I be jiggered," said Lacey, mild amazement in his slow voice. "She's taken to you and no mistake."

"Looks like she approves of Jewel, too," smiled Daisy.

Tom said nothing. He could not tell them that Becky's spontaneous gesture had taken him back to the days of their childhood on the ranch, when Becky had ridden fearlessly about the rolling grasslands, and had every horse on the *estancia* literally eating out of her hand . . . It somehow brought a faint mist of tears to his eyes, remembering that brave, untouched girl – and he turned away, ashamed of his weakness.

But Daisy was of sterner stuff. "If Garnet's accepted you, you *must* be all right!" she told Becky, laughing. "I reckon you could ride one of the others next time you come. What do you think, Lacey?"

"Ay," said Lacey, without hesitation. "She'll do."

It was high praise from the quiet farm hand, and Becky knew it. But she also knew better than to push her luck with Garnet, so she gave the gentle, thrusting nose one more soft pat, and turned away.

"Come on," said Daisy, also knowing that small miracles mustn't be made too much of, "let's have a look at the lambing pens . . . And then we'll walk up the hill."

The lambing pens were full of placid mothers and bawling lambs, most of them white and woolly and absurdly bouncy, but a few of them black and curly and even more bouncy. Becky loved all of them instantly, and was immensely pleased when Jim came towards them carrying a pair of fragile twins, and gave one each

114

to Daisy and Becky. "Take 'em up to the house for me, will you? Ruth'll know what to do."

"So do I," said Daisy, half reproachfully to her father. "You don't have to tell me!"

He did not answer that, but merely grinned at her and jerked his thumb towards the house.

The two women went off together, cradling the newborn lambs in their arms, and Tom stayed behind to talk to Jim – that is, if the busy farmer had time to talk. "Can I help?" he asked, though he was very much aware that he did not know enough about lambing to be much use.

"Nay, there's not much left for us to do now," said Jim. "Lambing's mostly done. Those two were late ones, see, and the poor old ewe's had a bad time with 'em . . . We might give her back one o' them when she's recovered a bit . . ." He leant comfortably against one of the metal struts that separated the pens. "Things'll get easier now," he said, with his eyes still following Daisy and Becky as they made their way up to the farmhouse door.

Tom wasn't quite sure whether Jim Bellingham was talking about the lambing season or not, but he rather suspected that the sturdy Yorkshire farmer understood a lot more than he said about Becky and her problems.

"Good air," he said suddenly. "Up on the moors. Put some colour back. She's a bit pale, like . . ." He smiled at Tom with great innocence. "Does you a power o' good – hill country."

Tom nodded. It was certainly true for him. He just hoped it would be true for Becky, too.

"Tell you what," said Jim, suddenly realising that Tom really wanted to make himself useful, "you could help lay out a few more straw bales. Keeps the wind off the little 'uns. Some of 'em are still a bit fragile-like."

Tom was absurdly pleased to be asked, and set about building windbreaks round the edges of the lambing pens, following Jim's laconic instructions as best he could.

"Coupla over here . . . Stack 'em in threes . . . Make an angle on the corner . . ." They worked companionably side by side until a loud bell began to clang outside the farmhouse door. "Dinner," said Jim cheerfully, putting down his last bale. "Reckon we've

115

earned it." And he led Tom back to the farmhouse in comfortable silence.

They found Daisy and Becky still feeding the new lambs from small but well-filled bottles. Becky's face was absorbed and fascinated, and she held the limp little curly-haired creature cradled in her arms as naturally as if she had always done it. Daisy held the floppy twin with more nonchalant ease, but then she really had been doing it, off and on, at lambing time for as long as she could remember. She looked up at Tom as he came in, and gave him a cheerful wink. "She's doing fine," she announced, smiling at Becky. "Might've been born to it!"

Ruth turned from the stove them, and carried a large hotpot over to the table, followed by a steaming dish of potatoes and one of mashed buttered carrots and swedes. "They've had theirs," she said, with a jerk of her head towards the sleepy lambs. "Now it's our turn."

Mango and Lacey came in then from their various chores, as they had the night before, and sat down at the table, silent as ever. But Lacey did not stay silent this time, and kept looking at Becky with puzzled admiration.

"Never seen owt like it," he said to Jim. "Puts her hand out and says 'What d'you think, mother?' – and Garnet comes to her like a – like a –?"

"Lamb?" said Daisy, grinning, and everyone laughed.

"Becky's always been good with horses," said Tom, well aware that this gentle praise was doing much for Becky's morale. She was looking quite pink and pleased.

"Thought we'd go up Drumhead Crag after dinner," said Daisy. "You can see all across the Vale of York from there."

"It's steep, mind," warned Ruth, dishing out more potatoes. "Don't tire Becky out."

"I like walking," Becky protested. "I – used to do a lot . . . once."

"If you go up to the top pasture," Jim cut in, covering Becky's slight hesitation, "keep a look out for Trudi."

Daisy grinned. "Has she gone off again?"

"Broke her tether – if she hasn't et it!"

There was a general rumble of warm laughter, and Daisy turned a smiling face to Becky. "Trudi's a goat – the most

116

ornery, cantankerous creature you could hope not to meet on a day out on the moors!" She glanced across the table at her father, still looking a bit mischievous. "But it's all right, Dad, we'll bring her home, if we can find her."

"If you can catch her!" growled Mango, and Lacey choked a little over his latest forkful of stew.

Tom was surreptitiously watching Becky, and he felt the whole complex web of anxiety about her health and her future begin to dissolve and slip from his mind strand by strand as he saw how relaxed she was, and how naturally she seemed to be fitting into this easy, friendly group of warm-hearted people.

Was it really possible, he asked himself, that it was going to be as easy as this? Surely something must go wrong? It was almost too good to be true.

But Daisy was looking at him now, and signalling unspoken reassurance with those candid grey eyes. "You never know," she said obscurely, "it's the kind of day for miracles – even catching goats."

No one seemed to think her remark at all odd, not even Becky, and everyone went on eating and talking and laughing in the sunny farmhouse kitchen as if there were no such things as shadows anywhere.

So after lunch (dinner, in farm terms) they did climb the steep path up to Drumhead Crag, and stood on its stony outcrop crest looking down at the chequered fields and woods and blue–green distances of the Vale of York.

"Beautiful," breathed Becky. "So wide – so much space!"

"That's what Tom said," agreed Daisy, smiling at both of them.

They stayed for a while, just gazing from north to south, from east to west, at the whole breathtaking panorama spread out before them.

"Like a snake's skin," said Daisy obscurely.

"What is?" Becky turned to her, puzzled.

"Up here –" Daisy waved an expressive hand, "where it's all pure and clean and empty – you can *shed* it, all that down there in the bloody old world. It simply doesn't exist!"

Becky smiled. "You're very clever, Daisy."

"No. It's true. Ask Tom. It's a *shedding* place – like a snake,

117

all new and shiny – or a sheep that's just been sheared . . . Isn't it?" She looked at Tom, willing him to confirm what she felt.

"Absolutely," agreed Tom, also smiling. "You can grow a whole new skin with a totally different pattern . . ." His eyes met Daisy's in perfect understanding, but before he could say any more, Daisy let out a shriek.

"Talking of new coats – there's Trudi!"

They glanced round, following her pointing finger, and, sure enough, there was the runaway goat, placidly munching at something soft and woolly that looked suspiciously like Ruth's best angora sweater off the washing line.

"Will she come if you call?" asked Becky.

"Not bloody likely," said Daisy, laughing.

"Shall we spread out then?" asked Tom, and began to edge sideways down the rocky outcrop at the top of Drumhead Crag.

Daisy edged round the other side, moving slowly and cautiously, while Becky, entering into the spirit of the thing, crept forwards, hiding behind clumps of gorse and tall heather when she could.

Trudi took no notice of them for a while, and simply went on munching chewed-up purple wool, but when they got dangerously close, she merely kicked up her heels and pranced off downhill, with the ruined sweater still hanging from her mouth.

Then the three of them charged, like an avenging army, tearing downhill, whooping and shouting and waving their arms in reckless abandon. Trudi was so startled by the noise and the pounding feet that she actually stopped to look round at them in amazement, and that was her undoing. Tom's legs were the longest, and in spite of his damaged knee his stride got him there first, so he flung himself headlong at the astonished goat and seized the broken halter still dangling round her neck. Almost at the same time, Daisy arrived, breathless and laughing, and flung her arms round Trudi's neck in a none-too-loving embrace. And close behind her came Becky, also out of breath and laughing, hands reaching out for the broken halter to help Tom to pull.

There was a brief struggle while Trudi plunged and kicked, but then, all at once, the fight seemed to go out of her, and she submitted quite docilely to being led home.

"Well," grinned Daisy, "you make good goat-catchers, you

two!" And they went on happily together down the heathery slopes towards farmhouse tea.

Tom wasn't sure how to approach Becky about the idea of her staying at the farm, but he found to his enormous relief that Ruth had done it most skilfully for him.

"Tom," said Becky, looking like an eager child again, "what do you think? Ruth's asked me to stay here for a bit – just till I get on my feet. She thinks it would do me good, and I would so love to. Do you think I could?"

Tom smiled his approval (and his secret thanks to Ruth, over the top of Becky's head). "I don't see why not – if Ruth would like to have you?"

"I could get back to see Dr Bradley if I needed to, couldn't I? But I feel so well out here on these hills, I don't think I should need to much." She glanced from Tom to Ruth a little anxiously, sounding absurdly humble: "I – I wouldn't be a nuisance, would I?"

"Of course you wouldn't," said Ruth stoutly. "And since you've rescued Trudi, you've already earned your keep!"

They laughed at that, and Daisy, who had been listening but carefully not taking part in the discussion, said smiling: "Mum'll keep you in order, mind – just like the rest of her charges!" and she waved a hand at the motley collection of lambs, ducklings, dogs and cats in the warm stone-flagged kitchen.

"I wouldn't mind being treated like the lambs," said Becky wistfully. "Lots of tender loving care, a place by the fire, and plenty of cuddles."

"Wouldn't we all!" muttered Jim, but he was laughing, too.

"Come here then," said Ruth, holding out her arms to Becky, "and we'll start right now!" And when Becky went, disbelieving into her warm, laughing embrace, she said, winking over Becky's head: "Take her home, Tom, and bring her back next week for as long as she likes to stay."

It was as simple as that, and Tom knew he need not say any more, or do anything else but obey. So he and Daisy took Becky home (in another borrowed farm car – "You can't bump about in that rattletrap of a lorry!") while she chattered on happily about the new foal Jewel, and the wonderful feel of a newborn lamb in her arms, and the view from Drumhead

Crag, and the capture of Trudi, in a long stream of happy gratitude.

Daisy let her talk and said nothing to dampen her ardour. Nor did Tom. (She has been alone too long, he thought. She needs to talk.) They were so amazed at the change in Becky that they did not dare to put any doubts into words, or even think them.

But when they had finally left her for her last recuperating week at Greenbanks, they stopped at a café in York to take stock. And to say a temporary goodbye. For Tom was going straight back to London to see if there was any news of Kit, and to collect a few more of Becky's belongings and bring her car back to Yorkshire for her. And Daisy was spending a few more days at the farm while she collected the remaining stores for her lorry before she returned to London for the final loading of the convoy lorries. Whichever way they looked at it, they were going to be separated for a while, and Tom found that he didn't like the idea one bit.

"I may not get back to see Becky installed at the farm," said Daisy, almost apologetically. "But she and my mother seem to get on fine. I don't think you need worry."

"I don't either," agreed Tom. "I didn't really try to thank her, Daisy –"

"Oh, she doesn't like fulsome thanks," Daisy told him bluntly. "She'll take it as read – I mean, said."

"All the same –" Tom didn't know how to express the relief that had overwhelmed him when Becky had agreed to the arrangement, and had even been convinced that she had planned it with Ruth herself. He smiled at Daisy, somewhat ruefully. "Words fail me! You've solved all my problems, between you."

"Not all," said Daisy, clasping her cup of tea in strong, competent fingers. "There's Kit."

Tom sighed. "If he's really missing – where do I start?"

Daisy considered. "The aid agency will have all the details up to the point when he disappeared. And they'll have been making enquiries. So will the UN and anyone else out there who feels responsible. You'd better start with them."

He nodded.

"But after that," Daisy went on, pursuing a thought, "you'll be on your own . . ."

"Yes. Asking questions, driving off to unknown destinations,

120

following up exceedingly slender leads – I know!" He thought for a moment. "You know about transport. Will I be able to get hold of a Jeep or something?"

"You might. Though they're like gold out there – and so is petrol. But if you convinced them that you were competent to mount a rescue, they might agree . . ." She grinned at him. "I daresay it could be fixed. Speaking the language – one of 'em – will be a bonus."

He groaned. "Oh Daisy, am I going to need your help! . . . And you've got your own job to do. I can't interfere with that."

"No," agreed Daisy, "you can't. But there are usually ways of getting round things. Let's face all that when we come to it."

They smiled hopefully at one another, already conspirators, and then Daisy said suddenly: "Tom. Can I ask an impertinent question?"

"Sure," grinned Tom. "When did being impertinent ever stop you?"

Daisy laughed, and then grew serious, even a shade embarrassed. "How are you off for money? I mean, I know you airily fixed it with Mum about Becky's expenses and all that – but can you afford it?"

"Oh." He smiled at her serious face. "Yes, I can. I had quite a big salary before I left the advertising agency, and I saved most of it. And then . . ." – he hesitated a moment – "the awful pharmaceutical company paid me a lot of compensation for my smashed knee . . . I think they paid Suzi's parents a lot, too." His voice was very dry. "They had a guilty conscience, and hoped to pay it off."

Daisy touched his hand gently, as if warding off evil spirits.

"I haven't touched it," said Tom. "It seemed like blood money to me. But I suppose in an emergency, with Kit and Becky involved, I would."

She nodded. "Fair enough." Then she glanced at his troubled face and added: "I only asked because you may need to bribe people out there. It goes on all the time."

He was not surprised. "Do *you* have to?"

"Oh yes. To get through the roadblocks – to scrounge more petrol. Not always money, though." There was a half-smile of impish amusement on her face. "Chocolate, cigarettes – a bottle of whiskey . . . I won't give them food, though, unless I'm forced to. That's for the people who are still really starving – and there are still plenty of them . . . But anything else that oils the works and gets us moving, that I will do!"

Tom was shaking his head at her, more in admiration than reproof. "Crazy Daisy – nothing daunts you, does it?"

"Not a lot," admitted Daisy. "No good being daunted. Life's too short."

How right you are, thought Tom, considering the risks you run. But he did not say it. He could not undermine Daisy's careless courage with doubts and dark warnings.

"It's all right," she said gently, laying her hand on his again in quiet reassurance. "I know the dangers. I don't take risks – unless I have to!"

Tom laughed. "Am I so transparent?"

"You are to me," said Daisy, and rings of meaning hummed round them like a spinning top as she spoke.

They looked at one another, almost in dismay. But at last Tom said, somewhat shakily: "Take care, Daisy . . . That's a different kind of risk."

She smiled at him, reckless as ever. "I know." Her voice was soft. "But it's much too late to worry about that."

He shook his head at her again, in helpless acquiescence. Then he leant forward suddenly and kissed her upturned face across the café table.

"Honestly!" she protested, rosy and laughing. "In a public café!"

"Where else would you suggest?" asked Tom innocently. "Shall I shout it from the housetops?"

"No!" grinned Daisy. "Don't shout it at all." She looked at him then, straight and serious again. "Keep it safe," she murmured, holding tight to his outstretched hand. "*Very* safe, Tom. Until there's time . . . It will keep."

He nodded, and lifted her hand to his lips in a last, rebellious gesture of declaration. "Yes," he murmured. "*Very safe.*"

When Tom got back to London he went straight to Greg's house, where he found a message waiting for him from the aid agency. Would he ring without delay?

"Did they tell you what it was about?" Tom asked Marian, who was looking distinctly anxious.

"No," she said. "Well, about Kit, obviously. But they didn't say what. Just, would you ring them soon?"

Tom nodded. "I'd better do it right away." He dialled the number and waited patiently for a reply, but when the cautious voice came on the line he was suddenly frightened – it sounded so careful and so deliberately calm.

"Oh yes, Mr Denholm. I'm glad you rang. We have some news about Kit Wade – but I'm afraid it isn't very good."

"What has happened to him?"

"I'm afraid we don't know. He is definitely reported missing now. Nothing has been heard of him or his lorry load of goods, since he disappeared on the detour road." The quiet voice paused, and then went on: "They are doing all they can out there to find him, of course – making all the proper enquiries, but the situation is so confused still, it is very difficult to get any hard facts out of anyone."

"I can imagine," said Tom. "Can you tell me the name of the place where he went missing? Or any place near to it . . .?"

There was another pause and then the cautious voice said: "They were making for a small village between Slavonska Posega and Nasice – aid convoys have been getting through to Osijek and its surroundings on that route, now that a cease-fire is in force . . . There's a road to it through the mountains and that's where they got held up by mines and had to go round the long way . . . The Serb forces are still very close all along there, and small flare-ups do still occur, in spite of the cease-fire . . . they are very unpredictable." There was another fractional pause and then the woman at the other end of the line, sounding slightly worried now, said: "If you were thinking of going out there to look for him, Mr Denholm, I wouldn't advise it . . . But if you did – I understand you've been there before in a war situation – the aid team on the spot would give you all the details they've got, I'm sure, and all the help they could. But you'd have to go through the Foreign Office and all the usual channels, of course."

"Thank you," said Tom. "That's very reassuring." He hadn't meant to sound so sardonic, but his voice came out much too dry, and he was just about to ring off, feeling slightly ashamed

123

of himself, when the voice suddenly became human and took on a name.

"I'm Rosamund, by the way. Ros to most people. I'm just a volunteer manning the phones, you know. It's not my fault that the information is so sketchy."

"No, of course not," Tom said, feeling even more guilty. "I understand that."

"It's very frustrating, I know." Rosamund's voice was quite sympathetic now.

"What's the situation out there at the moment, d'you know?" asked Tom, trying to get any extra pointers he could.

"I probably don't know any more than you," said Ros. "If you've been watching the news bulletins. There is supposed to be a general cease-fire at the moment, and most of it seems to be holding. Bits of the war seem to be over – but other bits suddenly flare up and there are atrocities, and in one or two places the mortars still haven't stopped . . . And I'm told there are stray pockets of armed soldiers who don't seem to be taking orders from anyone. Not a very stable situation, to put it mildly." She sighed. "But on the other hand, the UN has a bit more clout and is getting a bit more respect these days, especially since that British commander took over and got tough . . . So the situation is improving . . . but of course the ordinary people need the aid supplies as much as ever, and very few facilities – such as water and electricity – have been restored in the bombed towns yet." She hesitated, and then added almost shyly: "Is that any help?"

"Thanks," said Tom. "Yes, it is. I'll – er – let you know what I'm doing, and of course you'll do the same if there's any more news?"

"Of course."

"Well, thanks again, Ros," said Tom awkwardly. "I'll be in touch." And this time he did ring off.

Marian was waiting for him, still looking worried. She handed him a stiff drink, with the anxious words: "Well? What's the news?"

"Not good," said Tom, and proceeded to tell her what little the agency aid worker had known.

Marian was looking at him doubtfully. "You're thinking of going out there, aren't you?"

Tom sighed. "I think I'll have to. Someone's got to look for him . . . But I don't know whether I'll do much good – or whether I'll be very welcome. After all, the authorities out there are probably doing everything that can be done – and an outsider on a freelance mission could be a frightful nuisance."

Marian nodded. "But even so –?"

"Even so, I've got to try . . . Knowing a bit of one of the languages should help, though it depends what area is involved . . ." He rubbed a distracted hand through his hair. "I suppose I can't make things any worse."

"How will you get there?" Marian was nothing if not practical.

Tom was suddenly aware that he was reluctant to talk about Daisy yet, and he didn't quite know why, but he answered casually enough: "Oh, I may cadge a lift on an aid lorry . . . I know one of the drivers."

Marian's eyebrows rose, and she was about to ask "Who?" when Greg came in, looking a bit weary, and more drinks were administered.

Tom told them then about the Yorkshire farm and his arrangements for Becky, and to his relief both Marian and Greg seemed to approve of the plan.

"It sounds ideal," said Greg, smiling. "You've been very clever."

"Not clever," Tom told him. "Lucky."

And, my God, he thought, I *have* been lucky. Lucky to meet Daisy on a wild Yorkshire side road . . . Lucky to meet her parents, Jim and Ruth Bellingham, and lucky, so lucky, that they were as kind and welcoming as their daughter . . .

"It was Daisy who fixed it," he said, and forgot his caution and found himself telling them all about it.

"Well, well," murmured Greg, more than a twinkle in his eye. "And this girl – your Crazy Daisy – is *driving* out to Bosnia? Are you sure she knows what she is doing?"

"Yes," said Tom flatly. "She's done several trips before this." He saw Greg's sceptical expression and added honestly: "But of course that doesn't mean it'll help to find Kit. It's just a way of getting in – and Daisy knows the ropes. She'll at least be able to

125

point me in the right direction, and get me introduced to some of the right people."

Greg agreed with this, but cautiously. "Yes, that makes sense. But it's going to be a risky business."

"Oh, *risky*," said Tom, sounding impatient. "All life is risky." He grinned at Greg. "I don't suppose it's much worse than crossing Trafalgar Square in the rush hour."

Greg laughed.

"How did you get on down at Becky's house?" asked Marian, aware that Tom was not to be deflected, and deliberately moving the discussion on to another tack.

"Oh, I haven't told you about Holly," Tom said. "Holly and little Adam . . ." and he went on to describe his meeting with Holly and her lively young son.

"I think she's really fond of Kit," he concluded. "I hope to God there can be a successful conclusion to all this. There are more people involved than I realised."

"So it seems." Greg sounded thoughtful. "How much does Becky know?"

Tom looked confused. "About Holly? I told her a little, to prepare the way. I think they'd get on very well once they got to know each other . . . And it may be important that they should . . ." He stopped there for a moment, as a curious idea came into his head. But he did not pursue it then. Instead, he returned to Greg's question and went on steadily: "But about Kit, I haven't told Becky anything . . . I don't think she could take any more anxiety at present."

Greg nodded. "She'll have to know in the end."

Far away, Tom heard Daisy's sturdy voice saying: "*It might do her good to worry about someone else . . .*"

"Yes," he sighed. "I just hope the end will justify the means."

During the rest of the week, Tom set about putting his own house in order and trying to work out some plan of action for his Bosnian trip. He looked at maps, brushed up his own remembered knowledge of the language and the place – and talked to a friend of Greg's who worked in the Foreign Office and who was rather disapproving of the whole project but nevertheless had some helpful suggestions to make.

After this, Tom made two rather testy phone calls, one to Derek and one to Jenny in California. He felt he ought to tell them both that Kit was missing.

Derek was, predictably, unperturbed. "He'll turn up," he said, sounding off-hand and faintly impatient. "Boys his age do go off."

"I don't think you quite understand the position," said Tom. "This isn't a boyish prank. Kit is part of a well-organised team of aid workers."

"Not well organised enough, it seems," retorted Derek.

"This is a war," snapped Tom. "Not a picnic. No one can predict what a few trigger-happy soldiers may do."

There was a moment's silence, and then Derek said, rather incredulously, "Are you saying Kit might be in *danger*?"

"Yes, I am." Tom's tone was blunt. "I've no idea what I may find out there. He may just have got lost in the mountains. I hope so – though even that is dangerous enough." He paused, and then added crisply: "I just thought you should know. He is your son, after all."

"Does Becky know?"

"No. She's in no fit state for this kind of extra anxiety. If the news is really bad, of course she'll have to be told."

"Rather you than me," said Derek.

"So I gather." Tom was so appalled by this response that he couldn't think of anything else to say.

There was another uncomfortable silence on the line, and then Derek said, somewhat lamely: "Well, let me know what happens."

"Of course," Tom said, and rang off before he added something really rude. The conversation with Jenny (when he got hold of her; which was difficult) wasn't much better.

"What am I supposed to do about it?" she said, sounding almost as impatient as Derek.

"Nothing now," Tom told her. "But if there is bad news, Jenny, I think you should come home."

"Why?"

"Because your mother will need you."

"She's never needed me much before." Jenny's voice was flat and unsympathetic.

127

"That's not true, Jenny. She may not have said much, but she misses you and Kit a lot – especially now."

Jenny sighed on the other end of the line. "I can't get mixed up in all that, Uncle Tom. If Dad's gone off with a floosie, well, he's gone off. People do it all the time."

"Maybe they do," Tom told her, "but that doesn't make it any better for the one left behind."

There was silence while Jenny digested this. "I suppose not," she admitted at last. There was a fleck of unwilling sympathy in her tone which Tom did not fail to notice.

"What are you doing out there, anyway?" he asked. "Is it important?"

"I'm on a course at Berkeley. Yes, it is important – to me."

"When does it end? In June?"

"Yes."

"Then come home for the summer, Jenny. At least you could do that." He hesitated, and added more cheerfully: "I'll pay your fare, if that's what's worrying you."

"Thanks –" she began, but he could hear the reluctance still in her young voice.

"*Please*, Jenny," he begged. "It's important."

"I'll think about it," she answered, none too graciously.

"Whatever the news about Kit?"

"Ye–s." She knew she sounded lukewarm, and added more positively: "You'll let me know?"

"Of course."

He had to be content with that, and rang off, wondering how any girl could sound quite so detached. But then he remembered Holly's compassionate young voice saying: *They had a funny sort of childhood, expensive boarding schools and jet-set holidays . . ."* and he thought he understood a little of how they came to feel so separate and unconcerned about each other . . .

Sighing, he went back to his own problems, and hoped that these rather fruitless phone calls were an unnecessary precaution. But on the strength of these somewhat anxious thoughts, he also decided to make a will. It was something he had never thought about before, but there was quite a lot of money in his bank account and he thought he had better do something useful with it. So he left half of it to Becky – having checked first with Greg's

128

tough lawyer that events were moving towards a very reasonable settlement and Derek had caved in rather swiftly under pressure. Reassured by this, he left bequests to Kit and Jenny, and the rest he assigned to Daisy Bellingham, "to assist her in her charitable work". He didn't know if Daisy would ever accept it, but it was something he felt he had to do.

When all these tiresome arrangements had been made, he went down to Becky's house again to pick up her car and a few more possessions – and also to see Holly and Adam. For the idea he had in his mind was beginning to take shape. Before he actually went across to find Holly at her flat, he made a careful phone call to Ruth Bellingham at the farm. Then, happy with her response, he made his way down the road to the shrubby, neglected grounds of the old Rectory.

The first person he met was Adam, riding his tricycle furiously up and down the drive. "Hullo, Uncle Tom," he called, pedalling wildly towards him. "I'm a cowboy. Are you a horse or a cow?"

"Whichever you like," said Tom. "Perhaps I'd better be a steer. Then you can round me up."

"Good," said Adam, and pedalled even more furiously round him in circles. "Have you come to see my Mum?" he added, suddenly remembering his manners.

"I've come to see you both," said Tom, smiling at the blue-eyed small boy who was looking at him with such cheerful welcome.

Holly came to the door then, hearing their voices, and added her own brand of cheerful welcome to the occasion. "Come on in, Tom. Kettle's boiling, and I've just made some gingerbread men."

"How can I resist?" grinned Tom, and followed her inside.

But after Adam had demolished three men with currant eyes, and swallowed some orange juice, Holly sent him back to his tricycle in the garden, and turned to Tom seriously. "Is there any news?"

"Yes, Holly, I'm afraid there is. Or rather, there's some non-news, which is even more frustrating." He proceeded then to tell her what the aid agency worker had said, and went on with as much reassurance as he could: "But I'm going out there to get him back, Holly, and I'm sure it will be all right."

Holly looked at him levelly. "Ought you to go back?"

129

Tom blinked. "Yes, I ought. I've spent too long avoiding family responsibility." A long way away, he heard Sally Maguire's fierce voice saying: "*Family is family*!" and he half smiled at the memory. "And that's what I want to talk to you about."

Holly's eyes were a bit wary now, but she didn't look away. "Family responsibility?"

"Exactly. It's about Becky, really." He sighed, wondering how to put his suggestion in persuasive terms. "I haven't told her about Kit's disappearance, Holly, and I don't think I'm going to. Time enough for that later on, if – if the need arises. In the meantime, the less anxiety she has to cope with the better." He glanced at her, somewhat uneasily. "I hope to God the need won't arise at all."

Holly nodded. "So do I."

Tom took a deep breath of resolve. "This is where you come in, Holly. I want to ask a huge favour of you. Will you bear with me while I try to explain?"

"Of course." She spoke calmly, smiling a little, waiting to hear what he had to say.

Tom explained then about the farm and the arrangement with Ruth Bellingham, and how much Becky was looking forward to it. "But since I'll be away, and Daisy will be away too, driving her lorry – there'll only be Ruth to talk to, and she's a very busy farmer's wife. So I wondered if you would consider going up there to stay for a couple of weeks? Adam would love the farm, and you'd be company for Becky. It's high time you got to know each other properly anyway –" He paused, not sure how Holly was going to react. "Do you think it's a good idea?"

Holly hesitated. "Yes, but – what if Becky doesn't *want* to get to know me?"

Tom stared at her, hearing in her doubtful voice the insecurity and the long months of loneliness and isolation that Holly had suffered as a single mother struggling to bring up a small boy in an uncaring world. "But she will, Holly," he said gently. "And she'll simply love Adam . . . What Becky needs more than anything just now is a feeling of *family* security. Ruth Bellingham can give her a glimpse of it because she and Jim and Daisy are a close, affectionate family – but you could give her more."

130

Holly sighed, and looked at Tom with painful honesty. "But I'm not family."

"I think you are," said Tom softly. "Because you care for Kit."

There were suddenly tears in Holly's eyes. "It's not as simple as that."

"Isn't it?" Tom asked. In a life and death situation like this, he thought, only basic truth matters. He did not try to say it, but he thought Holly understood him.

"As regards expenses," he went on, swiftly turning to practical matters, "it would all be taken care of. I've made a sort of deal with Ruth Bellingham anyway. You wouldn't have to worry – it'd be like a free holiday . . ." He paused, and dared to sound openly appealing: "It would relieve my mind so much if I knew you were with Becky . . . She does so need support – and someone young and energetic to go around with . . . And think how Adam would like the lambs and the horses . . ."

"Oh stop!" laughed Holly. "Stop heaping coals of fire on my head! . . . Of course we'll go, if you think it would help. I suppose we can always come back here if Becky doesn't like it?"

"Of course," agreed Tom. "That goes without saying." He smiled at her still-doubtful face. "I thought perhaps Adam's school term ended soon? Isn't it nearly Easter?"

"Yes. It ends this week."

He nodded. "I thought so . . . Could you come back with me then? I'll be driving Becky's car up, and there's plenty of room."

Holly drew a long, rather shaken breath. "I – yes, I think we could . . . Can you give me a day to get ready?"

Tom laughed. "Two days, if you like. But I should go on Friday." He was serious again for a moment. "And I shall have to leave almost as soon as I get you to the farm, if I am to get to Bosnia with Daisy . . . It will mean rather plunging you in at the deep end . . . Will you mind?"

"I've faced worse," said Holly, a little grimly. But then she smiled and tried to make amends. "No, I won't mind, if Becky doesn't . . . It'll work out all right, I'm sure."

"Bless you," Tom said, his voice warm with relief. "I can't tell you how much it will mean to me to know you are there . . ." In

131

case of really bad news, he might have added, but at that point Adam came in and walked confidently over to Tom and leant against his chair. "Are you coming to supper again? Do you like sausages? We bought some in the shop."

"What do you think, Adam," said Holly, "we're going to stay on a farm . . ."

"Can Benji come too?" asked Adam promptly.

Holly looked from him to Tom in some doubt. She had almost forgotten the dog. How would he fit in on a farm?

"Yes, I'm sure he can," said Tom. "If you keep him in order!"

And when he saw young Adam's face light up with eagerness at Holly's description of the animals and the moors, he knew he had done the right thing.

But he had to find Kit and get him back to them all in one piece – or the whole complicated web of family commitments and affections would end in disaster.

When they got to York, Tom decided to leave Holly and Adam (with Benji firmly held on a strong lead) to have a look at the beautiful city, while he went to fetch Becky.

"I'll meet you in the park," he said, "in about an hour. I expect Benji could do with a bit of a walk."

"So could I," said Adam, sounding absurdly grown-up. He had been very good on the long drive north, but he was rather tired of sitting still. "Can we feed the ducks?"

Tom didn't even know if the park had a lake or any ducks, but Holly said firmly: "I'm sure we can. Come on, we'll buy them some bread on the way," and led Adam and Benji swiftly away. She understood very well that Tom needed a bit of time with Becky alone to explain their presence. She only hoped Becky would take to the idea and not feel resentful or upset about it. As it was, she felt that Tom was taking rather a risk presenting Becky with a fait accompli like this.

Tom watched them go off hand in hand in the spring sunshine, looking somehow heartbreakingly vulnerable and brave in the face of this new adventure. Then he turned away to face what he feared might be a difficult interview with Becky.

He had not really dared, even in his own thoughts, to admit the

132

real reason why he wanted Holly to be with Becky at this time. But he knew, deep down, that he was afraid Kit might have been killed out there in Bosnia, and his instincts told him that the two people who really loved the boy might somehow draw together and find comfort in each other – if it ever came to that. But it won't, he told himself sternly. It can't. He must be somewhere – and I'll find him, somehow. *I must.*

He was so immersed in his own thoughts that he had arrived at Greenbanks and walked through the open reception area of Becky's house unit before he knew it, and was just on his way through the corridor leading to Becky's room when the same tall boy who had been so worried about God came up to him again.

"Hallo, Tom," he said. "Have you come to take Becky to the farm? She told me all about it. Lucky her. But I've got another question for you before you go."

Tom's heart sank. He didn't want to be delayed just now, with Becky waiting for him, and so much to be said. But the boy's fierce eyes were as beseeching as ever, and he could not ignore them. "Well?"

The boy waved the book he was carrying, keeping one finger in the place. "This Donne someone lent me . . . You know – all that 'for whom the bell tolls' stuff . . .?"

"Yes?" Tom's mind suddenly snapped to attention. For he knew this passage all too well – who didn't? . . . And it was all too relevant for him.

"What I want to know is –" – the boy's extraordinary eyes seemed to blaze with entreaty – "If no man is an island – *where does the mainland begin*?"

Tom stood staring at him, arrested by the simplicity of the question. Where, indeed? . . . It said the whole of what Tom had been denying for so long, and he knew it. For a moment the two pairs of eyes seemed to be locked in challenge, and Tom did not know how to answer him.

"I've been asking myself the same question," he said slowly. But then his gaze softened and a curiously sweet smile touched him for a moment. "But I think you've just taught me the answer."

"I have?" The boy looked startled.

"Yes." Tom was still half smiling at him. "What's your name?" he asked gently.

133

"Justin. Why?"

"Because you're a *person*, Justin. Not just a question mark. And I think the Mainland begins right here." The half-smile grew oddly tender as he saw the boy's confusion. "Right here and now, Justin . . . Doesn't Donne go on: 'We are all part of the Main'?"

Justin nodded slowly.

"So it begins *here*," said Tom, holding out his hand. "And it took you to make me see it. Welcome to the club."

Shyly, the boy took his hand and held on to it as if he didn't know how to let go. "Well, thanks . . ." he said at last, and the fire of anguished uncertainty had gone out of his eyes. "I thought you'd know." And he wandered off again, apparently entirely satisfied with Tom's answer.

But Tom stood still for a long moment, curiously shaken by that encounter. It had brought him face to face with his own craven-hearted failure to acknowledge the truth. "'*We are all part of the Main*'," he repeated aloud, before going on down the corridor to find Becky's room.

He found Becky looking excited and remarkably cheerful. The prospect of life on the farm seemed to have given her something really positive to look forward to, and there was a new light of hope in her eyes.

"I'm nearly ready," she said. "I've just got to shut my suitcase."

Tom hated to quench her eagerness, and almost decided to say nothing and wait till they got back to York to pick up Holly and Adam. But he thought, no, that would be too sudden. And it would be too like taking things for granted. I want her to feel that she has the choice herself . . . He was just about to plunge into explanations, when he suddenly thought about the boy, Justin again, with his fierce eyes and desperate questions. And it seemed to Tom that the boy's need for reassurance was relevant to both Becky's and Holly's problems. So he said instead, with sudden decision: "That boy, Justin. He says you talk to him. Do you know his history?"

Becky looked surprised. But she answered readily enough: "Oh yes. He's a nice boy . . . It's a bit tragic, really. I believe he's very clever, worked too hard over his college exams and broke down . . ." Her eyes met Tom's for a moment of vivid

134

awareness. "He – tried what I tried, Tom . . . and failed, like I failed . . . And now they are trying to convince him that life is worth living."

Tom nodded. "I guessed it was something like that."

"The trouble is," Becky went on, sounding all at once very direct and frank about the problems she shared with the bewildered boy, "he's lonely. No one comes to see him . . . he needs someone to talk to – that's why he latches on to me, and to you!" She sighed, and her eyes met Tom's again with candid admission. "But most of all, I think, he needs to feel *wanted*. And some use to someone . . . No one seems to want him much."

Again Tom nodded, well aware that Becky was leading the discussion just where he wanted it to go.

"What did he want from you?"

"Reassurance," said Tom, and went on to explain exactly what the boy had asked, and what he had answered.

Becky was no fool. She looked at Tom hard and said: "We're all in it together, aren't we? The whole, bloody mess . . . Is that what you're saying?"

"Yes," said Tom. Then he took a deep breath, and went on to the real crux of the matter: "And because of that, I've got a big favour to ask you."

Becky looked at him warily. She knew that serious voice of old. "What is it?"

"I've brought Holly and little Adam up here with me . . . I thought they might be company for you on the farm . . . I don't know if you're going to like the idea, but I hope so."

He stopped to see whether Becky seemed annoyed or dismayed by the news, but she was still looking at him with the same questioning glance. "Why?"

He did not hesitate then. "Because she's lonely, too, Becky, and worried about Kit, just as you are . . . I thought maybe you could reassure her a bit. She and the child badly need some sort of family to belong to. It's no joke bringing up a small boy on your own."

"No," agreed Becky thoughtfully. "It can't be easy."

"And I sort of feel," went on Tom carefully, "that if you and Kit are going to get close again when he comes home, you'll have to accept his girlfriend, too. I think it may be

135

rather serious between them, really, though she's said little enough."

Becky nodded. "I've been thinking about that – since Daisy said she must care about him if she sent him away . . ."

Privately, Tom blessed Daisy for those wise words of hers that had put things in the true perspective for Becky. But aloud, he pressed home his advantage, sensing Becky's softened mood. "The little boy, Adam, is an endearing child. You'll love him – and he's so excited about the farm . . . You'll be able to show him everything." He smiled, seeing the beginnings of an answering lightness in Becky's gaze. "And to tell you the truth, I was afraid you might get lonely there on your own if Ruth got too busy with farm chores. Especially as I'll have to be away for a bit, and so will Daisy . . ."

Becky actually laughed. "You're a scheming devil, Tom, you know that? I'm not too stupid to know when I'm being manipulated!"

"But do you mind?"

Becky paused to consider the matter. "No," she said at last, "you are quite right. I ought to get to know Holly anyway. God knows I need some sort of family, too, to hold on to – whoever they are! What with Kit and Jenny at the ends of the earth . . ." She grinned at Tom's anxious face. "Stop looking so apprehensive. I'm not going to scream!"

Tom sighed with relief. "Holly's very humble about it. She promised to go home again at once if you didn't like the idea – and she meant it. I think being a single mum has meant a lot of rebuffs and a marked falling off of friends in her young life. She's terribly afraid of rejection."

"The poor girl," said Becky, her voice suddenly full of understanding. She knew what rejection was like, and what havoc it played with one's self-confidence.

"I thought you might – sort of take her under your wing?" Tom suggested, with the greatest innocence.

"You're very clever, brother mine," said Becky, smiling, "and I'm not taken in one bit. But it's all right. Let's go and find her, and tell her so."

So she left Greenbanks Hospital without a backward glance (and already furnished with a rôle to fulfil) and went cheerfully

136

with Tom to the little park in York to find Holly and Adam with Benji the dog.

When Adam saw them coming, he came running up to them with a small twist of paper in his hand and solemnly presented it to Becky.

"This is for you, 'cos you're Kit's Mum, and I like Kit, and Mum says it's a – a –?"

"A white rose," prompted Holly, laughing a little shyly. "A white rose of York."

"A white rose of 'ork," repeated Adam, manfully trying to get it right. "An' we got it in a special shop 'cos roses aren't really out yet, but this one is 'cos it comes from – from –?"

"The south of France," prompted Holly again, and by this time they were all laughing at Adam's breathless attempts at diplomacy.

"A white rose of York from France?" said Becky, impressed. "That's *very* special! Can you put it in my button hole?" And she stooped down, already beguiled by those blue eyes and that unruly blond head, so that Adam could reach the lapel of her camelhair coat. Then there was a great fuss about finding a pin, and they were all laughing again before she and Adam had finished putting the rose in place.

Above their two heads, Tom's eyes met Holly's in thankful relief and an unexpected sense of cameradie. All at once, it became a cheerful family occasion, and they set off for the farm full of hopeful anticipation.

"Come on, Benji," said Adam. "There'll be hills to run on."

"But you mustn't chase the sheep," added Holly severely.

Benji wagged his tail and put on an expression of angelic good will, assuring them that butter wouldn't melt in his mouth, and all sheep were his best friends, anyway.

But Tom didn't trust him an inch.

Ruth welcomed them all with open arms and a huge farm tea "to put them on a bit". Adam was so totally enchanted by the lambs beside the Aga that he could hardly be persuaded to come and eat at all. And Benji, to everyone's amazement, settled down humbly beside the old collie, Nell, and did exactly what he was told.

After tea, Becky took Holly and Adam with her and went to

see the new foal, Jewel, and her proud mother, Garnet, who were both still in the warm, straw-filled loosebox in the stable yard, with Lacey keeping a careful eye on them.

"Kept 'em in out of t'wind this week," he explained to Becky, as if she was an old friend who understood all about how he looked after his charges. "But I'll be putting them out in the paddock termorrer. I reckon you'd all like to see 'em kick up their heels, like?"

"Yes, please," said Adam, awestruck already as he looked over the loosebox door from the safety of Holly's arms.

"Hello, Garnet," crooned Becky, holding out her hand. "Your Jewel is even more beautiful today, isn't she? Aren't you a clever Mum?"

And, as before, the gentle, thrusting nose came out and pushed confidingly against Becky's outstretched hand.

Lacey watched, mesmerised as ever, and muttered grudging approval: "Reckon she's glad to see you!"

Becky was well aware that this was an enormous compliment in Lacey's world, and she turned to smile at him. "Yes, but you're the one she trusts," she said. And that made Lacey even more enchanted.

Mango came up then, not to be outdone, and took them all over to inspect his milking parlour and the cows who had come down for their evening milking.

"We only keeps a few," he explained. "Not enough pasture up here for a big herd, d'you see? But they do well enough." He patted one brown and white rump as he spoke. "Don't 'ee, then?"

Adam was fascinated by the milking machines, but while Mango was solemnly explaining the process, Jim Bellingham strolled up and took them all off to look at the lambing pens . . . It was clear that everyone had been briefed to make that first evening as eventful and welcoming as possible. There was no time to feel shy or awkward. There was too much to see and do – and beyond the immediate activities of the farm, stretched the wild, empty moors waiting to be explored.

Tom, meanwhile, had stayed behind to talk to Ruth for a few moments while the coast was clear.

"It's very good of you to have Holly and Adam, too," he said. "I hope Benji won't be a nuisance."

Ruth laughed. "The other dogs will keep him in order, don't you worry! And as for Holly and Adam . . . it's good to have the old place filled up a bit. We rattle about in it rather in the winter." She smiled at Tom's anxious face. "I'm used to numbers, you know. We often take six or eight bed-and-breakfast people in the summer."

Tom shook his head at her. "I don't know how you do it."

"I'm used to it," Ruth told him comfortably. "Nothing much fashes me." Her grin was almost as mischievous as Daisy's, and reminded Tom of things he ought to say.

"About Daisy – "

"Oh yes. She left you a note. Let me see, where did I put it?" She went over to the big kitchen dresser and took a folded sheet of paper from behind one of the blue china plates. "She was sorry she couldn't wait for you," she added, smiling.

"I'll be at the London Depot till Monday", said Daisy's clear, round hand. "Will wait as long as I can. Come soon. D."

Simple and to the point, thought Tom. Just like Daisy! I must get back to London tomorrow.

"How long can you stay?" asked Ruth, watching his face.

"Till tomorrow," Tom said. Then he looked swiftly round to make sure Becky wasn't in earshot, and went on urgently: "Ruth, the boy – Kit – is really missing. Daisy will have told you about him?"

Ruth nodded.

"Holly knows," he explained. "But I haven't told Becky. I don't think she could cope with any more at present." He paused. "But if –?"

"If the news was bad, I'm sure Holly and I could handle it," said Ruth tranquilly. "We'll take care of her, Tom."

Like Daisy, thought Tom. She grasps essentials and accepts responsibility with no fuss at all.

"I'll bring him back safely," he promised, somewhat bleakly, "if it's humanly possible."

"I know you will," said Ruth.

Later that night, when everyone had gone off to their rooms – the farm routine made for early bedtime and early rising – Tom went to check how his charges were coping with their new arrangements. He felt a bit like a headmaster inspecting the dormitories on the first night of term, with a sharp eye out for anyone homesick – but he had to find out if they were going to manage to get along together, before he went away.

He found Becky standing by her window looking out at a brilliant, moonlit landscape of silver and black shadow stretching away beyond the farm to the deep night sky above the hills.

"Such *space*," breathed Becky, as he came up to her.

"Are you going to be happy here?" he asked, putting an arm round her shoulders so that they both stood looking out together.

"Oh *yes*!" she assured him. "I'm going to love every minute of it – and Lacey's going to let me ride one of the horses!" She turned her head and smiled at Tom. "And you were right about Holly – we're going to get on fine."

"There's a lot more to her than meets the eye."

"I know." Her smile was faintly mischievous. "I've found that out already!"

Tom laughed. "What about young Adam?"

"A real charmer, that one." Becky was laughing, too. "I've fallen, hook, line and sinker."

Tom gave her shoulders a little squeeze. "I'm sorry I've got to be away. There's . . . some unfinished business I have to deal with – but I'll be back as soon as I can."

"Don't worry about me," Becky told him. "I've made up my mind to live from day to day at present, and enjoy every minute of it . . . I feel – a bit like a child let out of school."

"Good," Tom grinned. "Holiday time! Keep it that way till I get back!"

He thought, looking at her, that she really was calmer and more stable now – the nightmare shadows seemed to have retreated. She was almost back to the cheerful, outgoing, adventurous girl she used to be. Almost. He just hoped this mood of childlike euphoria would endure.

"Be happy," he murmured, and left her there, still admiring the silvered hills outside the window.

Then he went to tackle Holly, tapping very gently on the door in case he woke Adam or started Benji barking. "Is everything all right?" he asked, sounding absurdly anxious. Really, he thought crossly, I'm behaving like a mother hen.

"*All right*?" Holly turned a glowing face in his direction. "It's absolutely fabulous. I could hardly get Adam to go to bed at all, he's so thrilled with everything."

"And you?" The question was serious, and Holly understood it.

"Of course. I'm thrilled, too. And very relieved to find everyone so – so friendly and welcoming." She looked at Tom, knowing what his worries were. "I think Becky has quite taken to Adam . . . and she and I seem to have quite a bit in common."

Tom grinned. "Including Kit."

Her answering smile was luminous and sad. "Including Kit. But you mustn't take anything for granted . . ." Then she answered something in his eyes that he did not say. "And, of course, I'll do my best to be a – a support and comfort to Becky, if need be. You know that."

Tom nodded. "Yes. I know that." He grasped her arm for a moment. "Bless you for being here."

He went away then, having done all he could, said all he could, to reassure them. And because he knew he couldn't sleep with so much of the unguessable future on his mind, he went walking in the black and silver night.

In the morning, he got up very early and cadged a lift with the milk lorry that was driving down to York, where he caught the first train he could to London. It was time he got on with what he had to do. It could not wait any longer.

Part Three

No-Man's-Land

At the London depot, he found Daisy's lorry, almost completely loaded, but no Daisy. There were two tough-looking teenagers on guard beside it, one with a ponytail and three gold earrings in one ear and two in the other, the second boy with an almost-bald bristle haircut and a single silver nose ring. They eyed Tom suspiciously, but when he asked for Daisy, their belligerent expressions eased a little and the tense, lithe young bodies relaxed. Tom was glad to see this – he had almost expected to be attacked for even daring to look at the loaded lorry, let alone trying to loot it.

"She's up at the estate," volunteered Ponytail, nonchalantly leaning against the tailgate and fiddling with his earrings.

"Last minute extras," added Bristle-head, with an attempt at a thin, sardonic smile.

"Thanks," said Tom, looking round rather helplessly. What estate? Where?

"Down the Cut," directed Ponytail, jerking a thumb at a narrow grey slash in the brick wall at the end of the warehouse buildings.

Tom went across the litter-strewn parking lot and started to walk down the dark little passage, wondering uneasily how safe it was for Daisy to be wandering about here on her own. It was not a very safe-looking area, and when he came out of the Cut into the bleak concrete wilderness of the apartment blocks on the estate, it looked even less inviting. There were a couple of burnt-out car wrecks at one end of the square, and a silent knot of angry teenagers glaring at him from close beside them. Someone was shouting at someone else on one of the covered walkways outside the flats, and a scatter of children were playing football with a tin can and a chalked-in goalpost on the scuffed ground. The rest of the square complex of council flats looked blank and shuttered, with closed doors and heavily curtained windows, and a silent disregard for anything that might be going on in the street below.

Tom shivered a little, thinking how little anyone here would care about what was happening to his neighbour – if he even knew who his neighbour was. And where on earth would Daisy find extra supplies for Bosnian Relief among these tight-shut doors? But as he thought this, he saw Daisy coming out of a doorway, carrying an armload of small tins and packets, and calling out as she left: "Thanks, it'll be a great help."

Tom heard no answering voice, and the door slammed shut behind her, but Daisy came on, undaunted, juggling with the packages as she descended the outside concrete staircase. He got to her side just as the first few tins began to slip from her grasp.

"Here, give some to me," he said, his heart lifting to Daisy's instant smile of welcome. "I was just wondering where on earth you'd get anything out of this soulless place," he said, balancing some tins of corned beef against a large carton of cotton wool.

"Oh, were you?" growled Daisy. "Just you come with me, Tom Denholm, and be thankful I don't make you eat your words! There's plenty of soul around here."

She marched down the square and up the next set of concrete steps to another walkway and another series of closed front doors. Here she stopped, consulted a list which she clutched in her hand under the pile of tins, and rang the bell of No. 4.

After a few moments while nothing happened, footsteps came to the door, and a thin, child's voice called out: "Who is it?"

"It's me, Daisy. You've got some things for me."

There was a scrabbling sound of chains and bolts being withdrawn, and then a small, brown face came round the door. "Sorry, Daisy. Mam makes me keep everything locked while she's out."

"Don't blame her," grinned Daisy.

"They're in here," said the child, and led them into a narrow hall where a neat pile of boxes waited to be collected. "And Mam

143

said the Medical Centre where she works sent these. They're salesman's samples, mostly."

Daisy pounced on the packages of dressings and bandages, disinfectants and ointments, and non-prescription drugs with delight. "Oh Melly, you don't *know* how useful these will be!"

The little dark face split into a cheerful grin. "Mam's good at scrounging!" She darted into the kitchen at the back of the hall and returned carrying several empty carrier bags. "Will these help?"

"Sure," said Tom, and started pushing all the packages safely inside, enthusiastically assisted by the small Jamaican girl, her round head of neat pigtails bobbing with excitement.

"God bless, Melly," smiled Daisy, staggering out of the door with her loaded bags. "Thank your mam for me . . . Got a couple more calls to make. 'Bye!" and she was off along the outside passage, looking for No. 10.

This time it was an old, bent man with a quavery voice who handed them a bag of stores (which Tom privately thought he could probably ill afford); and in No. 17, a woman in a wheelchair handed over a parcel of knitted blankets and a brand-new pullover.

"Good luck, Crazy Daisy," they said. "Come back safe. We'll have some more for you next time . . ."

And so it went on, till they could carry no more, and then a couple of the scowling teenagers detached themselves from their silent, watchful group and came forward to help carry the bulging carrier bags to the waiting lorry.

"Soulless, my foot," rumbled Daisy, glaring at Tom.

"Sorry!" he laughed, clutching at his carrier bags. But he had to admit he was feeling thoroughly chastened. He gave one last, disbelieving look at the closed doors and empty walkways, and shook his head – more at himself than anything else. "Appearances are very deceptive!"

"They are," Daisy acknowledged. "But don't ever underestimate these people. They may talk tough, but they've got hearts of gold when roused!"

Tom did not add: Especially when roused by Crazy Daisy! – but he thought it, and he fancied the two unexpectedly helpful teenagers thought so too, as a fleeting grin passed between them.

It was at this point that a thin, scrubbed-looking woman in a

144

shabby raincoat came up to Daisy and said: "Excuse me asking, luv, but have you got any stuff from Mrs Parker today?"

"No." Daisy looked surprised. "She wasn't on my list this time." She paused, and then added slowly: "I did wonder why not . . . she was always so good – especially with her knitted blankets."

The woman nodded. "No one's seen her lately. That's why I asked."

Daisy exchanged a swift glance with Tom. "Shall we go and bang on her door? See how she is?"

"Why not?" agreed the woman. "Can't do no harm. She can always see us off for nosy parkers if she likes."

They reclimbed one of the stone staircases, and Daisy duly knocked on the door of No. 23. She rang the bell as well, and knocked again, harder. But there was no reply.

They looked at one another in mounting unease. "Perhaps she's gone off on holiday?" muttered the woman, sounding unconvinced by the idea.

"When did anyone see her last?" asked Daisy, trying to peer through the letter box.

Tom and the woman were trying to see through the window, but there was a concealing net curtain over it, and they could see nothing.

"I dunno." The woman considered. "Not for a coupla weeks."

"A couple of *weeks*?" Daisy's voice rose a little. She looked at Tom again. "I think we'd better do something."

"The police?" suggested Tom.

The tired woman in the raincoat looked alarmed. "Don't want the fuzz round here causing trouble."

Daisy sighed. "Look – it's either the police, or we break the door down ourselves – and how do we feel if it's a false alarm and we frighten her out of her wits? And who pays for the damage?"

The woman echoed Daisy's sigh. "See what you mean."

"Tell you what," said Daisy. "I'll get the sergeant on the corner. He's usually patrolling this beat – and he knows me. He's not too bad, as policemen go." She smiled reassuringly at the worried woman, and went off at a run to find her friend the sergeant on the corner.

He came back with Daisy, looking doubtful, but after repeated

145

attempts to make anyone hear, he finally put his shoulder to the door and burst into the tiny flat.

It was all immaculately clean. There was no litter anywhere – no dirty crocks in the sink – not even a newspaper out of place. The electric kettle still sat on the working top, but there was no water in it and it was not plugged in. When Tom tried a light switch nothing happened and they all realised the electricity had been cut off.

There was no food of any kind in the cupboard, not even a packet of biscuits; only a few unused teabags lying on a clean white saucer.

"Nothing here," muttered the sergeant.

And then they found Mrs Parker – sitting alone in her chair, in a small, quiet heap.

"She's alive," said the sergeant, feeling a faint pulse in the cold, thin neck. "Hypothermia, at least – and starvation, I shouldn't wonder." He took out his radio then and phoned for an ambulance.

"*How could she come to this*?" said the tired grey woman, in a voice of horror. "And we not know?"

Daisy and Tom looked from her to the shrivelled, lonely figure in the chair, and sighed. How could she come to this, indeed?

"It's these damn closed doors!" said Daisy fiercely. "Everyone shut inside, afraid to go out!"

She glared at her friend the sergeant. "You're supposed to keep it safe for them," she said, her voice full of reproach.

"I know," agreed the sergeant sadly. "But there's only one of me. And there ought to be dozens!"

He led them outside then, and said kindly: "You go on now. I'll see to everything here. You've done your bit, Daisy. And you, too," he added to the shocked woman who was still shaking her head in weary self-reproach.

"I'll stay with her, Serge," she said suddenly. "Till the ambulance comes . . . After all, we was *neighbours*!" Her voice was still bitter.

The sergeant nodded quietly, and gestured to Tom and Daisy that they were no longer needed. "I know you've got work to do, Daisy," he said, smiling at her. "Thanks for your help."

The two of them went rather sadly back down the stairs to

where the two teenagers were still standing guard over the rest of the stores.

"I take it all back," said Daisy, looking up in despair at the grey, faceless walls and shuttered windows of the council estate.

"No," Tom said gently. "It's the *place* that's soulless – not the people."

Daisy shot him a small, grateful grin, and they turned back to the task in hand. They stuffed the rest of the donated stores into the last few inches of space in the lorry, and then pulled the sliding back door down and locked it securely.

"A cup of tea," said Daisy, briskly grasping Tom's arm. "Come on. We need to talk."

They went back to the same little café, where red-headed Joe called out his usual greeting and brought over two bacon rolls and two mugs of tea without being asked.

"Now," said Daisy, looking at Tom hard, "how soon can we start?"

Tom looked back, smiling at her blunt, no-nonsense tone. "Whenever you say." He paused, seeing her surprise, and then added: "I've done visas and permits today – I knew what to do from last time, and Greg had a friend who hurried things up for me . . . But maybe the agency has other papers?"

"Yes." Daisy nodded. "I've got all those for you. Since you're going with me, it makes it easier."

Tom leant forward suddenly and laid his hand on Daisy's wrist, grasping it in firm fingers. "Daisy, I want you to promise me something."

"Yes?"

"Keep to your own schedule. Don't let me deflect you from your regular plans. I don't want you to take any unnecessary risks on my behalf."

She looked up at him, almost as if she meant to protest, but then, seeing his intent, serious gaze, seemed to acquiesce with a small, quiet shrug. "OK. No more risks than necessary."

"Just – point me at the right people to ask questions from," he went on, "and leave me to it. I don't want to get you involved."

She did protest then, gently. "But I am involved, Tom. You know that."

His hand tightened on hers. "*Please*, Daisy – try to understand.

I know you're brave as a lion and twice as reckless! But I – I caused the death of someone I loved already once, remember."

Daisy just looked at him. If she was startled by the implications of that phrase "someone I loved", she did not show it, and Tom seemed almost unaware of his own admission – or else he had already accepted it as an indisputable fact.

"You didn't *cause* it, Tom."

"I was responsible for it."

"No. We are only responsible for our *own* actions. Your Suzi *chose* to do what she did. It was very brave and probably very foolhardy – but it was her choice. Not yours." Her clear grey eyes were full of certainty, willing him to accept the truth. "It's time that ghost was laid," she added softly, and when Tom gave a faint nod of consent, she went on in a more robust and cheerful voice: "We've got to go into this with no built-in misgivings, Tom. We're going to succeed! You must treat it like an adventure. I always do – and mostly it is just that. Especially the first part of the trip – lots of scenery and a mildly sore bottom!"

Tom laughed, and the shadows suddenly retreated. Daisy was right. It was an adventure – and he was going to succeed. Of course he was. If Daisy said so, how could he fail?

"You off, then?" asked Joe, as they got up to go.

"Yes, Joe." Daisy smiled at his red and anxious face. "We're on our way."

Tom thought she looked like a modern-day Boadicea, setting off to battle, sword in hand and all banners flying.

"Mind how you go," Joe said, and turned to Tom rather fiercely. "You take care of her, see? She's someone special, is our Daisy!"

"Yes," agreed Tom. "I know."

Daisy was right about the journey out – it was mostly an adventure, and it was hard on the bottom. Even the best-sprung lorry in the world could not avoid all the potholes on the mountain roads, and they rattled and bumped up and down hills and round hairpin bends on the edge of fearful drops until Tom was almost dizzy with concentration as he swung the heavy vehicle safely past one hazard or another. But he had to admit that the scenery was spectacular.

148

In a way, this part of the trip was a rather special time for both of them. There was time to talk, time to discover a whole lot more about each other, time to let thoughts run free and private dreams take shape without interruption. Enclosed in their little world of the warm, humming lorry cab, a curious intimacy and cameradie seemed to grow between them. Tom told Daisy all about his wilderness days on Little Reward, prompted by her fascinated questions. Daisy had a feeling for wilderness country, and wanted to know every detail. He even found himself telling her about Sally Maguire's fierce prompting which had finally made him decide to come home: *Family is family* . . . and this led him on to a question which was very much in his mind at present.

"Daisy – what do you think of family life?"

She glanced at him somewhat warily, aware that there was a lot behind this innocent question. "I think it's important," she said. "And a lot of what's wrong with us all today is to do with the break-up of the family." She sighed. "But –"

"But it can be a tyranny, too?"

She laughed. "It could. If you let it." Her glance this time was a little mischievous. "I suppose I had a very happy childhood – even though I think my father would rather I had been a boy."

Tom looked startled. "Would he?"

"Oh yes. His right-hand man. Take on the farm after him –" She made a faint grimace. "Only, I wanted to go farther afield than that."

"Well, you certainly have."

"Yes, but I do go back, you know. I go home quite a lot – and I always try to be there at lambing time. Dad really does need help then."

Tom nodded. "But you need to escape?"

She shook her head. "It's not just to escape, Tom. I need to do something positive now and then – there's so much suffering out there –" She waved a hand in a vaguely forward gesture towards the war-torn country they were aiming for. "I just can't bear to – pass by on the other side."

Tom smiled. "I can't imagine you ever passing by anyone – or anything!"

Daisy grinned. "I know. I'm an interfering woman."

"So was Sally Maguire," said Tom. "And I loved her, too."

149

Daisy looked at him. "Tom –"

"No, it's all right," he said. "I'm just telling you – I love interfering women!"

They both began to laugh. But then Daisy said, more soberly: "You are really saying you have done your escaping, and now you've got to settle for family life, aren't you?"

Tom sighed. "It looks like it. Someone's got to give Becky a place to be and a rôle to fill. And then there's Holly and Adam, and probably Kit, if we get him home."

"*When* we get him home."

"Daisy –"

"My mother has always filled her house with people," said Daisy reflectively. "I'm used to it . . . I rather like an extended family." She looked at Tom, without dissembling. "All of us living in separate little boxes, trying to sort out our own separate problems, paying no attention to anyone else . . . It's a somewhat barren existence, isn't it?"

"But – what about privacy?"

"Oh, *privacy*!" said Daisy, grinning. "You can always shut the door!"

They didn't pursue it any further just then, but it seemed to Tom that an awful lot had been said about the future – and there would be time enough to say more later on . . .

They did not hurry too much on this outward journey, since Daisy told him severely that they would need to arrive rested and ready for anything. So they set themselves a shortish driving schedule for each day, and stopped off at various places where Daisy was known and welcomed on the way.

From Austria, they put the lorry on the train through the tunnel to avoid climbing up to the Alpine passes, and then it did not seem long before they reached Llubijana, and finally Zagreb.

In Zagreb, Daisy directed Tom to the headquarters of the aid agency. "All aid comes through Zagreb," she said. "We'll get news of Kit here, if there is any – and I shall get my instructions."

She took all her lists of goods and travel papers into the inner office, and left Tom sitting outside in the anteroom. "Remember," she said to him, smiling: "You are my interpreter, as well as my co-driver. *Very* important."

Tom looked troubled. "Not false pretences?"

"Believe me, Tom, they're *not*. You'll be enormously useful. In fact, you have been already. Usually, I'm flaked out with the driving before I start!"

Tom grinned, feeling a little better. He hated being any kind of an encumbrance to Daisy.

"Won't be long," she said, and disappeared through the pass door!

Tom saw that there was a large map of Bosnia and Croatia on the wall, with pins stuck into it, presumably marking places where the aid workers had managed to get their lorries through. He got up to have a closer look at it, and was still looking with respect at the difficult terrain and small mountain roads, when a voice behind him said: "Formidable, isn't it? Impossible, really, to reach everyone that needs help."

Tom turned. The woman who confronted him was tall, iron-grey hair swept back from a strong, pleasant face, and a general air of unfussy competence.

"I'm Esmée," she said, holding out a friendly hand. "And you're Tom. Daisy told me you were coming. But she didn't say you were Tom Denholm."

Tom stared. "You were here then?"

"Oh yes. Very much so."

Tom began helpless apologies. "It was a very badly organised trip."

"Yes." Esmée smiled at him with much kindness. "I know. Not your fault, though, was it? . . . And you got them out."

Tom looked surprised. "I – it was a very confused situation."

Esmée nodded. "It usually is. Shells falling everywhere. No one giving the right orders. Snipers behind every corner. And Serb commanders refusing to honour any cease-fires or promises of safe-conduct. It happens all the time."

Tom sighed. "Isn't it any better now?"

She echoed his sigh, a little wearily. "In some places, yes. Where the cease-fires actually hold and the UN have established so-called "safe" areas . . . At times, we think the war is really coming to an end, and then some trigger-happy hothead sparks off another flare-up . . . or some atrocity takes place somewhere, and the revenge cycle starts all over again." She looked at him a little grimly. "And then, of course, there are brigands."

Tom looked a bit grim, too. "It may take a long time to eradicate those."

"I'm afraid so." Her expression lightened a little. "I'm glad you're going with Daisy. It always worries us a little when she's on her own. She's a bit – er – reckless!"

Tom grinned. "I can believe it." Then he grew serious again. "But I – I don't know if I'll be much help. I mean, emergencies are so unpredictable. I couldn't save Suzi."

"You tried," said Esmée flatly. "And you were the one, I believe, who kept everyone together when they were too shocked to do anything – and talked yourself out of trouble at all the checkpoints in spite of a smashed kneecap."

Tom looked at her, astonished. "How do you know?"

"They told me. Afterwards. You kept quiet about it, I know. But they didn't." She paused, and then added curiously: "Tell me something – did you ever do the drawings they wanted? Official war artist stuff?"

Tom laughed, with some bitterness. "Oh yes. Before I resigned. But I'm afraid I made them so horrifically accurate that they were afraid to use them."

Esmée laughed, too. But neither of them was really amused. "There's still plenty here to draw," she said, with sudden emphasis.

Tom's eyes went wide. "What do you mean?"

"It's two years since then, Tom . . . Two years of privation, broken buildings, broken limbs, lack of food, lack of water, lack of heating, lack of everything. It grinds them down – the innocent victims of war . . . For them, things don't get better, they get worse – even if the fighting eases up, no one tries to help them. It will take years and years to get things back to normal – if ever."

"And?"

"Well, one of the ways of encouraging the aid to continue could be your pictures. More vivid than photographs – more immediate. You could have an exhibition or something in London, couldn't you? People's attention flags unless it is stimulated by something."

Tom was staring at her now with frank amazement. "Who have you been talking to?"

152

"Me, for one," said Daisy from behind him.

"And one of your camera crew who came out before . . . George, was it? He came back to help, you know." Esmée and Daisy were smiling at each other.

Tom swung round on them. "You've been ganging up on me!"

"'Fraid so," said Daisy, laughing. "And on the strength of it, I've brought you a sketch pad – in case you have time to spare."

"Honestly," groaned Tom, "you don't give me time to breathe as it is!"

Daisy and Esmée looked at each other, signalling cheerful things.

"Well, you've got a breather now," Daisy told him. "Here's what we're going to do." She laid her papers down and went over to the map on the wall. "One of the team who was with Kit is coming into Zagreb tomorrow. He'll report to his own aid agency first and then he'll come on here, and we can wait to see him in case he's got anything useful to tell us . . . Then we're going down to Slavonska Posega, and up to Nasice, and on to Osijek. The other three of Kit's team are still working from Osijek anyway."

"What about your schedule of supplies?"

"Some to Osijek itself, some to various villages around there – provided the Muslim–Croat agreement holds and the Serbs let us through . . ." She paused, with her finger on the mountain roads beyond Slavonska Posega. "And you can follow up what leads you can find from there." She turned and looked at him very straight. "It's difficult country to search, Tom. It could take some time."

"Yes," agreed Tom humbly. "I know."

"But still," Daisy added in a warm and cheerful voice, "you never know – we may strike lucky!" Her hopeful grin was somehow infectious and Tom found himself smiling back. And he could not miss that deliberately chosen word – "*we*".

"In the meantime," Esmée put in, also determined not to let Tom get too discouraged, "you'd better both stay the night with me. At least you can get one night in comfortable beds."

"And a hot meal?" said Daisy hopefully, and at Esmée's smiling nod, she laughed and added: "Now you're talking!"

* * *

153

The aid worker, Harry, when he came, told them all he could, which wasn't much. "We were trying to reach a village north of Nasice," he said. "No aid had got through there for some time, though the fighting had stopped. But the UN warned us that the road was mined, and there were still pockets of Serb resistance in the mountains, in spite of it being a 'safe area'. He sighed, and rubbed a tired hand over his stubbly face. "So we turned into the detour side road to go the long way round. We *had* stopped to consult each other, and Kit knew what was happening." He paused, and then added: "Normally, we drive in twos. It's safer in emergencies. But Kit's partner was off sick that day – dysentery from bad water." Once again he sighed, and looked rather anxiously from Daisy to Tom, almost as if apologising for something. "We thought Kit was following. It was difficult country and the weather was atrocious . . . lying snow and heavy mist on the mountains . . . It wasn't until we actually reached our destination that we realised Kit wasn't behind us."

Tom nodded quietly. He understood the situation very well. "What did you do?"

"We waited for him to turn up. We thought he'd just got delayed with a puncture, or a snowdrift or something . . . We often do get held up with one obstacle or another – or some uncooperative Serb commander . . ." He glanced at Daisy again, knowing she understood the hazards.

"When did you go back to look?" she asked, grasping firmly at essentials.

"The next day," said Harry, still sounding faintly apologetic. "We thought – till then – and for some time after, as a matter of fact, that he'd just turn up. But he didn't." He blinked a little, and then continued: "We went back to the crossroads where the detour began – and even tried to venture along the mined road a bit, but a UN patrol turned us back . . . There was no sign of the lorry, or of Kit . . . Just an empty mountain road and a lot of potholes."

"What do you think could have happened to him?" asked Tom, more or less calling Harry's bluff.

The thin, worried face with its dark shadow of stubble looked even more worried. "Several things. He could simply have got lost. There were minor turn-offs on that road, leading to God-knows-where in the mountains . . . Or the lorry could have been hijacked – by some maverick group of soldiers or other . . ."

"Then what would they have done with Kit?"

The question hung in the air between them, and Harry glanced wildly at Esmée and then at Daisy, as if asking for support.

"Better tell us the worst that could happen," said Daisy. "Then anything else will be good news!"

Harry gave her a rather desperate grin. "Well, they could have shot him and just made off with the lorry . . . Plenty of ravines to drop him in . . ." He paused, and shivered a little. "Or, they could have turned him loose and told him to walk home – wherever home is supposed to be. They've been known to do that before . . . Or they could have taken him prisoner . . ."

"Why would they do that?" Tom's voice was sharp.

"If they had a secret gun emplacement in the mountains, or a weapon store, or something – they might not want anyone like Kit to go back and tell the UN where it was."

"Yes, I see."

"Or what else?" pursued Daisy inexorably.

Harry looked weary, and visibly distressed by the whole dangerous scenario. "Oh well, I suppose the lorry could have broken down in some obscure spot – though we've searched almost everywhere accessible. Kit wouldn't want to leave it with a valuable cargo of aid on board. He'd try to mend it first – and then maybe give up and start walking . . ." He shook his head unhappily. "Or, it's possible he could have skidded and plunged the whole thing over a ravine . . . but I think that's *very* unlikely. We'd have seen the tyre marks . . ." He seemed almost to collapse then, and sagged against the table which he had been leaning across to point at the map on the wall. "I'm sorry – I can't tell you any more. The others are still trying to find out . . . They'll tell you all they can when you get there."

"Go and get some sleep, Harry," commanded Esmée. "You're flaked out."

He nodded sadly, and got to his feet. Then he turned to Tom with sudden intensity. "I wouldn't for the world have wanted anything like this to happen – especially to young Kit. He's such a good worker, and so uncomplaining. Much too good to waste!"

155

Tom smiled. "That sounds like a good testimonial."

"Well, I'm sure if anyone can find him, you and Daisy will," Harry told him, half smiling now. "Her ability to work miracles is legendary!" He held out his hand. "The best of luck, anyway."

"Thanks," said Tom. "We'll need it."

They were stopped at roadblocks and checkpoints several times on the way down to Slavonska Posega, but the various officials, soldiers, petty bureaucrats and commanders of small, belligerent groups seemed to know Daisy pretty well, and most of them waved her through with the minimum of truculence – especially when she produced her usual "gifts" of cigarettes and Mars Bars.

"Is this your regular route?" Tom asked, marvelling at how much Daisy's wide, cheerful grin could achieve. "They all seem to know you."

Daisy hesitated. "Not always. I've been up here in Croatia a lot of the time . . . And it's been easier since the Muslim–Croatian agreement, of course. But sometimes it was down in Bosnia. Just a different front line, with Muslims on one side and Serbs on the other . . . The needs of the beleaguered civilians are the same everywhere . . ."

Tom looked at her sideways. "Daisy, you didn't change your field of operations just for me?"

She shrugged. "There was a choice – north or south. Both areas need help. I chose north, that's all."

Tom was about to protest, but she forestalled him. "It makes sense, Tom. You *had* to come up here. What use would I be to you down in Sarajevo?"

Tom shook his head at her. "You promised to keep to your own schedule."

"Well, I shall. I've got a whole list of places to visit, sheafs of papers and bills of lading . . . I shall deliver every last package and bottle of pills, don't you worry!"

Tom laughed, but he was still a bit troubled by how much his own search was affecting Daisy's work.

However, at the next roadblock, much closer to the Nasice area, they were stopped by a group of tough and intractable Serbs, and Tom found himself talking like mad, and pleading for the cause of neutral, noncombatant aid workers who risked their lives to

156

bring relief to the innocent victims of war. He got quite lyrical and was surprised to find the angry little group of men listening to him with some respect. At length, they let them go on, with the shouted instructions to "mind the firing line".

"Phew," said Daisy. "You could talk the hind leg off a donkey."

"I know, I just did," said Tom, and they both began to laugh. After that, he felt better.

Tom had to admit to himself that he had been dreading his return to Bosnia (or even to the different war zones of Croatia). There were too many anguished memories of that last fatal trip, and the whole awful episode had somehow taken on a nightmare quality in his mind. He just hoped that facing up to the present reality of difficulty and danger would somehow cure him. He wasn't really a coward, he told himself, and crisis moments usually geared him up to behave better than usual. But it wasn't the danger or the difficulty that finally cured Tom – it was the people themselves.

Daisy took him straight to her first port of call before they ever reached Nasice. It was a smallish village, in which scarcely a house was left standing. It had been in the front line of the recent offensive, before the fighting moved on further south. Shells had demolished most of the walls, and the rest of the small houses had been gutted by fire. Atrocities had taken place here, Daisy knew. Muslims had been dragged out of their houses and shot – and now there was an atmosphere of helpless despair about the few people left trying to exist in the ruins. There wasn't a hospital here, of course, the village was too small – but a makeshift first-aid post had been set up to deal with what casualties had survived. They couldn't get to the town yet, as there were still Serb troops guarding the roads, and the villagers did not dare risk the shells and snipers if they tried to cross the Serbian line. Food was scarce, too, for the same reason, and they were mostly living on potatoes and beans and what stores they had left.

They greeted Daisy with cautious joy, emerging from their shattered houses in ones and twos, seeming almost afraid to indulge in too much rejoicing. But there were still a few children there, and they had no such reservations. They came running out to meet Daisy and the lorry, and Tom, too, since he seemed to be part of the setup. For a moment Tom was painfully reminded of that other child who had come running out, and Suzi bravely running out after him . . . But he sternly shut the memory down and concentrated on the immediate problems before them.

Following Daisy's example, he had filled his own travelling rucksack with bars of chocolate, cigarettes, and even a few chocolate easter eggs, remembering what children might expect to get in safe and affluent England. He glanced now at Daisy for permission, wondering if he was doing the right thing, and at her quick nod began to hand out the small, silver-wrapped eggs to each pair of eager hands. The children received them with a mixture of disbelief and delight, and one small girl reached up and put her arms round Tom's neck and hugged him as he stooped over her.

Then Daisy and Tom unloaded the allocated consignment of food and medical supplies, carrying them all into the makeshift clinic for distribution. The battered and emaciated villagers queued up patiently and with curious dignity for their small rations. No one pushed or tried to jump the queue. Most of them managed to say an English "thank you", and one young woman, who was the only nurse in the village and had been trying to tend the wounded with her inadequate supplies, turned to Daisy with tears in her eyes and said in her own language: "I cannot tell you what this means to us –" which Tom duly translated for her. Daisy merely smiled and went back to see if there was anything else she could spare from the lorry's precious cargo.

But the nurse had not finished with them yet, and she tugged at Tom's arm and begged him to come with Daisy to see one of her patients. It was another small girl, lying on a mattress on the floor and clearly very ill and feverish. But when Daisy and Tom bent over to lok at her, she stared up and suddenly smiled at them with enormous sweetness. It was only then that Tom noticed the thick, bandaged stump where her left leg should have been.

"I can't treat her here," said the nurse, urgently to Tom. "She will die. I can't get her to the hospital in Osijek. We have no transport – and the mortar shells keep falling beyond the road . . ." She turned fierce, desperate eyes from Tom's concerned face to Daisy's equally compassionate one. "Can you take her with you? Is it allowed?"

Tom turned to Daisy, repeating the question, not in the least knowing the answer.

"Is her mother here?" asked Daisy. "Or her father?"

The nurse shook her head. "Both killed," she said bluntly. "The child left for dead. We found her under the rubble."

Daisy was clearly considering the matter. "Do the other villagers think she should go?"

The anxious eyes of the nurse went from one face to another, waiting for their verdict as Tom translated. Several heads nodded, and one old woman said: "If it gives the child a chance, she must go."

"It is against the rules," said Daisy, "but we will take her. But only as far as Osijek . . . The UN officials will have to decide what to do for her then. I have stores for the hospital, anyway. I can deliver her there. But I don't know how much they can do for her; they have been bombed as well."

"It will be better than here," said the nurse.

The old woman came forward then and clasped Daisy's hand. "God is good," she said simply. Then she clasped Tom's hand, too, and smiled a cracked and toothless smile.

So Daisy and Tom, directed by the young nurse, lifted the sick child on to what blankets and cushions they could muster and laid her along the seat in the front cab of the lorry. They didn't like to put her in the back in the cramped space among the stores, in case some of the boxes fell on top of her. So they squeezed up very close in the driver's seat and just made enough room for her beside them.

"She is called Sonja," said the young nurse. "I have only the paper with her name and her father's name. Nothing else was left."

But the old woman spoke to her then in an urgent voice, and then handed something to Daisy, with a whispered: "It was her mother's . . . Please take it." And when Daisy looked down she saw that it was a rather beautiful string of old amber beads.

Tom half expected her to hand it back, but Daisy did no such thing. She accepted it gravely and said in a gentle voice: "I will take good care of it for her . . ." and smiled with great warmth and understanding at the tired, war-weary face before her. She's seen it all, Daisy thought to herself. What more can

159

I say to her? Nothing is left to her now, except hope for the children . . .

Then she turned to Tom briskly. "Come on. The sooner we get her there, the sooner she will get treated," and she turned the lorry round and drove off, to a flutter of waving hands and a chorus of something that sounded like "God speed".

It was a narrow mountain road with a steep rock face on one side and a sheer, dizzying drop on the other. Tom drove while Daisy cradled the child against one arm and held the outspread map in her other hand. It was an unfamiliar road, even to her, and she followed the map reference carefully. It wouldn't do to get lost in these mountains. One lost aid worker was enough.

"We're all right," she said. "It's only a few miles to Nasice."

Tom was just about to answer with a cheerful "Oh good", when there was a kind of dull thud above them on the mountainside and something whizzed over their heads and landed with a loud explosion far below.

"Mortars," said Tom. "I thought this was a UN 'safe area'."

"It was," agreed Daisy. "Still is, I expect. But that doesn't stop the odd gun crew going it alone."

Tom grunted. "Better get out of here," he said, and went down the next stretch of road and round the next bend rather too fast.

"We're not in their range," protested Daisy. "That was over the top."

"You're telling me!" grinned Tom, and swung round the next curve on a wing and a prayer.

At the bottom of the next incline, they met a Serb roadblock.

"Talk, Tom," said Daisy. "They mean business."

"So do I," said Tom, and began to talk.

The Serb captain was not impressed. "You should not be on this road."

"No one told us," Tom explained, spreading his hands out in a gesture of innocent bewilderment.

"And why is that child here?" The captain seemed about to lean into the cab and yank the little girl out on to the road, when Daisy leant over her protectively and said in a cool, dangerously pleasant voice: "We are taking her to hospital. Translate, Tom. No one makes war on children, do they?"

160

This was clever of Daisy. Everyone knew perfectly well that all three sides of this terrible civil war – Muslim, Croat and Serb – made war on children. They were always the innocent victims. But no one liked to admit that it was true. Especially of their own side. It was always the other side that committed the atrocities – as everyone knew.

Dutifully, Tom translated. The Serb captain looked doubtful.

"And anyway," pursued Daisy, still looking at Tom for interpretation, "since this sector is now declared a 'safe area' and you have withdrawn your heavy weapons, why is someone still shelling the road? Surely your soldiers would not disobey you?"

Again, Tom translated. The Captain looked even more confused by doubt.

"The siege is over," pointed out Daisy. "And supplies are low, as you know. That is why we are bringing aid. And taking an injured child to the local hospital is *not* an act of war."

This time, Tom could see, the Captain's resolve was weakening. "Daisy Bellingham is known everywhere for her humanitarian aid," Tom added, off his own bat. "She has UN authority to enter places under their control. Are you countermanding their authority?"

The Serb's perplexed and unpredictable mind considered this, and his better judgement seemed to prevail. "Very well," he conceded. "But do not stray from the road."

Daisy smiled at him with dazzling gratitude. "They need the stores in the town," she said, waving a hand at the back of the lorry. "Though of course you could take them all if you chose . . . But I have some chocolate and cigarettes to spare. Would they be acceptable?"

Tom translated with alacrity. It seemed they would. The Serb's face almost smiled. And as if to reinforce Daisy's sunny acceptance that all was well, the child, Sonja, suddenly woke up and smiled, too, with the same heart-rending sweetness as before, and said in disbelieving tones: "Everyone is kind . . ."

That somehow clinched it, and Tom drove on with an audible sigh of relief.

"Wow!" breathed Daisy, when they had got round the next bend in the road. "That was touch and go."

"If the siege is really over," said Tom, puzzled: "Why are they being so belligerent?"

161

Daisy shrugged. "The *war* isn't over – not for them, anyway. They simply move a little further down the line and attack somewhere else." She sighed, and added thoughtfully: "It's the *land*, you see . . . Each side thinks it is theirs. There's nothing like defending your own patch to keep you fighting mad!"

Tom nodded. Territorial, he thought sadly. We are all territorial animals. I suppose I would fight for my own patch, if I had to . . . But which patch would that be, I wonder? Little Reward, or a certain hillside in Yorkshire . . .?"

"Daisy," he said suddenly. "Would you fight for your own patch?"

She was silent for a moment, and then said slowly: "Yorkshire . . .? I suppose so – if I had to. It means a lot to me – and even more to my parents . . ." She looked at him sideways. "Would you?"

Tom echoed her sigh. "Yes . . . We are all the same, under the skin." But they were coming into the town now, and there was a UN checkpoint ahead of them. The first part of their journey was over.

But in Nasice, where there were only a few UN observers, and the amenities were even fewer, the friendly official Daisy approached said sadly: "We have no authority to do anything for the child here, and no facilities, either. You'll have to take her on to Osijek. I don't know if you really ought to be taking her anywhere, but it's fairly obvious you've got to do something. Even in Osijek the amenities will be limited, I'm afraid. They've been bombed almost out of existence."

Daisy sighed, and both she and Tom looked anxiously at the feverish child in their charge. It was bad enough getting her this far. (Especially without official UN permission.) Would she survive another fifty kilometres of bumpy, shell-pocked roads?

"We'll have to try," murmured Tom.

Daisy did not hesitate. "Yes. We must." She looked up at the UN official, frowning with concentration. "I have stores to deliver here. But I think we'd better get on with delivering Sonja first. I'll come back later."

The friendly face opposite her smiled doubtfully. "Mind how you go, then. And try to get back here before nightfall, or else stay in Osijek overnight. The roads are difficult enough by day, let alone at night."

Daisy nodded, and they drove off again, after another anxious glance at Sonja's pale, half-conscious face.

To their relief, there was only one roadblock and checkpoint on the last stretch of the road – and that was a UN one. They were waved on by a smiling young official who knew Daisy from earlier visits and who said cheerfully: "Go on, then, Crazy Daisy. I don't know what the hell you're up to this time, but we're not stopping you!"

She and Tom looked at each other and laughed, and thankfully drove on into the shattered outskirts of Osijek.

"The Serb front line is very close just here," she said. "Or it was. The town is supposed to be safe now, but the zone is very narrow."

As if to confirm this, there was a sudden explosion not far away, and a plume of smoke and dust rose into the air beyond the straggling houses on the edge of the town.

"Come on," said Daisy. "We might as well get there in one piece!"

Tom grinned, and followed her directions at top speed.

They took Sonja to the hospital, and Tom carried her in to a dark and overcrowded ward, where at least she was able to lie on a fairly comfortable bed. But the conditions in the shattered hospital were, at best, primitive, and at their worst, appalling. There was no glass left in the windows. Electricity was nonexistent, though a generator worked sometimes for a few hours. Water was scarce and intermittent. Drugs had almost completely run out, and anaesthetics were in desperately short supply.

The tired, overworked doctors and nurses greeted Daisy and her stores with thankful relief, and even a few tears – especially over a consignment of antibiotics. But the weary young doctor who examined Sonja said sadly: "We can do little for her here – except use some of your precious antibiotics. She needs to go somewhere better equipped than we are today."

Daisy nodded. "I was afraid you would say that. We will talk to the UN and see what they can do." She looked round the hospital ward and added sorrowfully: "And she is only one of many . . ."

The young doctor looked at Daisy and smiled. "We do our best . . . And so do you."

Tom, meanwhile, had been looking round the roomful of pitiful casualties, his face getting grimmer by the moment as he saw their plight. He had known it would be bad – but as bad as this? It was beyond belief. Sighing, he shook his head in wordless grief, not knowing what to say or how to help.

"Don't despair," said the doctor, rightly interpreting Tom's expression. "A lot of them will get well."

Tom shot him a grateful glance. But once again it was the quiet, uncomplaining dignity of these suffering people that moved him most.

"They are so patient!" he murmured.

"Yes. Patient patients," smiled the young doctor. "And this little one is the same." He ruffled Sonja's tangled hair and gave her a special smile.

The child smiled back, and held out thin arms to Daisy and to Tom to say goodbye. "Thank you for bringing me," she whispered, and sighed a little and shut her eyes.

"She's very tired," Daisy murmured to the doctor, and saw his quick nod of assent with relief. He clearly understood the situation.

He looked from Tom, who was still hesitating by the child's bed, to Daisy who was also reluctant to leave her, and said in as comforting a voice as he could muster: "We will do what we can for her."

Tom turned away them, with tears in his eyes, but Daisy leant over the small girl and put the necklace of amber beads round her neck. "It came from her village," she explained to the doctor. "It may be worth something . . ."

He smiled. "We'll see that she keeps it with her." They exchanged a brief glance of understanding, and then Daisy also turned away to follow Tom.

"How can you bear it?" he said to Daisy, as they went in search of a UNPROFOR official.

Daisy looked at him with faint reproof. "You have to be tough," she told him. "It's no good letting it defeat you. That way, you'd never get anything done." She gave him a small, hopeful smile. "Concentrate on essentials. It's the only way."

Tom's answering grin was rueful. "I know. It was the *gratitude* that threw me."

Daisy agreed. "Makes you feel awful, doesn't it?"

"Don't you ever want to take one of these children home with you?"

"Yes. Often. But I know I can't. It has to be done by the UN – through the right channels. In spite of the carnage, both sides are fussy when it comes to shipping out one of their nationals . . . One or two people have tried to go it alone, and once or twice they've got away with it. But it usually causes more trouble, and the situation is tricky enough for everyone, including the UN, as it is."

Tom saw the sense of that. But a rebellious part of him still wanted to charter a plane and cram every injured child he could find into it and fly them out to a safe, warm world.

Fool, he thought. Sentimental fool. You couldn't do it. Stop daydreaming and get on with what you've come here for. Find Kit. Get him home. That's your first priority.

"We'll find the aid workers next," said Daisy, reading his mind. "If they're still here."

But the UN official said they were off on another small relief expedition that day, and wouldn't be back till the next day. He did, however, promise to do what he could for little Sonja. "Though there are others whose needs are just as urgent," he said, sighing. "But if we can get them out, we will."

Daisy and Tom looked at each other doubtfully. "We'll have to stay here for the night," she said. "But that won't be a problem. I've got friends here."

Tom nodded, and waited to be told what to do. His own search would have to wait, at least till the aid workers got back. So they spent the rest of the day distributing the food stores that were on Daisy's schedule to the central depot in the town.

In the evening, Daisy directed Tom to another quarter of the town that was slightly less battered, and found her way to a block of flats that seemed to be comparatively unscathed.

"We'll get a floor to lie on, if not a real bed!" she said, smiling!

They parked the lorry as close to the sheltering walls of the apartment block as they could, locked it securely in case of looters, and went up the steps to knock on one of the doors. But before they could lift a hand to the knocker, the door flew open, and a jumble of people almost fell out on to the landing.

"Daisy!" they cried. "Welcome back! . . . We heard you were coming." They all seemed to manage a little English, and an excited jumble of words fell about them like summer rain.

Daisy emerged from several large embraces, and introduced Tom. "How did you hear we were coming?" she asked curiously.

"The aid worker, Geoff, told us. And about your friend, Tom." The head of this little household, Drago, a thin, wiry man with steady watchful eyes, spoke for them all. He turned to Tom courteously and added: "We are sorry your friend is missing . . . But Geoff will help all he can . . . So would we, if we knew how."

Tom smiled and nodded hopefully. It was clear that everyone wanted to be helpful. It was the delay that fretted him. But there was nothing he could do about that till the next day, so he followed Daisy into the crowded little living room and tried to join in the general rejoicing. Daisy had brought them a few special gifts out of her private store, and when she and Tom assured the family that they had already eaten at the aid depot canteen, Irena, the hospitable housewife, was content to offer them some precious coffee.

"They love to be hospitable," Daisy whispered to Tom. "You have to let them do something. It's a matter of pride."

Tom nodded, and refrained from offering them more than two bars of chocolate and one pack of beer from his own rucksack. He also, suddenly remembering Esmée's conversation about drawing these people to promote interest back home, surreptitiously got out his sketchbook.

But when the family even tried to give up their own beds, Daisy smilingly refused. "We have our sleeping bags," she said cheerfully. "Give us some floor space. That's all we need."

There were still occasional crumps of gunfire from the surrounding hills, but the family took little notice of them, except to listen and judge how far away they were. There was no electricity on that evening – it came on sporadically, as the engineers managed to mend it, so life after dark was mostly lived by candlelight and people went to bed early. Both Tom and

Daisy were thankful for this, as they suddenly realised they were bone weary. It had been a long, anxious drive, in fairly perilous conditions, and they fell into thankful sleep almost as soon as they climbed into their sleeping bags on the living room floor.

The next morning, they said goodbye to their friendly, affectionate hosts, after breakfasting with them on some English tea (from Daisy) and some real bread from the baker who had now got some flour to use.

"Come back again," they cried, and Irena, as much head of the family as Drago, added earnestly: "Not for aid, Daisy. But because we love you."

Daisy did not reply to this in words, but hugged her hard instead, and the lined face of the woman softened. She clearly understood.

They had to wait about for most of the day till Geoff and his team returned, and Tom tried (somewhat vainly) not to fret any more about the delay. There were still things Daisy had to do, and he helped her unload a few more stores, and repack the rest of the lorry load a bit more securely.

They also visited the hospital again to ask after Sonja, and found her sleeping but much more comfortable, and the doctor told them he thought arrangements really were being made to evacuate a few of the more serious casualties, and Sonja would be among them.

They both sighed with relief at this, and both stooped to smooth down the child's still tangled hair before they left, admitting to themselves (but not to each other) that they had got mysteriously fond of the brave little girl.

In the afternoon, the three aid workers arrived in their mud-caked lorry and came to talk to Tom. "We can take you back to the crossroads where we last saw him," they said. "The detour is still in force. The mines haven't been cleared off the road yet."

The leader of the group, Geoff, looked at Tom with anxious eyes. "We've combed the area pretty thoroughly," he said sorrowfully, "but we might've missed something . . ." He hesitated, and then added seriously: "I think I should warn you that the media may have got on to it . . . We kept it as quiet as possible at first, because we didn't want to make things worse by assuming

167

that there was something wrong. If you start accusing people out here, repercussions can be pretty deadly."

Tom agreed. "I can see that."

"But now – it's been too long. Something *must* have happened to him." He turned a worried face from Tom to Daisy. "The trouble is, we don't know where to look. But we'll keep trying. Everyone is looking for him now." He grasped Tom's arm kindly. "We'll go down there first thing tomorrow – Serb patrols permitting, OK?"

"OK," said Tom, and managed a hopeful grin. "Thanks." He realised he had to agree to their plan of action. It was yet another delay, but they were clearly too tired, and it was too late, to do anything more today.

But Daisy surprised him then by saying abruptly: "All right. We'll go back to Nasice now. I have stores to deliver. We'll meet you at the crossroads tomorrow." She got out her map to confirm the meeting place and the time, and then turned briskly away. Mystified, Tom climbed into the lorry beside her and drove out of Osijek on the road to Nasice. He glanced at her once or twice rather questioningly, but Daisy did not choose to enlighten him then.

After several more roadblocks and arguments, they arrived back in Nasice almost too late to distribute any stores. But Daisy seemed to have some driving force pushing her on, so they off-loaded what they could at the aid depot as the light was fading, and then made for their next night's shelter.

As before, Daisy had friends in the town – people who had offered her hospitality, or anything else they had left to give, in exchange for the aid she brought and (more than material aid) the friendly contact she offered. So now she took Tom across town to the side nearest to the mountain road where the shells had fallen most frequently in the long, hard siege. Many of the houses were nothing but blackened shells by now, but there were a few still standing, in small, tangled plots of land on slightly higher ground away from the general destruction.

"They were *inside* the range," she explained, leading the way towards a small house that stood alone at the end of a narrow path. "They told me to come here at the depot," she added. "I hope they are able to cope with us."

168

As she spoke, the door opened and a woman came out, smiling, with arms outstretched. "Daisy!" she cried. "You come back! Milan," she called over her shoulder, "come quick! It is Daisy – she has come back!"

A tall, thin man came out then, also smiling, and there was general rejoicing all round. Tom was introduced. Daisy produced a few more special packets out of her private store, including some coffee powder and a bag of biscuits – and Tom produced some more chocolate and another four-can pack of beer. (And his sketchbook.) It was instantly a party again, like it was in Osijek, and in no time at all they were all sitting round the table in the small living room, drinking coffee and beer and exchanging news.

When Daisy had explained to them about Tom's search for Kit, the reason for her choice of this particular household for a night's shelter became apparent. They had been talking in a mixture of English (which the woman, Nina, spoke haltingly and understood better) and Tom's translation of Milan's laconic comments. But now Daisy turned to Tom and said: "Ask Milan if he knows of any other small roads or tracks off the main one, where a lorry could be driven away and hidden . . . He knows the mountain well. He has sheep."

Milan listened attentively while Tom made Daisy's request, and then nodded with slow deliberation. "There are such places – but they are not on any map . . . I could show you, but the Serb guns are up there now. They do not permit us to go near them." He made a slight grimace of disgust. "Not that we want to – there have been too many guns in our lives already . . . But," and here his eyes lingered on Tom's face for a moment, "I do have to fetch my sheep down – when I can."

Tom nodded, understanding him very well.

"Tomorrow," said Daisy, "we will follow the aid workers to the crossroads where the detour begins . . . If you came with us, maybe you could point out a few likely places to Tom? . . . The aid lorry would bring you back."

Once again Tom translated, and Milan listened. Then he nodded again, more decisively this time. "Yes. I will come."

Daisy smiled dazzlingly at him, and then at Tom. "There! At least we've begun!"

Tom's answering smile was full of gratitude. But there was a certain anxiety behind it which he did not voice till they were alone for a moment while Nina and Milan were shutting up their house for the night. Security was difficult these days, there were looters about, and the few houses still standing intact were obvious targets – for them as well as the guns.

"Daisy," Tom began, "you can't just drop your own work and stay with me on this search."

"No," agreed Daisy tranquilly, "I know." Her smile was still open and without reservations. "But I can *start out* with you – and then we'll have to make plans to meet."

"Where? I don't know where I'm going."

"There are only a few places you *can* go to, in the end," Daisy said, unperturbed. "And I am visiting *all* of them with the lorry. They are all on my list." She looked at him, with a hint of mischief behind her smile now. "D'you think I'm going to let you out of my sight for long?"

Tom began to laugh, somewhat despairingly. "What am I to do with you?"

"Bear with me," said Daisy. "It's easier in the long run!"

So the next morning, the small procession set off. The three aid workers took their lorry, with its Aid Relief logo clearly marked on the sides, and Daisy, Tom and Milan climbed into their own lorry and followed the others up the mountain road. At Daisy's request, they went very slowly (it would have been difficult to do anything else, anyway, on those steep gradients) so that Milan could point out any paths he knew that might be wide enough to take a hijacked lorry. Tom noted them all, with the practised eye of an old campaigner in high mountain country.

At the crossroads, they all got out and stood in a small, anxious group while Geoff, the leader, explained the situation as far as he knew it.

"The main road goes off that way – where the mines are. There are also, I suspect, Serb heavy guns concealed along there, though they were *supposed* to have handed them over to the UN." He turned then, and pointed the other way, up the mountain road. "We went on that way, straight to the next village. There didn't seem to be any other turning on the way."

Daisy looked at Milan. "Could we all go on that way a bit further . . . as far as Milan's knowledge of the countryside goes?"

"Why not?" agreed Geoff. "As long as there aren't any more roadblocks . . . You can never be sure."

So they went slowly on, up the winding road, and once again Milan pointed out any places where it might be possible to secrete a stolen lorry. Finally he said to Tom, with genuine regret in his voice: "I do not know the mountain any further . . . From here you would have to look for a gap in the rocks yourself."

Tom nodded, and once again they all got out and conferred. And Tom asked Geoff, rather fiercely because he was so anxious for any sort of clue: "Can you remember where it was you last looked back and actually *saw* Kit following?"

Geoff consulted with the others, and then said: "Yes. About two miles back, before that steep bend where the derelict hut is . . ."

"And when did you next look back and see that he *wasn't* following?" pursued Tom.

Geoff looked round him, trying desperately to remember. It had been a terrible day, with swirling fog coming down over the snowy slopes of the mountain, obscuring the road in sudden walls of whiteness . . . "I think . . . it must have been about here," he said. "Or maybe a little further on . . . Not much, though, because we began to worry about him long before we got to the next village."

"How far is that?"

"About ten kilometres from here," said Daisy, looking at her map. "I know, because it's the next place on my list."

They all looked at her with respect. But Tom knew what was on her mind and reached for his rucksack in the cab of their own lorry.

"What are you proposing to do?" asked Geoff, looking a trifle alarmed.

"I am driving on to the next village," said Daisy crisply. "You are taking Milan back with you – and many thanks for all your help." Her smile was brave and cheerful as usual, despite her own misgivings. "And Tom – "

"I am going to do a spot of walking," said Tom. "I know where

171

the key rendezvous places are. I shall get back to one of them, I've no doubt."

The others looked at him doubtfully, but Milan simply patted his shoulder and handed him his own sturdy shepherd's walking stick. "Probe for drifts," he instructed. "There is still snow on the mountain. Good luck."

"Good luck," echoed the others, still looking very dubious about the whole affair. It was probably totally against UN orders to wander about alone on the mountain. But eventually they all climbed into their lorry, and Geoff leaned out to say: "Watch out for stray Serb soldiers. They can be unreasonably belligerent!"

Tom laughed. "I can believe it."

"Don't get lost," added Geoff, still anxious about him. "We don't want two of you on the missing list . . . And come back and let us know what else we can do to help."

"Yes," agreed Tom. "I will."

They waved then, and drove off, leaving Tom and Daisy on the road with the lorry between them.

"I know what you're trying to do," Daisy said. "I hope it won't be a wild-goose chase . . ." But she did not try to dissuade him. "Just take care, will you?"

"And you," said Tom.

"I'll probably wait in the village for one day," she said. "Or maybe two. It depends on how much there is to do." She looked at him steadily. "Meet me there. Or failing that, go back to Nasice – or on to Osijek."

Tom nodded, and suddenly Daisy's arms were round him, and they were hugging each other like frightened children.

"I'll be waiting," she said.

"I'll be coming!" he retorted.

And though they both laughed into each other's tangled hair, they both knew that much more important things had been said.

Then Daisy got into the lorry and drove away, leaving Tom standing on the road, staring after her.

Becky had been riding that morning. Lacey had been as good as his word and saddled up one of the horses as soon as he judged she was ready to venture out alone. Morello was a quietish mare, her black coat shining with good health and her alert, intelligent

172

head full of good temper and calm enjoyment of the day, in spite of her dancing feet in their neat white socks. Lacey didn't have any worries about her with Becky, once he had watched them together for a bit, though, as he told Becky gravely: "All on 'em needs exercising. We uses them to round up the sheep sometimes, just to give 'em a run like – specially on the rough tors where the Jeep won't go and they stray too far for walking . . ."

He gave the mare a gentle pat on the rump, and Becky went off joyously on to the wide, free moors. It felt like being a child again, in those far-off, unspoilt days on the ranch in South America with her brother, Tom . . . She was feeling well today – amazingly well. Her mind was clear and without any shadows, and the gentle life of the farm seemed to have banished all worries about the future from her thoughts. She was doing what Tom had asked – living each day as it came – and getting very fond of Ruth Bellingham in the process. And of Adam and Holly, too.

She was surprised about Holly. In spite of her assurances to Tom, she had still sustained reservations about the girl – nice though she was – being a suitable long-term partner for Kit. An unmarried mother, with all the responsibilities of bringing up a small boy on her own did not seem the ideal choice. But, somehow, all these doubts seemed to dissolve when she got to know Holly better – and the small boy, Adam, ceased to be a problem and became a real, affectionate, fun-loving companion who filled her days with laughter and small, cheerful adventures. It was all much better than she had dared to hope, and she found herself thinking as she rode back to the farm under those windswept skies: I am happy! Just think – after all that hassle, I am happy!

She came down into the farmyard, and saw Holly and Adam playing with Benji in the home meadow. Adam was running about laughing in the sun, trailing the brightly coloured tail of a kite behind him, and Benji was leaping up and down trying to catch it. Holly was only a little behind them, breathless and laughing, too. When she saw Becky coming, she waved and called: "Come and join us. We're hopeless at kite-flying."

Becky stabled Morello, and was just about to rub her down and find some feed, when Lacey mysteriously appeared from nowhere in the way he did. "I'll see to her," he said, smiling his approval that Becky cared about the mare's welfare before her own, as a good horse-woman should. "You go on – the boy was asking for you."

"Was he?" Becky was pleased. She gave Lacey an answering smile of gratitude, gently rubbed Morello's nose, and went to join the others in the field.

"We ought to go higher up on the hill," she said, panting and running with them, full of laughter. "It would fly better from there."

"Adam wanted to wait for you," said Holly, observing Becky's cheerful, relaxed mood with approval. Becky was so clearly better, improving in confidence and natural enjoyment of life day by day . . . Tom would be pleased to see it when he came home. *When he and Kit came home* . . . But she carefully did not let herself go on with that thought. Worrying would not help Kit – or Tom either. Better believe with all her might that it was going to be all right, and they would come home safe and sound . . .

"I have to go to York this afternoon," said Becky. "Just for a check-up, and to get some more pills. But I don't think I really need them any more . . ." She looked at Holly, smiling. "Would you and Adam like to come?"

"Yes, please," said Adam, who was mostly polite when he remembered. "Can we buy some more string? Benji's chewed up most of this." He held out a tangled, chewed-up ball of soggy string that ought to have been wound round its holder, but had somehow escaped.

"I think we'd better," agreed Becky, laughing. "That looks like a bird's nest!"

"Can Benji come?"

"If you tie him up in the back and stop him bouncing."

"OK," agreed Adam, sublimely confident that he could.

So they set off for York, feeling cheerful and adventurous, the two women as much like children out on a treat as Adam. They looked at the shops and bought some string, and all of them had ice cream cones from the stall near the park – and then they went on to Greenbanks for Becky's appointment.

"I won't be long," she said. "Why don't you and Adam take Benji round the grounds?" She knew she didn't need to explain to Holly that she did not want Adam to go inside those enclosing

174

hospital walls – however open and free each pleasant unit was supposed to be. "I'll come and find you," she said, and went in through the door.

The interview with Bradley was short and friendly – and encouraging. He agreed that she seemed very much better, and that probably she didn't need her pills any longer, but he would give her one more week's supply, just in case. And he said, patting her arm as she got up to go: "I am so glad to see you looking like this. Those Yorkshire moors seem to have their own magic, don't they?"

"Yes," agreed Becky happily. "They do."

She left the small consulting room, and was just crossing the main entrance hall, when the door of the television lounge opened, and a patient came out. The news bulletin was on, and something about Bosnia made Becky pause to listen.

". . . It is confirmed that a young aid worker, Christopher Wade, has been reported missing in central Croatia . . . A search is being instigated . . ."

Becky stood staring at the television screen, rooted to the spot. Kit? *Missing*? . . . It couldn't be true. *Could it*? But then she remembered how Tom had gone off without explanation, leaving her at the farm, when she had hoped and expected that he would stay there with her . . . And how he had brought Holly and Adam up to keep her company. Had he known then that Kit was in trouble? Yes, she thought, remembering Tom's grave, shuttered face, and his unexplained words: . . . *There's something I have to do*.

The news bulletin had finished now, and someone else in the room had switched it off. Becky stirred out of her frightened thoughts and rushed out of the door into the grounds.

I must go and look for him myself, she thought. I can't leave it to Tom and a lot of strangers. I'm his mother. I've got to find him!

Forgetting all about Holly and Adam in her distress, she ran to her car, put her key in the ignition and started to drive away.

But Adam, walking decorously with Benji on a string, saw the car coming down the drive and began to run. "Becky!" he cried. "Don't go without us! Stop!"

And Holly, mystified by Becky's actions, ran after the car as well. Adam and Benji got there first, and somehow managed to

175

trip over each other and the tangled lead so that they landed in a heap on the grass verge almost under the wheels of the car.

Becky slammed on the brakes automatically and the car screeched to a halt.

"What is it?" said Holly, seeing at once that something had upset Becky terribly. Her face was white, and the old look of frightened uncertainty had come back.

"It's Kit," Becky said, shaking with reaction because she had nearly killed Adam and Benji as well as being distraught about her own news. "He's missing."

Holly's heart sank. After all Tom's efforts to keep the news from Becky, this had to happen. How was she going to be able to keep her happy now?

Swiftly, she climbed into the car beside her, and made Adam and Benji get in behind. At least if they were all together, Becky wouldn't be able to go off on her own and do something rash and foolish. "Tell me what happened," she said. "Don't drive on for a moment. Let's all get our breath back."

"It was the t–television," stuttered Becky, finding that her teeth were chattering. "They said his name . . . and that he was reported missing in – in central Croatia."

Holly sighed. It did not necessarily mean that things were any worse, she realised. Only that word had somehow got through to the media. By now, Tom was probably well and truly in the midst of his search . . . And he would be bound to find him . . . It would be all right.

"Did Tom know about this before?" said Becky suddenly, turning somewhat wild, accusing eyes on Holly's anxious face.

Holly took a swift decision not to prevaricate more than necessary. "Yes. He knew there was some doubt about Kit's whereabouts . . . that's why he went out."

"He should have told me!" Becky was suddenly rather angry.

"He didn't want to worry you."

"But I'm his *mother*. I ought to go out there, too." She still sounded wild and irrational. "I should be looking for him, like Tom."

"*No*." Holly spoke with sudden firmness. "No, Becky. Leave it to Tom. He knows the country – he knows what to do. You'd be no use out there."

"I'm no use *anywhere*," said Becky bitterly.

"That's not true." Holly drew a deep breath and tried to call in all her big guns to match the far-distant ones of the threatening Serbs. "You are needed here – by Adam and me. Tom sent us up to you because he knew I would need someone to depend on – and so would Adam – while Kit couldn't be with us . . . He hoped you and I would be able to cheer each other up and stop each other worrying . . ."

"Did you know as well?"

"Only as much as Tom told me – that the aid people were worried about Kit's whereabouts. That's all." She turned to look at Becky with candid eyes. "I was worried about him, Becky – even before Tom said anything . . . And now – we'll just have to be patient and wait for Tom. He'll find him, I'm sure – he and Daisy between them."

"But I ought to be there," Becky persisted.

"No. To begin with, you'd never get in. Tom only managed it by going in with Daisy as an extra aid worker. And then, it's very tough out there, Becky. Your health would never stand it – and that would mean you'd be a liability to everyone, not an asset." She hoped, profoundly, that she was not being too tough herself. "I know it's hard to be the one left behind waiting for news – but we can't help Kit by getting in the way and being a nuisance, can we?"

Becky shivered. "No, I suppose not . . . But waiting for news is awful."

"It is," agreed Holly. "But it's all we can do now. When they get home, there'll be plenty of things we can do for them. Let's concentrate on that."

"What does 'missing' mean?" asked Adam, following the conversation as best he could.

Holly looked round and smiled at the inquisitive small boy. "It means getting a bit lost," she said carefully. "And Uncle Tom and Daisy have gone to find him. D'you remember getting a bit lost with Benji the other day, and Becky and I came to find you?"

"When me and Benji went to look for fossils?"

"Yes. And we found you, safe and sound, and we brought you home."

She glanced at Becky, hoping she would believe what Holly was really telling her. But to her surprise Becky said unexpectedly: "It must have been hard to keep it to yourself all this time . . . I suppose Tom told you to?"

"Yes. He thought you'd got enough on your plate already."

Becky laughed, a little grimly. "Well, at least we can worry together now." She smiled at Holly with sudden warmth. After all, they were in it together, she thought, and it was somehow clear to her that the girl really did care about Kit.

"Uncle Tom will find him," said Adam, with supreme confidence. "He can do *anything*."

Becky's laugh was more natural this time. "There's sublime faith for you! D'you know, Adam, I believe you are right."

"'Course I am," said Adam. "Can I have another choclit biscuit?"

"Let's all have a chocolate biscuit," said Holly, watching Becky's colour slowly return as her panic subsided. "And let's all go and have a coffee to wash it down before we go home."

So Becky allowed herself to be persuaded to leave the car where it was for a moment and go back to the little coffee house on the lawn and drink something hot and sweet.

Holly sighed with relief. The immediate crisis was over. But she would have to think of some way of keeping Becky occupied with plans for Kit and Tom in the future . . . That way, she could probably be persuaded to believe quite firmly that they were coming home.

In the end, they drove home to the farm, with Becky more or less reconciled to the waiting game, but still showing signs of momentary flashes of panic.

But, finally, it was Ruth Bellingham who thought of the solution. "I was wondering," she said tentatively, with an eye on Becky's strained face, "if you'd be interested in the farm cottages . . .?"

"What?" Becky looked uncomprehending, but Holly began to see the point at once.

"It occurred to me that you might want a place to yourself once Tom and your son Kit got home . . .? And Holly and Adam might, too?" (And Daisy and Tom certainly will, she thought, half smiling to herself, if I know anything about it. But she did not say so.) "There's three of 'em in a row," she went on. "Standing empty. Since Lacey and Mango go home at night, we don't need them at the moment . . . The farm doesn't need extra workers – except at lambing time." She was watching Becky's face as she spoke. "Not that you're not welcome to stay here," she added cheerfully, "as long as you like – but maybe a little privacy might be a good thing, later on?"

Becky opened her mouth to speak, but Ruth went calmly on: "They need a bit of doing up – a coat of paint wouldn't come amiss. The roof's sound, and there's no damp – but they're a bit shabby . . ."

"We could paint them," said Holly, following Ruth's lead. "Couldn't we, Becky?"

"Can I help?" asked Adam hopefully. The idea of sloshing on dollops of lovely paint sounded enormously appealing.

"Not on your life!" answered Holly, and then seeing his disappointment, she relented: "Well, maybe you can a bit – if you do what you're told!"

"And a few more sticks of furniture," added Ruth, blithely continuing in the face of Becky's silence. "You could make them really cosy to come home to . . ."

"Ruth," said Becky, "you're a genius!" She turned a suddenly glowing face from her to Holly. "When can we start?"

Tom walked back to the bend with the derelict hut on the corner where Geoff said he had last been sure Kit's lorry was following – and began from there. Each time there was any opening or track leading off into the foothills, he went up it a little way, looking for tyre marks or ruts made by the Serb guns or tanks – anything that might suggest a place where a lorry could be hijacked and driven off.

At first, none of the small tracks seemed wide enough or suitable for any vehicle, and were merely sheep runs on the mountainside. But then he came across one that looked more promising, and followed its winding path quite a long way up into the hills. But it petered out into an empty quarry full of fallen boulders, and he had to abandon that course and come back down to the road.

All this time, he had not met anyone either on the road or the hills but just before he emerged this time on to the rocky

179

verge, he heard a rumble of tanks or gun-carriers coming along, and the raised voices of soldiers on the move. Not wanting to be stopped and questioned, however innocent his intentions, he dodged behind a rock and waited for them to go by. He didn't understand this war – or the so-called peace initiatives and cease-fires. People still seemed to be fighting – shells continued to fall on defenceless towns and even more defenceless civilians, and there seemed to be danger everywhere. Better keep my head down, he thought. No good courting even more trouble. So he kept still and waited for the ragged column to pass.

When they had gone and the curiously empty mountain silence had returned, he came down again on to the road and went steadily on, looking for the next opening in the rocky side of the steep incline. The first one he came to was too small for a lorry, and the one after was blocked by a rockfall so that no vehicle could possibly squeeze through, but the third one he approached had some curiously flattened grass and one or two broken shrubs, as if something heavy had passed over them. He stopped to have a closer look, and decided that this really did look a bit like a place where a lorry could be seized and driven away. There were even faint signs of feet trampling in the mud-caked ground, though the recent rains had almost washed them away. Of course, he told himself, it could just be where that column of tanks and guns had come from – but something made him persist in climbing a bit further up the slope to investigate.

He had been following the track for about ten minutes with no result, when he came across another patch of churned-up mud, and one clear imprint of a lorry tyre. But beyond that point, the ground got hard and rocky again, and there was no special sign or indication that anything had passed that way. Nothing at all – until his sharp eyes caught sight of something white in the rough grass. He went across to have a look, and found that it was a small, soggy tablet of aspirin. *Aspirin*? With the name stamped on it? He turned it over in his hand, whereupon it fell to pieces, dissolved by the damp, but he put a little on his tongue to confirm what it was. Yes, it was clearly aspirin . . . And the aid truck had been carrying medical supplies . . .

He cast about in the grass then, like a questing dog, wondering if he would find any more, and sure enough, a little further up the

180

track there was another . . . and still further, apparently dropped carelessly on the stiff mountain grass, a third . . .

I believe the boy is laying a trail, said Tom to himself, jubilantly. He's got more sense than we thought! . . . And he followed slowly on, searching each tuft of rough grass or clinging shrub as the track got higher and more rocky. The trail of soggy little tablets continued sparingly as he went, but then suddenly ceased, and there was another ominous flattening of grass and churning up of mud, and one alarming scorch mark on the turf just below a new, bright chip on one of the rocks above the track. Someone fired something here, he thought. Oh God, I hope they didn't shoot him . . . Where the hell are those aspirin tablets now? Have they stopped altogether?

He searched around again, to and fro across the trampled space and the adjoining scrub, and tried further up, and further sideways, but there was no sign now of anything that might lead him on.

Just a minute, he thought. If there was something of a row here, or a struggle, and shots were let loose, wouldn't the fugitive run away *down*hill, to get away more quickly?

Following his own line of reasoning, Tom turned sideways, away from the scorched grass and chipped rockface, and began to search the thicker scrub that led away from the track diagonally down the slope of the mountainside. After about a hundred yards of nothing, he found another small white tablet lodged under a clump of grass. I was right! he said, a lurch of excitement touching him now. He *was* running away, down this slope. I've only got to keep on watching out for pills. I hope they don't run out!

The tiny trail went on, patchily, for some time, weaving in and out of sheep tracks and rocky twists and turns on the shaly flanks of the hillside – but gradually the distance between one small white clue and the next got longer and longer, and finally ceased altogether.

There was one place where the grass and small clumps of herbs seemed to have been squashed and broken, as if someone had fallen or lain down on them, and there was a suspicious-looking rusty stain on some of the grass stalks, but after that there was no indication of anyone having passed that way, and nothing for Tom

181

to go on. Only an empty hillside, and another rumble of trucks or tanks far down on the road below.

Tom looked round him, desperate for any sign that might lead him in one direction or another, and was just about to sit down on the rocky ground and rest his aching knee while he thought what to do next, when something caught his eye. It was a thin plume of smoke from a cottage chimney just beyond the next rise in the hilly terrain. A cottage? he thought. Refuge? Would he risk it? Would they be Muslims? Or Serbs? . . . Friendly or aggressive? . . . But a desperate man, running away, would risk anything, wouldn't he? Anyway, *I* shall have to risk it. I must ask them if they've seen him – or seen anything . . . They may be able to help, at least.

So he plunged on, over the scree and scrub and tangled grass, till he came to the edge of a tiny cultivated patch of ground, and one beautiful wild cherry tree just coming into blossom – and beyond that a small stone cottage with a smoking chimney, and a donkey tethered in the stony patch by the door. Somehow, the sight of that cherry tree, so frail and perfect in the midst of war, brought a lump to Tom's throat. Was this little island of tranquillity really safe to enter? Or would he be blown to pieces by a Serb gun for daring to set foot on enemy ground?

As he stood hesitating at the edge of the cleared patch of ground, a man came out of the cottage with a pitchfork in his hands, and stood squarely in front of his door, clearly nervous but determined to protect his property if he could.

"It is all right," said Tom, hoping his Serbo-Croat was the right language for the occasion, "I'm English . . ."

The man stared at him, and then slowly put down his pitchfork. "*English*?" He actually used the English word, and Tom smiled and came forward, holding out his hand.

"Not an enemy," he said, making it clear. "No danger. I'm looking for someone."

The man was still staring at him, but this time the wary expression seemed to change a little. "A friend?"

"Yes. A young aid worker. Someone who came out here to help your people." He paused, waiting to let that first bit of information sink in before he went on. "He got separated from his team of workers, and now he is missing . . . We are afraid

182

something may have happened to him." Once again he waited to see whether his words were being understood and accepted. Then he asked the crucial question: "*Have you seen him*? We think he may need help."

The man's gaunt, weather-worn face did not change, but the brilliant anxiety in the dark eyes seemed to cloud and diminish as he slowly nodded his head. "Yes," he said. "He does need help. He is here."

A great wave of thankfulness swept over Tom. Kit was found! He was safe. He was *here*!

"I am Branko," the man said gravely, at last taking Tom's hand in formal courtesy. "Come with me."

He led the way inside the cottage, where a fire of broken branches burned in the chimney corner, and a woman was bending over it, lifting a heavy, blackened kettle off the flames. Beside her, drawn up close to the warmth of the fire, was a long, thin sofa, and on it was lying an equally long, thin man.

"Kit?" said Tom, restraining himself from rushing forward. "Is it you?" Though, in spite of the boy's gaunt, unshaven appearance and air of wary exhaustion, he did not need to ask.

The figure on the sofa looked at him incredulously, and then began, weakly, to laugh. "Now I *know* I'm delirious! Hallo, Uncle Tom!"

Tom came forward then, and stood smiling down at him. "You've led us a pretty dance!"

"Sorry," mumbled Kit. "Got lost . . ."

"And got hit?" asked Tom, seeing the bandaged shoulder with the ominous stain of blackened blood showing through.

"Not a lot," Kit reassured him. "It's mending. Branko and Ana have been wonderful . . ."

Tom turned to the woman, who was smiling at him, now that she understood he was no threat to her charge. "Ana?" he said, holding out his hand. "I am the boy's uncle, Tom . . . Thank you for taking such good care of him."

"It is nothing," she said, the dark eyes, like her husband's, warm now with relief and welcome. "He was sick and in trouble . . . We could do no less."

Then Tom sat down rather suddenly before his knee gave out altogether, unloaded his pack and offered Branko and Ana everything he had got left, including some coffee powder, a tin of corned beef and the last of the chocolate. "I think we should celebrate," he said, smiling happily and hazily at everyone. "Will these help?"

So there was yet another small party among quietly rejoicing friends, while Tom tried to piece together what had been happening to Kit since he disappeared.

"They came down out of nowhere," said Kit. "Half a dozen Serbs – armed to the teeth and very belligerent . . . I don't know if they were regulars, or strays on their own. But they meant business – and they simply took the lorry and drove it away up the mountain, and made me follow on foot with the men."

Tom nodded. "That's what I thought. And then –?"

"Some kind of argument broke out. I think some of them wanted to keep me prisoner – maybe as a hostage or something? . . . And some wanted to shoot me. And some simply wanted to get rid of me, one way or another. I was a nuisance."

"And which of them won?"

Kit laughed. "Well, I'm still alive, aren't I? . . . One of them – perhaps the nicest – jerked his thumb at the mountain and told me to go, but as I went, one of the others let fly with a gun. They're frightfully trigger-happy, you know. It didn't hit me direct, but I think it ricocheted off the rock and caught me in the shoulder . . . I went on running for a long time before I dared have a look."

Tom's face was grim. "Lucky for you he was a bad shot."

"I'm not sure he even meant to hit me – probably just to scare me and keep me running! But I got hopelessly lost trying to escape . . . Did you find the aspirins?"

Tom grinned. "I did. Every soggy one of 'em . . . It was a damn good idea."

"I only had one bottle . . . and a convenient hole in my pocket," said Kit. "But they ran out . . ." He sounded suddenly vague and tired. "And I – I think I wandered round in circles for quite a while before Branko found me."

"He was lying in the bushes by my field," explained Branko. "I thought at first he was dead."

Ana broke in then, anxiously: "He had a fever . . . from being out on the mountain with that wound . . . We knew he couldn't go further till he was stronger . . . That is why we kept him here. The Serbs are still all round us – we never know what they will do."

Tom nodded. "You did absolutely right. He could not have moved on in that state." He smiled at her with great warmth and gratitude. These two unassuming people in their isolated cottage had offered Kit a refuge and everything they possessed, which in these days of war and hardship was little enough to begin with. And now Ana was almost *apologising* for having kept him safe! "I can only thank God," he said to them seriously, "that you two were here to help him."

"You will be able to take him on with you tomorrow," said Branko, glancing out of the cottage door at the lengthening shadows on the mountainside. "It is too late tonight."

Tom realised that this was true. He could not climb down to the road with Kit after dark, and there would still be quite a long walk to the village where Daisy might or might not be waiting for him . . . He would have to wait till morning before attempting the rest of the journey.

"We will have more coffee," announced Ana. "And Branko will play. He plays his violin when his hands are not too tired . . ."

Branko held out his gnarled brown hands and looked at them critically. Wresting a living out of this stony mountain ground didn't do them much good, he reflected. But they still worked all right, unless the weather was very damp. "They are not tired tonight," he said, and reached for his fiddle.

In the morning, Branko tried to offer them his donkey for Kit to ride on, but he refused, saying stoutly that he was perfectly able to walk. Tom was not so sure, looking at the boy's white face and slightly clumsy movements, but he said nothing to discourage him. Nor did he attempt to discover how bad the wound in his shoulder might be, deciding that it was probably best left untouched till he could get him to a hospital for professional treatment. Tearing off blood-dried bandages would not help. So he contented himself with tying Kit's arm in a makeshift sling and draping an extra jersey out of his own pack round the thin shoulders. It was the best he could do for the moment, and he just hoped the descent to the road wouldn't be too steep.

They said goodbye to Branko and Ana – with real affection

185

and regret on Kit's part, for they had been very good to him – and set off down the scrubby slopes towards the road below.

Just before the cottage disappeared from view behind the hill, Kit turned to look back, and saw the two old people still staring after him. He lifted his hand in farewell, and two hands also lifted and waved back. "They have no sons now," he explained to Tom. "They were both killed in the fighting . . . I think that's why they were so kind to me . . ."

Tom nodded. "A proxy son?"

"Sort of." He sighed. "Family life matters to them."

"Doesn't it to you?"

It was a deliberate question, because Tom thought it was time he talked to Kit about Becky, and about Holly and little Adam . . . Family life was going to have to matter to Kit soon, whether he liked it or not.

Kit was no fool, even if he was still a bit hazy after the fever, and he looked at Tom out of alert blue eyes that were very like his mother's. "Yes, Uncle Tom. It does." He grinned a little. "Even apart from the fact that I've just been rescued by a dutiful gallant uncle who didn't want to come out here in the first place – I mean, the *second* place."

Tom glared. "How did you know that?"

"Oh I – surmised." He laughed, and then suddenly grew quite serious. "I've been doing a lot of thinking, lying about up there –" He jerked a thumb vaguely in the direction of Branko's cottage.

"And –?"

"And Ana and Branko are right. Families matter."

Tom smiled. "So?"

"So I made up my mind there were two things I wanted to do if I ever got back – and one was to give my mother a hand in building some kind of new life, instead of opting out like I did before."

Tom looked at him hard. "What about your father?"

Kit almost tried to shrug, and made a face instead. "He's got his bit of fluff, hasn't he? He doesn't need me . . . As a matter of fact, he never did need me much. But I think my mother does."

Tom nodded approval, and put out a hand to steady him as he stumbled a little over a clump of tangled bushes. "That sounds like good sense. And the second thing?"

186

Kit's expression changed a little and became curiously gentle. "Pipe dreams . . ." he murmured, sighing again.

"They wouldn't by any chance be connected with Holly and Adam, would they?" Tom's voice was entirely innocent.

It was Kit's turn to glare. "What do you know about that?" he asked. But he was more astounded than angry.

"Quite a lot," said Tom. And he proceeded to tell Kit all that had been happening since he went away, and about the Yorkshire farm and Becky's slow but continuing recovery.

By the time he had finished explaining, in between guiding Kit over the worst of the bumps and hazards, they had reached the edge of the road. They both looked up and down it warily, but there was no sign of any movement – no Serb troops on the move or a UN convoy, or even any refugees driven out of their homes by one faction or another.

Tom made Kit sit down for a moment, half hidden behind a rock and some tall grasses, while he considered what to do next. The village to which Daisy had been going was some nine or ten kilometres to their left, he thought. But would she still be there? And if they got there, would there be anyone to help Kit, or any transport to go further, or even a working telephone? On the other hand, if he went back to Nasice, to their right, he might miss Daisy altogether – and would the facilities in the town be any better? Really, he needed to get the boy back to Zagreb – or at least to Osijek where there was a hospital, even if it had been badly knocked about in the fighting and was still desperately short of supplies.

For a while the various options seemed equally unpromising, and Tom stood there in perplexed silence, trying to weigh one possibility against another. But at last instinct prevailed. Daisy had said she would wait at least one day, or possibly two, before leaving the village. Well, it was only one day so far – and he and Kit would get there by the afternoon if Kit's strength held out . . . So, they would go on towards the village, and hope for the best.

Tom had filled his water bottle before they left, but Ana had also insisted on filling up his small thermos with weak tea, and packing up a wedge of cheese and two cold potatoes for them – the best she could offer out of their meagre store. So now he persuaded Kit to rest and eat a little and drink the still-hot tea from the flask before they moved on.

"I'm all right," protested Kit, when Tom looked at him somewhat anxiously as they set off again.

"Is that shoulder bothering you?"

"Not more than your knee, I should think," retorted Kit, and they both began to laugh.

"Honestly, talk about the blind leading the blind!" spluttered Tom, and handed Kit an extra bit of chocolate which he had suddenly come across in his pocket.

They were walking along the grass at the edge of the road, where Tom hoped the going might be slightly less jarring for Kit's shoulder, when they heard the sound of a lorry grinding up the hill behind them.

"Better get off the road," Tom said urgently, "in case it's those trigger-happy Serbs again!" And he thrust Kit down behind him against another sheltering outcrop of rock, and lay down full length beside him.

The lorry stopped. A door slammed. Footsteps approached. And a voice said: "Well, really – I didn't know I was *that* frightening!"

"Daisy!" breathed Tom, and leapt to his feet.

"Daisy?" echoed Kit, bewildered, and began to scramble up beside him.

"In person," said Daisy, and held out her arms so that Tom could walk straight into them. Which he did. "You found him, then," she said unnecessarily, while they were both getting their breath back. "Welcome back, Kit. *Where the hell have you been?*"

And somehow they were all laughing (or was it crying?) on the dusty side of the road.

"But you were coming up the *wrong way*," said Tom, when they were all bowling along in the lorry, making for Osijek.

"Tom Denholm," said Daisy severely, "if you thought I was going to sit on my backside and wait for you to turn up, you've got another think coming!" She glanced at him, smiling. "I was up and down that damn road four times last night – and four this morning. The UN patrol thought I was mad."

"I think you were mad, too," said Tom. "But I'm glad you were!"

"Hear, hear," agreed Kit woozily. He had rather collapsed when they finally got him in the lorry, but he was still game.

Tom glanced at him sharply. There was a note of exhaustion in the young voice that worried him.

"I'm sorry to be such a nuisance," said Kit suddenly. "Fat lot of use as an aid worker . . ."

"Nonsense!" Daisy sounded even more robust and positive than usual. "You've done a lot of good trips since you came out. The others told me."

"Did they?" He looked vaguely pleased, as if praise could not quite reach him. "I ought to tell them I'm OK," he added, remembering his responsibilities with an effort.

"That's just what we're going to do," Daisy told him. "They're in Osijek at the moment – and so is the hospital."

"I don't need –" began Kit.

But Daisy interrupted him. "Yes, you do. Get it looked at. Then we can decide how best to get you home."

Tom thought the boy looked as if he would like to cry at this. "Can't I come with you?" His voice was absurdly plaintive.

"Depends," said Daisy. "If they think it won't do you any harm, you can. Otherwise, we may have to fly you home."

"No!" protested Kit fiercely. "I can't do that."

"Why not?" Tom was surprised at Kit's reaction.

"I'm an aid worker," Kit said piteously. "Or I *was*, till I made a mess of it."

"You didn't make a mess of it," retorted Daisy. "The Serb bandits did."

Kit shook his head. "I lost a valuable cargo – and got myself made useless into the bargain . . . How can I take up a place on a plane when they are still trying to fly out casualties?"

Tom laid a gentle hand on his good arm. "Let's wait and see what the doctors say. I don't think you need blame yourself – I'm sure no one else does."

Kit looked at him rather desperately. "I've seen such horrors, Uncle Tom . . . Children with bits blown off . . . shrapnel splinters in their eyes . . . And the old people – too shattered

189

even to know what has happened to them . . . *How can I –?*" He broke off, suddenly choked with helpless grief.

Tom knew he was very near the edge at the moment, what with the shoulder wound and the days of fever and anxiety, and all the atrocities and traumas of war that he had witnessed. He was still very young, after all, and until this revealing trip had experienced very little of other people's tragedies. It would not do him any harm in the long run, Tom thought. But now the boy needed reassurance from someone, and some rest.

"Kit," said Daisy, in her firmest, no-nonsense voice, "we've *all* seen awful things. And we've *all* been trying to do something about it – in our own small way. The best thing you can do now is get yourself well and make the people at home a bit happier! Charity begins at home, after all!"

Tom laughed. Trust Daisy to say what he hadn't dared to say.

"You can laugh," said Daisy, sternly repressing a twinkle. "You're just as bad. *There's plenty to do at home!*"

The two men looked at Daisy and then at each other. They couldn't think of a word to say.

In the end, the hard-pressed doctors at Osijek decided that Kit's shoulder could wait for more specialised treatment in London. They could only clean it up and put on a new dressing and a firmer sling. Kit was secretly very relieved, but Tom and Daisy were not so sure that the long, bumpy journey home would do him much good.

The three remaining aid workers of the team were enormously thankful to see Kit arrive back more or less in one piece, and Geoff, the leader, did much to restore his self-esteem by telling him he had behaved very well, especially in managing to lay some sort of trail for Tom to find, and he was not in any way to blame for being kidnapped by a bunch of maverick Serb soldiers.

They tried to give him a fine send-off, in spite of protests, and also made a great fuss of Tom and Daisy, his rescuers. Daisy, by this time, had distributed all the aid packages on her schedule, and assured Tom when he asked anxious questions that she had nothing else to do now but go home. But when Kit explained to Geoff painfully that he could not really face a party when things were still so fraught for the people of

190

this town, they understood, and kept the rejoicing deliberately low-key.

However, there were one or two people who felt otherwise – the battered citizens of the town that the aid workers, including Daisy, had come to help. Two spokesmen for these came forward to thank them all, bringing small gifts and a beautiful hand-written scroll of appreciation in return.

"You have done much for us," said one of them – a short, stocky man with a damaged leg and a lined and weary face. But his smile was still warm and gallant as he made his little speech. "And risked your lives on our behalf . . ." He came forward then, and took first Kit's hand, then Tom's, and last Daisy's, and finally, laughing a little out of shyness, kissed her on both cheeks. "Thank you," he said simply, "and God guard your journey home."

Daisy waited till the cheerful applause and general talk had died down a little and then said urgently to Tom: "For God's sake let's get that boy to bed before he passes out."

So they sneaked quietly off and found that the aid workers had arranged three comfortable beds for them (a luxury in this battered town), and firmly ordered Kit to bed, so that – as Daisy put it – she and Tom could crash out too and stop worrying.

It was one small room that they were all sharing, and another camp bed had been set up in one corner for anyone extra who might need shelter, so there was not much privacy. But Tom and Daisy were used to this by now, and merely dumped their belongings on the floor and climbed under the army blankets fully dressed. They were both suddenly aware of being enormously tired – Daisy probably from her acute (but unconfessed) anxiety about Tom and her fruitless patrols up and down that road waiting for him to emerge, and Tom from his perilous descent from the mountainside with a wounded and slightly weaving Kit in his charge and their nervous progression down that same empty road . . .

"Well," said Daisy, sounding warm and drowsy, "you've done what you set out to do."

"Let's get him home first before we start rejoicing," he answered, but somehow he could not help smiling.

"And then what?" asked Daisy, seeming almost asleep.

191

But Tom was not fooled. "You were right," he said. "Plenty to do at home!"

Daisy chuckled like a naughty child into her blankets. "Such as what?"

"If you don't stop asking silly questions, I'll come over and tell you what's what," said Tom, and turned over on his side and fell asleep, laughing.

In Zagreb they stopped to report back to the aid agencies, who had already been told the news of Kit's rescue, and Tom managed to get a phone call through to Greg in London, asking him to relay the good news to Ruth at the Yorkshire farm. He did not, of course, know that Becky was already aware that Kit was missing, so he was careful to make Greg promise to speak to Ruth and no one else. Then, having done what he could to relieve everyone's anxiety (especially Holly's), he climbed into the lorry with Daisy and Kit, and began to drive.

"It's a bit sad," he said, waving a hand at the passing scenery.

"What is?"

"This. All this beautiful wild country, and I never really even looked at it . . . except once when I saw a cherry tree in bloom."

Daisy nodded. "Beautiful country, lovely medieval towns and ancient buildings and bridges –"

"All smashed to bits," put in Kit, to whom it was all still too immediate to accept calmly.

"They'll rebuild it all – one day." Daisy's voice was curiously tranquil. "Those that are left . . ." She glanced at Kit's troubled young face, and smiled. "Things will heal in the end – they usually do."

Kit was silent. He was not convinced.

"Will you go back?" asked Tom, hoping to turn his thoughts to other things.

Kit was silent again for a moment. Then he said slowly: "I – I don't think so, Uncle Tom. I want to marry Holly – and that means getting a steady job and settling down."

Tom nodded. "I thought that might be the way of it." He didn't dare ask Daisy if she would be going back, because he was afraid of her answer.

192

But Daisy said in a quiet, reflective voice: "A different kind of future . . . but just as rewarding."

Tom looked at her then, not sure whether she was referring to Kit or perhaps to something else unsaid.

But Daisy just smiled at him as if she knew his thoughts.

Part Four

Homeland

In London, they took Kit to hospital, where the doctors decied to keep him in for a couple of days for a check-up. They also told Tom they thought there was a bullet or a bit of shrapnel left in the wound and they would probably have to dig it out. However, Kit seemed very cheerful, and arranged to ring Becky and Holly at the farm on the portable telephone.

Promising to return to see him that evening, Tom then left with Daisy to deliver the lorry and report to the aid agency. There was plenty to tell them, what with the transfer of the little injured girl, Sonja, to the Osijek hospital (and, hopefully, on to somewhere more equipped to deal with her), and then the rescue of Kit and his journey home.

"I hope they aren't cross with me for overstepping my duties," said Daisy, only half seriously.

"Could they be?" Tom sounded a bit incredulous.

"Oh yes. The UN don't much like outsiders muscling in on the act. All their negotiations are so complicated and so tricky – they see us go crashing in where angels fear to tread, and are afraid we may wreck the whole delicate operation."

Tom nodded. "Yes, I can see that." Then he grinned at her sideways. "But that doesn't stop you, does it?"

Daisy laughed. "Not bloody likely."

They arrived at the depot and Daisy made her report. But to their surprise they were both treated as something approaching heroes and congratulated on their achievements, even if they were breaking the rules.

"Phew!" said Daisy. "I'm glad that's over!" And she stood for a

194

moment uncertainly beside her own smaller lorry which she would be driving back to Yorkshire. "What now?"

Tom had so many things to say to Daisy, he didn't know where to start, but instinct told him not to rush it. Let them all get safely back to the farm before they thought too much about the future.

"Let's go back to your old café," he said. "And then I think we'd better stay with Greg and Marian. That is, if we're waiting to take Kit with us?"

"Sure we are," agreed Daisy. "Might as well finish the job."

When they walked into the café, Joe let out a whoop of delight, and came over with arms outspread. "See the conquering heroes come!" he cried, grinning from ear to ear. "What's all this I hear about rescues and dodging shellfire?" He kissed Daisy soundly and held her back to look at her, and then thumped Tom even more soundly on the back. "Bacon butties on the house!" he said, and rushed back to the counter to oblige.

Daisy and Tom grinned at one another and sat down thankfully in these undemanding, familiar surroundings. It was good to be home. Even this small bit of home. And they suddenly realised how tired they were, and how much the anxiety about getting Kit safely home had weighed on them.

"It's all right," Daisy murmured, seeing Tom's slightly worried expression. "Just getting my wind back."

Tom laughed. "I never noticed you'd lost it!"

They looked at each other with a mixture of rueful admission of weakness and sudden unexplainable joy. It was wonderful to be sitting here in this shabby café, doing nothing but drink strong tea and eat bacon butties, with absurd happiness welling within them like a tide of light.

"Wow!" murmured Daisy. "There's nothing like a cup of good old English tea!" But her eyes, looking into his, said many other things and were filled with thankful recognition.

At Greg's house, Tom lost no time in ringing Becky at the farm, and Daisy talked happily to her parents.

Becky sounded extraordinarily cheerful and practical. "It's wonderful about Kit," she said. "He talked to me a little while ago. He sounds fine."

"Yes, we'll soon be home," said Tom, and something registered and settled in his mind as he said that word "home". That one small farm on a Yorkshire moor was truly home.

"I'm so grateful, Tom – I can't tell you . . . And Holly's over the moon. She's been marvellous over this, you know . . . I'll tell you all about it when you come." She paused, and then added soberly: "Have a good rest first. You and Daisy must be exhausted."

Tom noted, with secret relief, that Becky was thinking positively of other people now, and was no longer entirely wrapped up in her own problems. "You sound awfully well," he said, in a pleased, affectionate tone.

"Yes, I am. Oh Tom, I *am*! This place – and Ruth and Holly, and little Adam – they've done *wonders* for me. You don't have to worry about me any more." She laughed a little over the phone, still sounding shy and pleased. "Go and relax. And come home soon. We'll get the red carpet out!"

She rang off then, leaving Tom smiling into the phone, and he turned to see Daisy watching him with affectionate sympathy.

"I take it all's well?"

"All's very well," agreed Tom, still smiling. "That mother of yours is a miracle worker."

"I know," said Daisy cheerfully. "She always was."

Marian came into the hall and said then: "I've run a bath for you, Daisy – and one for Tom downstairs. And then a large meal, I think?"

"A hot bath!" breathed Daisy, starting to climb the stairs. "What bliss!"

And Tom and Marian stood looking after her, laughing.

When Greg came in, he put an affectionate arm round Tom's shoulders and hugged him hard, saying: "Mission accomplished!" and then hugged Daisy, too. About Derek, he reported, the lawyers had done their job, and Becky would be well provided for. He added, somewhat wryly, that it was the threat of bringing in the American lawyers concerning the Californian condo property that had finally sent Derek running for cover.

"The American laws on maintenance are much tougher," grinned Greg. "They'd have taken him for every cent he earned – and that's quite a few!"

Tom laughed. "I take it he'll still have enough to keep his new girl in the style to which she is not accustomed?" Then he grew serious for a moment and added: "That reminds me, I suppose I should tell him Kit is safe."

Greg agreed. "Though he may know already. It was on the news."

"Was it? When?"

"Lunchtime today." He smiled at Tom. "At least you all got home before the story broke . . . I suppose news filters through slowly out there."

"Communications are dicey, yes . . ." His eyes were sombre for a moment, remembering the television crews trying to film in the littered, shell-torn streets and the broken walls of the hospital . . . But then he went over to the phone again and rang Derek. He was entitled to know about his son, whatever his private life was like.

"Oh?" said Derek coolly. "Turned up, has he? Told you he would . . . No, I didn't hear the news. All right, is he?"

"Not entirely." Tom's voice was crisp. "A bullet hole in his shoulder, and an unspecified fever brought on by exposure. He was wandering in the mountains for quite some time before he found shelter."

"Oh." Derek sounded a bit nonplussed – as if he did not quite know how to react. "Where is he now, then?"

"In hospital. Just for a check-up and a rest . . . And they told me they may have to dig out a bit of bullet or shrapnel. Nothing serious."

"Good." There was a moment's silence, and then Derek said, mustering the old breezy tone which to Tom's ears sounded a bit false by now: "Well, glad everything's all right. Tell him to ring me when he's better." He paused again, a shade uncertainly, and then added: "Thanks, Tom. You did a good job there," and rang off.

Tom was a bit mystified. But he began to suspect that Derek was not so callous or unmoved as he made out. He was just acutely embarrassed about the whole sorry story – and in particular about his own unruly emotions. It was never easy for a man like Derek, Tom realised, to express his feelings. He had been brought up not to – and had expected his children and his wife to be the same. It took a naïve and somewhat obvious girl like Moyra to make him

197

break out of his straitjacket of correctness and self-control. Maybe she was the right person for him, after all. She might be able to thaw that icy self-sufficiency and complacency. Becky certainly couldn't.

Sighing, he began to turn away from the phone, and then remembered Jenny in California. "Greg," he said, "I think I ought to ring Jenny, too. What time is it out there?"

Greg glanced at the clock in the hall and worked backwards. "About three in the afternoon. Will she be in?"

"Probably not," sighed Tom. "But I'd better try."

However, it was late in the evening before he managed to get hold of her. She sounded unexpectedly glad about Kit. Maybe there was some family feeling between them after all, Tom reflected. The cool young voice had sounded genuinely relieved and pleased. Then she surprised him still further. "Uncle Tom, I've been thinking about what you said . . . I've decided to come home for the summer. *Just* for the summer, mind. You see, I – I've got commitments out here."

Tom smiled into the phone. "That's good news, Jenny. Becky will be pleased. Why don't you ring her and tell her that yourself?"

The clear, hard little voice seemed to hesitate a little. "Yes – I might. Now that Kit's safe, it'd be all right to talk to her, wouldn't it?"

"Perfectly all right." He heard the doubt in her voice and went on quietly: "She's much better, Jenny. It won't be difficult."

"Oh . . . Oh good." The words were pitifully inadequate, but Tom understood the anxiety and reluctance to have a scene that Jenny felt.

"And as to your – er – commitment . . . why don't you bring him over with you? I'll gladly pay the fare."

She began to laugh then. "Oh, Uncle Tom. Am I so transparent?"

"You are a bit!" He was laughing, too. "But I mean it – if it would help?"

"It would mean no separation," she said wistfully. "I must admit it sounds tempting."

"Then do it," said Tom. "Let me know when you're coming, and I'll fix it. All right?"

"All right!" she agreed, sounding young and jubilant all at once. "Thanks, Uncle Tom – I will."

Tom rang off then, suddenly weary of all these difficult, fraught relationships, and realised that an enormous weariness was fast catching up on him.

"Come over here and have a drink," said Greg, smiling at him. "And then I think I'm going to order you to bed. Daisy's almost asleep in her chair already."

"No, I'm not," said Daisy, eyes flying open and fixing themselves, smilingly, on Tom's face. "I'm just *luxuriating*!"

"So am I," agreed Tom, falling into a chair. He smiled hazily in Marian's direction and added: "It's all your fault for having such a welcoming house."

But behind his eyes he still saw the tiny cramped rooms and shattered windows of the houses he and Daisy had stayed in, the half-wrecked block of flats, the isolated cottage on the mountainside where he had found Kit, and the extraordinarily warm-hearted welcome he had been given everywhere he went. That was mostly Daisy's doing, he told himself drowsily, they all loved her. But it was also the people themselves – brave and uncomplaining, and unbelievably kind to a stranger in spite of all that had happened to them.

"Amazing . . ." he murmured to the room at large. "Amazing what people have to offer . . ."

And his eyes met Daisy's in perfect understanding.

"You're a glutton for punishment, aren't you?" Daisy smiled sideways at Kit across the cramped space of the lorry cab as they drove up towards the moors on the last stage of their journey home.

"Who, me?" Kit was dozing a little, and sounded vaguely puzzled.

She laughed at him gently. "You could have gone home by plane from Zagreb, and you refused. You could have gone up to York by train, and you refused. Do you actually *like* being shaken to bits in a springless lorry?"

"Not entirely springless," protested Tom, also laughing. "You're slandering the poor thing."

Kit looked from one to the other of them in mute protest.

"I wanted –" he began, and then broke off. It was too difficult to say.

"To finish the way you began," nodded Daisy, smiling at his mutinous face. "You're still an aid worker, Kit."

"Am I? I feel like a very useless passenger at the moment." His voice was full of tired self-reproach.

Tom looked at him rather sharply. The boy was still very white and exhausted, even after his two days in hospital. But the doctor had warned Tom that he might be, what with the general anaesthetic to tidy up his shoulder, and the chest infection that was only now beginning to clear up with the antibiotics. "It'll take a bit of time," the doctor said. "Especially as we don't know quite how long he was out on that mountain before he was found, or how bad the chest infection may have been . . . But he's young and strong. He'll mend."

"You've done your bit," Tom told him gently. "Stop reproaching yourself."

"We've all done our bit," agreed Daisy, backing him up. "And now it's time to relax and enjoy ourselves." She glanced at Tom and added softly: "Nearly home."

Kit roused himself to look out at the rising hills all round him. The moors were in smiling mood, sunlit and laced with cloud–shadow, as Tom had first seen them, tawny–gold like crouched mountain lions close above them, and blue–grey with mysterious distance where hillside merged with sky.

"It's wonderful country," he said, sighing with a curious sense of relief. "So calm – and so much space."

Tom and Daisy glanced at one another again, but they did not need to speak. Let the boy make his own discoveries.

The lorry turned off the main road then, and Tom let in the gear to climb the last winding hill towards the farm. He was conscious of a strange mixture of gladness and terror inside him as he approached the end of his journey. For he knew that somehow all the different strands of his life were coming together at this point, and he had no idea how he was going to arrange them in a coherent whole that could possibly be the best for everyone . . . He only knew one thing clearly at this moment – Daisy was beside him, and he never wanted her to go away from him again . . . But how he was going to achieve this he did not know.

"Here we are!" said Daisy, sudden joy in her voice which she could not disguise. "Welcome to Jenks Farm!" And the lorry rolled into the yard and came to a halt by the door.

The whole welcoming committee tumbled out to greet them. There was Becky, smiling and looking much younger, waiting with arms outstretched. And beside her, Holly, looking strangely luminous with happiness and rather shy – and young Adam jumping up and down with excitement and not looking shy at all. Then there was Ruth just behind them, with a smile as wide as theirs but infinitely calmer – and even Jim Bellingham had found time to be home for a moment and managed a creaky smile as well. And, of course, Mango and Lacey had somehow contrived to be hanging about the yard when Tom drove up, and their smiles were even wider.

"Oh *Kit!*" said Becky, embracing him a little cautiously, afraid to jar his injured shoulder. "Oh *Tom!*" And this time she wasn't afraid at all, and hugged Tom with all her might.

Then it was Holly's turn, and she stood still, hesitating, until Kit took the initiative and hugged her soundly before them all, and then drew Adam close as well with his good arm.

By this time Daisy had managed to give her father a brief squeeze of the shoulder and a fleeting grin before going over to have a quiet word with her mother. Ruth was cheerfully unruffled by all the excitement, and led everyone inside to a celebratory farmhouse meal. It was easier to feed everyone than to try to sort out all their various problems.

Tom was wondering, though, how she could manage to house all these extra people, and whether he ought to try to make some other arrangements, but Ruth clearly saw and understood his concern and smiled at his troubled face.

"Leave be, Tom," she murmured, under cover of passing him the potatoes. "It's all in hand."

Tom looked up at her gratefully, and smiled back. Trust Ruth to take things in her stride.

Adam was allowed to stay up late for this one festive occasion, and kept looking from Kit to Tom with large, star-struck eyes. Having two heroes at once to admire was almost more than he could handle.

"Was there *guns*?" he asked suddenly.

Kit answered at once, sounding cheerful and reassuring. "Yes, but I didn't have one. Nor did Uncle Tom." He grinned at Adam's anxious face.

"Aid workers don't carry guns," said Daisy, also trying to allay the fears of one small boy.

"But someone had one," pointed out Adam, with irrefutable logic, "'cos Kit got shot."

Kit laughed. "Only a bit. And even that was a mistake. I can't play cricket with you yet, but I can play football. Will that do?"

"Tomorrow?"

"Tomorrow," Kit promised solemnly.

Adam seemed satisfied by this. "Smashing!" he said.

"Not smashing, please!" protested Daisy, laughing. "Say 'magic' instead."

"Magic!" Adam repeated obediently. After all, it did seem to say what he really wanted to say about the whole exciting homecoming.

Holly clearly agreed with him, and feeling that enough awkward questions had been asked, announced firmly that it was Adam's bedtime, especially if he was going to play football tomorrow.

"I think it's nearly Kit's bedtime too," said Tom, somehow realising that neither Becky nor Holly would want to appear too fussy about his wellbeing. "Since he's only just out of hospital." And to his surprise, Kit agreed quite readily and got to his feet.

"Becky, you know where his room is," said Ruth, and sat back calmly in her chair, while Kit and Adam were put to bed by their respective mothers. Her eyes met Tom's with guarded amusement. "Let them sort each other out," she said. "They'll enjoy it."

Tom glanced from her to Daisy and sighed happily. "Honestly, Ruth, you resolve all my problems for me without even being asked!"

But there was one problem Ruth could not solve for him, and he did not dare even think of that yet.

"Tomorrow," murmured Daisy. "Not only football . . ." She smiled at him with sudden dazzling certainty straight into his bewildered eyes.

And nothing more was said that night.

*   *   *

202

Tom got up very early next morning and went for a walk on the moors to clear his head. He knew the time for decision-making was coming, and he tried vainly to sort things out in his own mind before the day began.

The world up here was all blue and gold this morning – sunlight glistening on gorse after rain, and every small leaf of new bracken and thrusting frond of young heather abrim with light. The air was pure and clear, and set his heart racing with inexplicable joy – it was so good to be alive that he wanted to sing like the mounting lark that rose up at his feet and climbed into the sky. Yes, he told himself, it's wonderful to be alive, after all I've seen – and to have got Kit back safely, and to have come home here with Daisy beside me . . . But it doesn't solve anything, just walking about and rejoicing!

Sighing, he turned back towards the farm, his reluctant feet taking him steadily across the springy turf to the problems of the day. In the yard he met Lacey cleaning out one of the looseboxes, and stopped to admire the alert, clever head of Morello looking at him over the stable door.

"A gradely lass is your sister, Mr Tom," said Lacey, grinning a welcome. "And a right wizard with the horses. Or should I say witch?" and he gave a mischievous cackle of creaky laughter.

Tom laughed, too, and was moving off towards the house when Daisy came up to him, smiling. "Oh, there you are." She took his arm and led him firmly past the farmhouse door, out of earshot, and stopped to look up at him severely. "Tom Denholm, you're the world's worst worrier. I think you'll find that Becky has a surprise for you, and everything's going to work out fine."

Tom gazed back at her, half laughing at her absurd confidence that all would be well. "You've been talking to your mother."

"Why d'you say that?"

"Because she's a sublime solver of problems – and I rather fancy you take after her."

"Could be," said Daisy carelessly, a little smile still hovering round her mouth. "Come on, breakfast's ready. And after that, all will be revealed."

Farmhouse breakfast was substantial, and always early, after the first chores of the morning were done but before the real work of the day began.

Mango and Lacey settled down to large plates of porridge, followed by bacon and eggs, both of them grinning at Tom as though they shared a perennial joke, and Jim Bellingham came in soon after and nodded briefly at everyone.

Holly and Adam were already there, Adam eating "a boiled egg with soldiers" – his favourite food, he told Tom in a confiding whisper; and Becky arrived almost at once, with Kit just behind her, laughing.

"I told him to stay in bed and be waited on hand and foot," she said, "but he wouldn't hear of it."

"Not on your life!" said Kit, still laughing. "Miss a farmhouse breakfast! How could I?" He stopped to ruffle Adam's hair, and a summer-lightning glance passed between him and Holly as he sat down beside them.

Becky looked across at Tom and announced: "After breakfast, we've got something to show you – Holly and I." She turned then to Ruth for a moment, as if asking permission, and smiled when Daisy's mother nodded and murmured cheerfully: "It's all yours."

Mystified, Tom looked from his sister's incandescent face to Holly's, and then to Daisy's – but though they all seemed particularly pleased about something, they gave nothing away. Oh well, he thought. Let them have their fun. It's marvellous to see Becky looking so vital and decisive anyway, whatever the reason.

Ruth, seeing that everyone was now satisfied, stopped bending over the Aga and sat down herself, next to Jim. Tom, watching her with smiling affection and admiring the way she made sure all her charges were happy, saw her glance rather anxiously at Jim, as if he was the one person she had somehow failed to put at ease . . . And, come to think of it, Tom told himself, Jim was certainly a bit more silent and taciturn than usual – friendly, as ever, of course, but unsmiling and extra quiet . . . I shall have to ask Daisy about it, he thought. She will know.

But Becky was getting to her feet, like an excited child. "Come on, everyone. Follow me." She turned once more to Ruth, a shade anxiously: "Aren't you coming?"

"No." Ruth smiled at her. "You do the honours. You can all come back and fire questions at me later."

So, still uncomprehending, Tom and Kit followed the women across the yard, up the hill a little way and across a corner of the home field to a narrow track between high banks of furse.

The farm cottages stood squarely against the hillside, backs to the wind, their newly polished windows gleaming in the sun. All three doors stood open, with glimpses of clean white paint and scrubbed wooden stairs within.

"There you are!" said Becky happily. "Holly and I have worked very hard. I hope you like them."

"I worked too," said Adam, jumping up and down. "I cleaned the taps with brasso!"

Becky looked at Tom, almost pleadingly, words tumbling out of her. "It was Ruth's idea – and we thought, Holly and I, that it would solve things for everyone for the moment . . . Ruth says we can have them as long as we like. The rent is absurdly small – and there's room for everyone. It would – it would give us all a base and a breathing space – till we know what we're doing. What do you think?"

Tom and Kit were almost speechless, and didn't know what to think. But Becky gave them no time to speak anyway. "I thought Kit and I could have the first one, and Holly and Adam the next – at least for the summer. We neither of us want to go back to a London suburb after this. And Tom, you could have the end one, there's even an extra room with a skylight that would do as a studio . . ." She paused, suddenly unsure, afraid her plans were all too previous and too well worked out for them to bear . . . But it had been such fun getting everything ready for them and trying to put some order and sense into everyone's plans for the future . . . "I know I've been a bit – well, managing," she began again, "but it all seemed so *right*, somehow. And I began to feel that at least I was doing *something* useful for the family at last. But if you don't like it –"

"Oh, Becky, stop!" said Tom, laughing. He went up to her then and laid a comforting arm round her shoulders, hugging her hard. "Of *course* we like it. Just give us time to get our breath back!"

"I thought –" she was almost stammering now in her relief, "I thought we all needed a b–base – or a few roots . . . And there couldn't be anywhere b–better than this, could there?"

"No, there couldn't!" Kit agreed suddenly, and came up to

205

Becky's other side and added his own one-handed hug. Then he looked at Holly, a quirk of tender amusement making his mouth seem suddenly older and wiser. "But I may not be living in your bit for very long, because Holly and I want to get married."

Tom and Daisy looked only faintly surprised, and Becky not at all. "I thought you might," she said, smiling. "Well, that won't be difficult, will it?"

"When did this happen?" asked Tom, also smiling. But he did not dare to look at Daisy.

"Last night," said Kit. And Holly, looking shyer and more luminous than usual, said in a small, happy voice: "He refused to go to bed till I'd said 'yes'!"

"Quite right, too," said Daisy drily, and everyone laughed.

"Will that make Kit my Dad?" asked Adam hopefully.

"It will, indeed," Kit assured him. "Your very own special Dad."

"Oh, that's all right, then," pronounced Adam, as if that solved everything. Which it probably did, for him.

But Becky was still looking at Tom, not sure even yet if she had been too precipitate. "I – it need only be temporary," she said nervously, "until you know where you want to be."

"Oh, I know that already," said Tom. "And you were absolutely right." He grinned. "This is the real kind of 'extended family unit' I believe in!" Then he turned to Daisy and added, quite calmly: "But there are a few other things to discuss. We'll see you later." And he marched off, with Daisy's hand firmly in his.

"It's all too easy," he said to her, as they sat high up on the moors looking down.

"No, it isn't," Daisy contradicted. "Life's never going to be easy with Becky – or with Kit and Holly, come to that."

"Or with us?"

"I didn't say that."

"I'm too old for you," Tom blurted out.

"You are not! I'm thirty-six. No chicken meself! And you're forty-five, aren't you?"

"How did you know that?"

"Becky told me. It's a perfectly respectable age ratio. Men

mature later than women, anyway!" She wrinkled her nose at him. "Stop making excuses!"

"And I haven't got a settled job."

"Do you want one?"

He paused. "Not really. But what about money?"

"Do we need any?"

He shook her gently. "Be sensible."

"Why?"

"Oh Daisy," he groaned. "You're such an idealist."

"Am I?" She considered the matter. "I might want to go off sometimes, you know."

"Yes, I know," Tom agreed. "But I make one proviso."

"What's that?"

"If it's dangerous, I'm coming too."

Daisy laughed. "That's blackmail."

"Take it or leave it." He glared at her, and then relented, smiling. "I'm sorry, Daisy – this tempting fate business is too much for me." He clutched at her suddenly. "When you went off in the lorry –"

"And left you on the road –" She clutched him back.

"*Daisy* –?" he asked, surprised.

"OK, then," she agreed, looking into his face, all pretences gone. "Together or nothing."

"Done!" said Tom, and kissed her then, long and hard. But there were other implications in this surrender, too, and he needed to get them clear. "What about children, Daisy? Wouldn't they rather cramp your style?"

She looked at him seriously, and paused before she spoke. "I used to think – especially on the aid runs and in the refugee camps – that there were too many children in the world, anyway. Too many people altogether. And I ought not to add to the problems of overpopulation . . . But –" she looked down at her hands, almost shyly, and then up into his face again with her usual brand of candid honesty, "I've changed, Tom . . . since I met you, everything has changed . . . And I *do* want children – as long as they're yours."

Tom was almost too moved to speak then, so he just folded her close in his arms again and murmured: "Oh Daisy . . .!" and could not add another word.

207

It all seemed to be resolved so simply that Tom was a bit dazed. He knew he would have to ask Ruth and Jim for their blessing – they were those kind of people – but he thought they would give it, especially if Daisy pushed them hard enough. They found it hard to refuse Daisy anything, he knew.

Time enough for that when we get home, he thought dreamily, and walked on with Daisy's hand in his over the sun-dappled turf.

They were crossing the curve of a hill above the farm, when Daisy suddenly stopped and pointed upwards. "What's going on up there?"

Tom shaded his eyes against the sun and followed her pointing finger. The sheep all seemed to be bunched together in one corner and he could hear the sound of a frantically barking dog . . . and close to the huddle of sheep, something brownish and humped was lying still.

"Is that one of your dogs?" he asked sharply.

"Yes," said Daisy, and began to run.

Tom ran too, and together they hurled themselves up the hill and arrived, panting and breathless, where the frightened sheep stood huddled beside the barking dog, and Jim Bellingham lay in a crumpled head on the grass.

It was all nightmare, then. Daisy stayed with her father while Tom ran for help. An ambulance came – as near as it could get – and they carried Jim down to it on a stretcher.

Ruth, white faced but still calm, went with him to the hospital, leaving Tom and Daisy in charge. "He's still alive," she said. "People do recover from heart attacks. Keep hoping!" and she was gone.

Heavy-hearted, they summoned Mango and Lacey, and told them to carry on as best they could. "Daisy and I will help," Tom told them. "If you'll tell us what to do . . . We may have to manage like that for some time."

The two men nodded soberly. "Ay. We'll see the boss right," they said, and went back to work.

It is such a shame for the others, thought Tom – when everything seemed so right, and they were all so happy . . . And I said to Daisy that I was afraid of this tempting fate business, and I *am* . . . But he concentrated all his private sources of hope and optimism on supporting Daisy just then. She seemed curiously shaken and bewildered. The steady, untroubled life of her parents had always been the rock she leaned on.

"I never told him I loved him," she said bleakly, as she went out to feed the hens as Ruth always did at tea-time.

"He didn't need telling," said Tom. "He knew, anyway."

Becky and Holly, with Kit and little Adam, had stayed on up at the farm cottages for the time being, feeling that they were probably better out of the way. But they were all anxious, too, and Daisy decided to bring them all back to the kitchen for tea, and try to keep them all as cheerful as possible.

"I can cook, too," said Becky, pathetically anxious to help. "Let me give you a hand."

The phone rang then, and Daisy went to answer it, terror in the glance she shot at Tom.

"He's holding his own," said Ruth's voice, a little tremulous now. "The doctors think if he can hang on tonight, the worst will be over . . . I'll stay over, Daisy. Can you cope?"

"Of course," Daisy assured her. "You stay with Dad. We'll keep things ticking over here." She paused and then added: "Get yourself something to eat, Mum. Or at least a coffee. *You* mustn't collapse."

"Oh, I'll be all right," said Ruth, and sighed. "I'm tougher than Jim." And once again there was a slight tremor in her steady voice.

"Give him my love when he wakes," said Daisy.

"I will – I'll let you know . . . when there's any more news . . . God bless," added Ruth hurriedly, and rang off before Daisy could really hear the tears in her voice.

Jim hovered for two long days and nights between life and death, while his family went greyer and greyer with anxiety. But on the third day he suddenly rallied, said he felt better and it was silly to go on lying here, and demanded an egg for his tea.

"He's coming back!" said Ruth, who had never really allowed herself to doubt it. "He's actually hungry!"

And everyone waiting in this farmhouse kitchen for news breathed a huge sigh of relief.

"Ought we all to go away?" asked Becky, anxious as ever

about whether she had done the right thing to bring all the family together in this way.

"Don't be silly," said Daisy. "You'll all be a great help. Mum will need to concentrate on Dad a bit more – so we can take over some of her chores, can't we?" She smiled at Becky's worried face.

"My shoulder's nearly right," volunteered Kit. "I'll be able to be a farm hand soon, at least."

"That reminds me," Tom said, keen to turn Becky's anxiety to other channels, "what exactly are you and Holly going to live on?"

"I've got it all fixed," Kit told him happily. "I'm going to do two jobs."

"Where?"

"In York." He grinned at Tom's incredulous face. "The aid agency have offered me an admin. job. I wanted to go on with it somehow if I could – and I'm good at organising things on computers and finance and such."

"Oh, are you?" Tom still sounded a bit sceptical.

But Daisy laughed. "Give him the benefit of the doubt!"

Tom shot her a suspicious glance. "What do you know about it?"

She looked a bit embarrassed at this, but Kit spoke up for her.

"As a matter of fact, I asked them in Zagreb on the way back. It was after you'd told me all about Yorkshire and Holly, so I knew where I wanted to be based, if I could . . . And of course when I said Yorkshire, they referred me straight back to Daisy."

Tom looked at her reproachfully. "You didn't tell me!"

"There was nothing to tell," said Daisy airily. "Not till Kit got back and went to see them. I only told him who to contact . . . He did the rest himself." She turned to Tom with the utmost innocence. "I couldn't say anything till it was certain, could I?"

Tom shook his head at her, but he couldn't help smiling. "Oh Daisy! – Conniving, contriving, crazy Daisy!"

"And then," added Kit, amid the laughter, "I did a deal with my old college."

"What kind of deal?" Tom was still suspicious.

"Well, while I was there, I set up a computer database for them. It was part of my course in business studies – and they were very

210

pleased with it. So I made them promise to recommend me to any other university that might want its courses programmed or something . . ."

Tom stared at him. This was a side of Kit that he didn't know. "So you suggested York?"

Kit looked smug. "It was a brain wave, wasn't it? . . . And it worked. It's a year's work, setting it up and running it in. That'll give me time to look round, won't it?"

Tom was impressed. "When was all this?"

Kit looked a little embarrased. "Oh, when you and Daisy were so busy with the farm . . . I thought I must do something positive about the future – one less thing for you to worry about. Besides –" He looked at Holly and smiled: "I've got responsibilities now!"

Becky was smiling too by this time. "He didn't even tell me till it was all fixed."

Tom and Daisy exchanged a glance which only they could interpret. It said that they, too, had a future to plan, but could not begin to think of it until Jim Bellingham was back on his feet.

"It'll keep," murmured Daisy, knowing his thoughts. But Tom wondered how long that would mean.

Ruth came home that night for a rest, looking drawn and pale, but reasonably optimistic. "He'll need to take it easy," she said, sitting down with a sigh of weariness while Daisy fetched her a late supper and a blessed cup of tea. "No more staying up all night at lambing time –"

"Can you stop him?" asked Daisy.

"We must try," Ruth said grimly.

"He'll need help," said Tom. He looked at Ruth with sudden appeal. "Could I learn to be a sheep farmer?"

"I don't see why not," said Ruth. "Would you like it?"

Tom nodded. "One of the few professions I would really like to be good at."

"Lots of hard work, and not too much money?"

"Suits me," said Tom.

He and Daisy looked at Ruth, wondering how to tell her what was in their minds.

"When are you two getting wed?" Ruth asked suddenly, confounding all their careful evasions.

"When Dad's better," replied Daisy stoutly.

211

Ruth nodded. "Better tell him then."

They looked doubtful. "Should we? Now?"

"Yes, you should." She was quite definite. "Give him a filip. Something to plan for." She looked at them, almost roguishly. "He's always wanted grandchildren!"

Tom and Daisy burst out laughing. "Jumping the gun?"

"Not at all," said Ruth. "Hurry up, that's all. Go and see him tomorrow." She put down her cup then, and got rather hazily to her feet. "I'm bushed now, Daisy . . . Think I'll go up." She looked at them both with sudden affection. "I think it's a gradely idea!" Then she patted them both, and went away up the stairs.

So the next day, they went to see Jim Bellingham together, carrying some fruit and a bunch of buttercups and daisies from the home field, which, Daisy said, was always what she had given him on special occasions since she was a child.

They found him sitting up in bed, looking somehow smaller and frailer, but still indomitable.

"Lot of fuss about nothing," he grumbled. "Right as rain in a day or two."

Daisy made no comment on that, but Tom said, with meaning: "Could you teach me, Jim? You could do with a right-hand man."

Jim nodded slowly. "Even a left-hand man would do," he agreed, and then shot a shrewd glance at the two of them. "Permanent?"

"Yes!" said Daisy joyfully, speaking for both of them.

"Glad to hear it," growled Jim. "Too many fly-by-nights these days." A faint grin touched the corners of his mouth. "Village church?"

They both nodded solemnly, struck speechless again by the way Jim took everything for granted.

He grinned at them a little more broadly. "All the trimmings? Can see our Daisy with these in her hair." And he waved his hand at the bunch of wild flowers on his table.

Tom was amazed. The grizzled farmer was a poet and a romantic – just like his daughter.

"'Singing, singing buttercups and daisies'," sang Daisy softly, smiling at her father. "You old fraud – I never knew you liked all that flummery."

"There's flummery and flummery," said Jim severely. "This is important!" His blue eyes, a little too bright with tiredness and strain, rested on them briefly. "Go on home and get it fixed," he said. "Nothing to wait for, is there?"

They looked at each other. They supposed, at last, that it was true. "Right, then," said Daisy. "But you get well first, you hear me? You've got to walk me up the aisle."

His eyes met hers squarely then. "I'll be there," he said.

It didn't really seem possible, but all at once they were in the throes of arranging a wedding. Tom had rather wondered if he ought to suggest making it a double one, with Holly and Kit, but Kit told him seriously that he and Holly had decided to wait till Jenny came home in the summer. It would give them both time to get the little cottage organised and bring up both Holly's and Becky's things from London.

"Then we'll all feel like a family rallying round Mum," he said, a shade awkwardly – for he was not much given to sentimentality. "It'll give her a boost."

Tom nodded. "Good idea."

"Anyway," said Kit, "you and Daisy need to get off alone before that. You've done more than enough of waiting for other people to get themselves sorted out."

"We had to get sorted out too," admitted Tom.

"Well, you have!" Kit was laughing at him. "So get a move on. Adam's dying to be a page."

So they got a move on – in spite of the fact that Jim was still very far from well and needed a lot of holding down from going back to his farm work too soon.

Ruth had arranged with another local farmer to lend Jim an extra farm hand for the summer, and it was only this arrangement that had made Daisy and Tom agree to go ahead with a late spring wedding.

"Small," Daisy pleaded. "Only family. Flummery or not, I don't want lots of people gawping!"

"Small it is," agreed Ruth. "Better for Jim."

"Not so much catering," put in Becky. "But Holly and I will do it."

"What can I do?" asked Kit, not to be left out.

"You can usher," said Daisy, laughing. "Not that anyone will need ushering. But you can make Mango and Lacey sit in a pew instead of skulking at the back."

"No, he can't," said Tom. "He's going to be my best man."

"Am I?" Kit looked pleased.

"What does a page do?" asked Adam, eager to help.

"In the old days," said Kit seriously, "he held his knight's sword."

"Will you have a sword, Uncle Tom?" Adam looked at him hopefully.

"'Fraid not," said Tom. "Maybe you could hold up Daisy's train."

"Will you have a train?" Adam asked, wondering what trains had to do with weddings.

"'Fraid not," said Daisy.

"Then what *can* I do?" demanded Adam, lower lip beginning to tremble.

"A banner," said Tom suddenly remembering how he had first thought of Daisy heading off for Bosnia, reckless and gallant, with all banners flying. "We'll have a banner – and you can carry it up the aisle."

"Depicting what?" asked Becky, instantly seeing a job she could do.

"A sheep rampant, I should think," said Daisy, and everyone giggled.

And in the end that was exactly what they chose for Daisy's banner – a white woolly sheep with a gambolling lamb, and some buttercups and daisies, to please her father. (And if she and Tom privately thought they had put their swords away and turned them into ploughshares, they did not say so.)

"Jim *will* be chuffed," approved Ruth, smiling. Then she looked at the two of them severely and said: "I haven't heard any word about a honeymoon yet."

Daisy began to protest: "Oh, but with Dad so ill, we thought –"

"Well, you thought wrong," said Ruth. "A couple of weeks away on your own won't cause a crisis here. We've got *lots* of help now. So go away and plan it." She glared at them, and then changed it to laughter at their chastened expressions. "Start as you mean to go on," she added darkly. "Flummery or no!"

Tom and Daisy went away and thought about it.

"D'you know what I'd really like," Daisy said, looking suddenly a little shy and uncertain.

"What?"

"I'd like you to take me to your island."

"To Little Reward?" He looked startled. "Are you sure? . . . It's very primitive."

"So am I," said Daisy, grinning at his astonished face.

"Why, Daisy?" he asked. Though he thought he already knew the answer.

"Because you loved it," she said simply. "And I want to be sure –"

"Sure of what?"

"That you really want all this domestic bliss, and not the wild wilderness . . ."

He smiled. "I learnt something in Bosnia, Daisy. I don't care where I am, so long as you are with me."

Daisy nodded. "That's what I wanted to hear."

"Do you really need telling?"

"Not really." She leant against his arm happily. "But I don't mind hearing it."

"All right," said Tom. "I happen to love you, Daisy Bellingham, and you can go to Little Reward, or anywhere else you like, provided I can come too. Will that do?"

"Perfect," said Daisy.

Before the day of the wedding, Becky took Tom aside and seriously began to thank him for all he had done for her.

But he cut her short. "It's meant a lot to me, too, you know – to see you well again . . . And the whole of my own life has changed because of you, really."

She smiled, but she was not to be deflected. "I nearly did something awfully silly, you know, when I heard about Kit being missing. But Holly stopped me. She's a really strong person, Tom. I think she'll be good for Kit."

Tom nodded. "Kit's grown up a lot."

"Yes, he has." She hesitated, and then went on: "He rang up Derek, you know – to tell him he was all right. And he – he said I was *marvellously* well and building a really happy new life here. I

215

think Derek was rather surprised." She took a determined breath and added: "So I – I actually spoke to him on the phone and told him I was fine, and I wished him and Moyra well!" She looked at Tom anxiously. "I – I thought it was time I did."

Tom hugged her hard. "I'm so glad. That means he's got no power to hurt you any more."

"Yes. I thought you'd like to know." Her smile was a little tremulous. "One more weight off your mind." Then she went and fetched him his wedding present.

"What is it?" he said, smiling, and feeling the flat package with curious fingers.

"It's an easel," said Becky. "Daisy said you'd be painting again soon . . . when things were off your mind!"

They looked at each other and laughed, and then Tom gave her an extra hug. "There's nothing on my mind right now," he said, "except wedding nerves!"

So then it was the day. Daisy, walking up the aisle on her father's arm, with a wreath of buttercups and daisies in her hair, and a plain white dress that scorned all flummery – but such vivid happiness in her eyes that Tom was almost frightened. Could he make that incandescent glow of certainty last?

There were a few extra neighbours, in spite of Daisy's plea – farmer friends who wanted to support Jim Bellingham, especially now when he'd had a bit of a jolt.

Lacey and Mango had squeezed into their best suits and looked suitably scrubbed and solemn. Becky and Ruth had both dressed in their best, and even Kit had found a decent suit to wear since he was acting as Tom's best man. And Adam, resplendent in a real page's outfit, carried Daisy's sheep-rampant banner all the way up the aisle of the little church without tripping once. Even Benji was wearing a white bow on his collar, but he had to wait outside while they sang "We plough the fields and scatter" and the little organ wheezed through the wedding march.

There was a splendid wedding breakfast at the farm, and everyone went on eating and drinking local cider and toasting Daisy and Tom with misty eyes until it was nearly dark and they saw that dear old Jim was looking tired.

Then Daisy and Tom hugged everyone in sight, with a special

216

extra embrace for Jim covering the whispered words: "Mind how you go . . ." and they were off.

Tom had carefully laid on a taxi, a train, and a flight to St John's in such swift sequence that they had hardly any time to worry about anything – let alone feel anxious about those they had left behind.

"It's *us* now," said Tom, smiling into those clear, dauntless eyes. "Just for a little while. It's just us two – alone!"

"Hurray!" murmured Daisy. "About time, too."

And before very long, they were driving up to Reward Cove in a hired car, and Sally Maguire was coming out to meet them.

"So there you are!" she said, echoing Daisy. "And about time, too!" She gave Tom a huge hug of welcome, and then did the same to Daisy. "Any friend of Tom's is welcome," she said, smiling. "And a wife is doubly welcome – except that you've dashed all my hopes!"

"But you've got one husband already," protested Tom, grinning.

"Can't have too much of a good thing, can you?" countered Sally, grinning back. Then she led them both down to the little harbour where Tom's old boat still sat at its berth, tied to the jetty.

"We took some stores over," she said, and there was a decided air of mischief in her glance. "And your wedding present is there, too. You can't miss it!"

"Sally, what have you been up to?"

"You'll see," she told them, laughing. "Better get on, before the light goes."

And she helped them stow their small amount of gear into the boat and pushed them off.

Daisy was looking round her with delight. It was a totally different landscape from any she had known before. The great black rocks stood tall round the little bays and islands, and a myriad seabirds flew up and settled on their sharp crags. A soft bloom of spring growth – blueberry and silvery herbs – lay across the crowns of the cliffs, and the light on the sea was so clear and pure it almost hurt.

They landed on Tom's small beach at Little Reward without mishap, and stood for a moment looking back at the sea.

"I wonder if Ollie's still there," murmured Tom, and as he spoke he thought he saw a small round head lifting up through the swell to stare at the island rocks with inquisitive eyes. *Oh, there you are,* it seemed to be saying to him. *I thought you'd come back one day . . .*

"It's beautiful," breathed Daisy, tucking her arm through Tom's. "No wonder you love it."

He tightened his arm against hers. "Not as much as I love Daisy Denholm," he said, smiling. "Come on. I want to show you the lighthouse – such as it is."

Arm in arm, they wandered up the path, put the old, heavy key in the lock and pushed open the door. The downstairs room looked much as he had left it, except that there was a new small table with some packets of stores laid out on it.

"Lovely," said Daisy. "No clutter *anywhere.*"

"You can say that again," grinned Tom. "I told you it was primitive. Wait till you see our bedroom!"

But when they got upstairs to the room with the narrow built-in bunk beds, Tom stopped and stared – and then began to laugh.

For, placed squarely in the middle of the room, was the most beautiful old carved and gilded four-poster bed with what looked like its original silken hangings in pale, shimmering gold.

"Good grief!" said Daisy, laughing too. "What's *that*?"

They went over to inspect it, and found a note in Sally's large, bold hand pinned to the elegant matching coverlet.

This here is an old French bed. Probably from a wreck long ago. But the mattress is new, and so are the sheets! Happy dreams – from all at Reward Cove.

"Honestly," said Tom, touched beyond words at the unexpected gift. "Aren't people marvellous?" He fingered the hangings with an awestruck hand, and then turned, smiling, to Daisy. "What more could we want?"

"What more, indeed?" agreed Daisy, smiling back. But her eyes were serious as she looked at him. "Only – it isn't *all* we want, is it?"

Tom's eyes softened as they looked back into hers. "Of course not," he murmured, drawing her close. "There's a whole world out there, waiting for us to come back. But *now* – this time is ours!"

"Ours," she echoed, like a sigh of homecoming.

And beyond the old lighthouse walls, the voice of the sea spoke to them only of peace.

218